D0479413

40 THINGS
I WANT TO TELL YOU

40 THINGS I WANT TO TELL YOU

ALICE KUIPERS

HARPERtrophyCANADA™

40 Things I Want to Tell You
Copyright © 2012 by Alice Kuipers.
All rights reserved.

Published by Harper*Trophy*Canada™, an imprint of HarperCollins Publishers Ltd

First published in Canada by HarperCollins Publishers Ltd
in an original trade paperback edition: 2012
This digest paperback edition: 2017

Flan recipe on p. 241 from *Mexican Cookery* by Barbara Hansen,
reprinted by permission of the author (www.EatMx.com).

Harper*Trophy*Canada™ is a trademark of HarperCollins Publishers Ltd

HarperCollins books may be purchased for educational, business, or sales
promotional use through our Special Markets Department.

HarperCollins Publishers Ltd
2 Bloor Street East, 20th Floor
Toronto, Ontario, Canada
M4W 1A8

www.harpercollins.ca

Library and Archives Canada Cataloguing in Publication information
is available upon request.

ISBN 978-1-44340-588-1

Printed and bound in the United States
LSC/H 9 8 7 6 5 4 3 2 1

For my dad—for believing in me

40 THINGS
I WANT TO TELL YOU

PART
ONE

CHAPTER 1

"THERE'S SOMETHING I'VE BEEN MEANING TO TELL YOU." I LEANED back in my desk chair, resting the phone between my cheek and my ear, and doodled on the pad of paper by my computer. There were ten items on my to-do list and I scratched a pen line through the fourth: ~~Tell Cleo.~~

"Did you and Griffin do it?" Cleo squealed.

I giggled. "My birthday. Not till then."

"How do you *cope*? You've got so much self-control."

I imagined Cleo sitting on her king-size bed, probably painting her long nails while talking with me, her gorgeous black hair and dark skin contrasting with the cream-and-white design of her luxurious room. I said, "So. Okay. It's not exactly a secret. Well, it is."

Cleo's voice dropped. "What do you mean? What secret could you possibly have that I don't know about?" I could tell she was teasing me.

"It's no big deal."

"Oh my God, Bird, just tell me already."

"Well, about two months ago I set up this website." I paused, feeling stupid. I was making way too big of a drama over this. "I sort of didn't want to tell anyone because it's an advice thing, so it seemed best to keep it secret, but, well, it's getting lots of hits and I'm thinking about it loads and I was just reading a question that a reader had sent in about how to deal with a crush—"

"You're, like, an Internet advice girl! That's so perfect. What's the address? I'm looking you up."

I told her and heard her clicking on a keyboard. There was a long pause.

"Hello," I yelled. "I'm still here, like, talking to you."

"Calm down," she said, "I can still hear you. It's superb. I love it. People really write these questions to you?"

"Honestly? I made up the first couple, but then, after that, people started writing in. I try to answer when I've got time and something to say. I don't answer everyone." I spoke fast— thinking about the site got me animated like that.

"How do you know what to *say*? Oooh, I'm reading it now. I like the way you do it—clever. And I love your onscreen name."

"I do research and use experiences from my own life. I choose questions I feel like I'll be able to answer. I started this never imagining it would become so, you know, popular, so quickly."

She said, "Sex advice from you."

"Shut up. Okay, so no experience there. Yet. That answer was research-based. Plus, I listen to you."

She laughed. "If you'd only get on and do it with Griffin, then you'd be a real expert. Sexpert." She fell quiet again, then she burst out, "Oh my God, you should totally pay me for that line: *A bad boy might be attractive, but he's always trouble and he won't change for you. I told you that.*"

"That's why I had to tell you about the site. You *know* stuff. How can I write to this girl about dealing with a crush when I've never had a crush, not since I was, like, a little kid and into some guy in a boy-band?"

"Why would you need to have a crush when your boyfriend is right next door? Plus, having a crush would be, I dunno, way too out of control for you. It would be *wild.*"

"I can be wild," I shot back.

"If you say so."

"I just crossed off an item on my to-do list. That's pretty wild," I joked. "Anyway, you like it?"

"Stop talking: I'm still reading. Wow, Bird, it's really good. Why was it secret from me? I wouldn't have told anyone."

"I figured I'd put it up there and no one would be interested and then I'd feel like an idiot if anyone knew."

"I don't care if you do idiotic things."

"I didn't know I'd want to keep the site going."

"As if you ever give anything up when it's not finished. What made you start?"

I tapped my pen against the page. "I guess I find it fun. It's pretty great when someone asks me something and I can figure out the answer and tell it in a way that might help them get their own life under control. I dunno. I guess I want to *fix* things for people."

"Well, you're certainly my go-to girl for advice. You know, if you can give advice on sex, you can probably handle the girl with the crush, but I'm flattered you want my help."

"I just wanted you involved. So any thoughts?"

"Hang on, does Griffin know?"

"Of course he doesn't know. It's a *secret*—I wanted my site to be anonymous so the people writing in could say whatever they wanted to say."

"Okay, well I'm honoured to know your alter ego. Now, Miss Take-Control, you have to tell me what to do about Xavier. I'm seeing him tonight."

"You know what I think about him. Oh, Griffin's calling. I gotta go. Quickly, advice on a crush . . ."

"Cold turkey. Stay away. Remember, you'll get over him. Do other stuff, et cetera. If he's not into her, then it's his loss, right?"

"Perfect." I ended the call and then answered Griffin's.

"What's up? Did you get all your homework done?"

His soft voice said, "Most of it. Sort of. Just wondering if you want to come over. We could . . . study."

"You should finish all your homework, remember? You've got to study hard this year." I was half teasing, half reminding him to stay focused.

I looked out my window and saw him standing at his, smiling over at me. Our bedroom windows faced each other—and when we were little kids we wrote each other messages to read through the glass, or tried out semaphore, or communicated by turning lights on and off. With phones and Internet, and now that we were sixteen, we hadn't used sign language in forever. Still, I automatically checked the window whenever he called.

He wore his usual white shirt and jeans. He was classically handsome: milk-white, baby-smooth skin and vivid blue eyes.

He was tall, muscular but slim. He worked out, worked hard at school, had few friends but the ones he had were close. He radiated calm. With his pale skin and dark hair he had that sexy-vampire thing going for him. A couple other girls occasionally glanced him up and down, but he never looked at any of them, never even seemed to notice their stares, because he loved *me*. If he could haul himself out of bed at a decent hour, he'd be practically perfect.

I said, regretfully, "I can't, G. Too much to do." I looked down at my list.

Read chapter for History
Learn subjunctive of twenty new verbs for Spanish
Upload new photos to computer and file them
Tell Cleo
Essay for English
Read through emails for website and answer the crush question
Start "Top Tips" section
Online Pilates workout—45 mins
Write list of Christmas presents for everyone—get ahead on this
Tidy room and pack bag for school tomorrow

He pouted at me through the glass.

"Don't be like that," I said, smiling over at his sweet puppy-dog expression. "Look—" I held up my Spanish textbook. "I'll get this done, but why don't you come over tonight? Mum's making a roast, as usual. I'll go ask her if it's okay."

"Sure. Give me a call. I feel like we've hardly seen each other recently."

"You're seeing me right now."

He wrinkled his nose. "Yeah, I guess. You look really pretty today, by the way."

"Do I? Thanks." I was wearing my favourite pair of jeans and a blue turtleneck, also super comfy. I'm five-foot-six, not quite as slim as I'd like to be but just about okay in the figure department—not like Cleo, who is stunning. I'm curly-haired (well, frizzy, which is why I straighten it), freckle-faced, and I sort of like my eyes, which change blue/green/grey with the weather. People are always telling me I look *just* like someone they know.

He said, "So give me a call when you figure out this evening." He waved and hung up.

I turned away from the window and read over my list, deciding to start with my website. I opened up the crush email and got to work. I had a smile on my face. I loved being Miss Take-Control-of-Your-Life. Loved it.

Sun 3 Oct

Dear Miss Take-Control-of-Your-Life,

Theres a guy in my school who doesnt know I exist. He doesnt even know my name but I think about him all the time and I wish I could get him to notice me but its crzy because he already has a girlfriend . . . I cry at night because I know we cant b together and I take it out on my friends because I think about him all the time . . . This is taking up my whole entire universe . . . I wnt him out of my head so I can get on with my life . . . help help help!!!!

Mercedes, 12

Dear Mercedes,

Tips to Take Back Control

Cold turkey. Stay away.

Remind yourself you're worth a guy who sees how great you are, *and* who doesn't already have a girlfriend.

It might seem like he's the only boy in the world for you, but I *promise* that will pass. Soon you won't remember what you saw in him.

When you find yourself thinking about him, force yourself to think about something different. Like another guy. Or one of your friends' problems. Or homework. Or *anything*. Keep talking to your friends—don't get mad at them. By sharing your thoughts, you'll stop feeling like you're going to explode.

From one teen to another . . .

Miss Take-Control-of-Your-Life

I got my essay done, learned all the verbs for Spanish, uploaded my photos and did the Pilates workout. I folded my clothes and put out what I was going to wear for the next morning. Supper was off as Mum said she wasn't cooking—weird for a Sunday—and because I wanted to use the time to get on with my Top Tips section for the site, I made a sandwich to eat at my desk and texted G to cancel.

He texted right back.

All okay? Sure?

I replied.

Course. C U 2moro xxx

My phone buzzed.

Is this about the sex thing?

9

My throat tightened. *The sex thing*. I reread the text a couple of times. Wow. That had come out of nowhere. As I was figuring out an answer, he texted again.

What's wrong???

I called him straight away. "Nothing's wrong, G," I said as he picked up. "Everything's fine. This has nothing to do with . . . with sex."

He said, "Why can't we just hang out even if your mum isn't making her regular roast? Also, you've been going in to school early for the last couple weeks, so we don't, I dunno, hang out like we used to. I figure—"

I stared out my window but he wasn't looking at me. He was being really . . . whiny. "Griffin, you're being weird. Nothing's wrong, I promise."

"It's normal for a guy to want to have sex with his girlfriend."

My cheeks flushed. "Where's this coming from? We talked about my birthday."

"That's ages away. You're putting me off."

"I'm *not*. I'm just busy with school. You *know* what I'm like, G."

"I know. It's just— I feel like I saw you more before you became my girlfriend, which isn't how it should be—" He broke off. Then I heard a muffled "Mom, careful." He said back into the phone, "I've gotta go. Love you."

I hung up, a grumble of disquiet starting low in my belly. Griffin was my best friend, and becoming his girlfriend three months ago had been easy—at first. But cancelling dinner wouldn't have been such a big deal before. Now he was acting almost clingy.

I lingered, looking at the heading of the homepage where my onscreen name loomed large. *Miss Take-Control-of-Your-Life.* Getting focused always helped when my brain was stressing about something. I began to set up the new section I'd been planning. Every time I wanted to add to it, the words *Top Tips* would pop up to direct readers to a new permanent sidebar on the homepage. Once I'd done the coding, I typed in:

> It's time to start my new Top Tips section for you, like I've been planning. Top Tips are things I want to tell you, things you might appreciate, extra bits of advice . . . Enjoy! Find them <u>HERE</u>. More Top Tips soon.

Now it was time to write out a tip. I tapped my fingers on the desk. I read through some quotations online to inspire me. I wanted to get this first one exactly right. I came up with a few: *There's always another story . . . When in doubt, don't . . . Count to ten before you say something you regret . . .*

I read each of them over. Then I remembered something my dad often said to me that felt like the perfect way to start my new project. These were words that made me excited about the future.

TOP TIP 1: YOU NEVER KNOW WHAT'S COMING NEXT— EMBRACE THE UNEXPECTED

CHAPTER 2

Mon 4 Oct

Dear Miss Take-Control-of-Your-Life,

I need some advice fast. I think my boyfriend is going to dump
me and I don't want him to. He never answers my calls and
he treats me like he doesn't even like me. What can I do to get
him to fall back in love with me?

Nikki-M

Some of these questions were really hard. I wasn't sure I had
anything to say to Nikki about her situation—it sounded *complicated*. What if *she* was calling *him* a hundred times a day?
Maybe he was right not to always answer her. I went to get myself a cup of coffee and came back to sit in front of the screen a
little longer. I could do this. I could figure out how to fix things
for Nikki.

Dear Nikki-M,

<u>Tips to Take Back Control</u>

You can't get him to feel anything he doesn't already feel.

If he's changed and he used to be more loving and kind, then perhaps try to talk to him. Maybe something else is going on his life that he hasn't talked to you about yet.

Be wary. By treating you as if he doesn't like you, he's probably trying to show you it's over without facing up to telling you directly.

Don't let him call the shots. Walk away with your head held high.

From one teen to another . . .

Miss Take-Control-of-Your-Life

I posted my reply. I had gotten up early, as always, and after I'd finished with the website, I showered, straightened my hair, dressed in the clothes I'd laid out the night before and collected my bag.

As I pulled back the curtains, I noticed that the clouds outside were thick and stormy. Surprisingly, Mum was standing by the front gate with her camera in her hands. She had the same wild blonde curls as me, and they bounced around in the wind. She was curvy, with milky skin and freckles. Looking down at her, I realized how much we looked alike, even down to our changeable eyes and almost invisible blonde eyebrows. Both of us were often told by people that we *needed a little sun*. This morning, Mum wore a plain black dress and wool coat that bleached her out even more than usual, making her look ghostly in the faint light that was finally coming up. She held the camera to her face and snapped a shot of the front of the house. I waved down at her but she didn't see me. I tried to remember the last time I'd seen her taking photos. Forever ago. I felt weirdly sad. Huh. Glad she was back at it.

I scooted downstairs and hurried past Dad, who was reading the newspaper online in his office. He grunted something about coffee, but I was on my way out the door. I called over my shoulder, "See you later, Dad. Love you."

I stepped out of our brick house and was whipped by the wind. I looked around for Mum, but she had vanished. I noticed that Griffin's curtains were still shut: lazybones. Pulling my jacket tight, I tried to tuck away strands of my hair, silently begging the rain to hold off until I got to school. At Coffee Grounds—my favourite local café—I ordered my usual non-fat latte, which I drank as I dodged the traffic to get to the small park near my school. The sound of cars and the morning rush hour faded as I hurried along the path by the lake. The water danced in small metallic waves, shaken up by the approaching storm. The clouds grew darker as I darted from the park into the small front entrance of the stone block where the sixth form classes were held. Just inside, I turned right to get to the first-year sixth-form Common Room of Harton's High School.

I said hi to Neen Patel and Gracie Atkins—this early there were only a few students around—threw some stuff in my locker and went to do a little reading at the library.

About half an hour later, Griffin came over and covered my eyes with his cool hands. "Guess who?"

I pushed back my seat and kissed him. He tasted of minty toothpaste. I said, "How was the morning?"

He swept his black floppy hair off his face. "Same old. I miss walking with you."

"G, I *told* you: it's not personal. I just want to get in early to do a bit of extra work."

"I don't understand why you can't study at home and then walk in with me like we used to."

"I explained it already: the library's a good place to work. I want to take this year seriously. You know the plan."

"Right, the plan." He grimaced.

"What?" He was the worst person in the world at talking about what was wrong—he just liked to pretend everything was okay all the time. Things with his mum were a perfect example of that. "Tell me."

"Be honest, Bird." He put his hand up to the side of his neck, his fingers lightly touching the skin. I knew the gesture meant he was nervous. He sighed, and then the words came out in a rush. "You didn't want to see me last night, and again this morning. Like you don't think it's normal for me to want us to . . . you know?"

"Griffin, nothing's *wrong*. This isn't anything to do with *sex*."

He gave an exasperated sigh. "If you're not ready—"

"That's not the issue."

"Well, I don't get it, Bird."

The conversation was starting to slide out of control. God, we were having our first real—uh—*disagreement* as a couple.

I snapped, "It doesn't help having you pressure me all the time." Wow, I was being a total bitch. Griffin didn't deserve me being so grumpy. I looked up at him and the muscles of my face smiled automatically. "Sorry. I didn't mean it."

"I know you're stressed about school and applying to Oxford and everything. But by telling me we have to wait until your birthday, well, I was thinking about it and it's not very— Well, it's not very spontaneous."

"Why does it have to be spontaneous? This way we can look forward to it."

He softened. "You're so . . . so *you*, Bird. So predictable."

Predictable. That was me.

He bent close. "Come here. Give me a kiss. We'll figure it out."

The bell rang. The word *saved* popped into my head. Some of what Griffin had said was still sneaking about uncomfortably under my skin. I kissed him lightly, grabbed my books and said—perhaps to reassure myself as much as him—"It's all fine, I promise. Come on, we'll be late."

IN FIRST CLASS, MRS. LIVERMORE WAS SAYING IN HER HIGH VOICE, "You need to think about your exams. This isn't about fun. This is about the future."

No one was really listening. I doodled in a notebook, jotting down some ideas for my website.

It took a second to register that something was going on, but quickly the ripple of interest in the room made me pay attention. I raised my gaze to see a guy lounging against the open doorway. I couldn't help but notice that he was *really* hot. I glanced at Cleo, who was sitting there with an expression of pure admiration on her face. I swivelled back to the guy. He was older than us. He wore jeans and a black shirt with the words *Born to Die* scrawled over it. His sandy blond hair hung slightly long, like he hadn't got round to cutting it, and he had stubble on his jawline. He managed to look like he didn't care about his appearance at all, yet he was one of the— No, he was *the* most gorgeous man who'd ever walked into our school. God, the last thing I needed was a teacher like him around. Totally distracting. I'd have to work doubly hard to concentrate if I had any classes with him. I wondered who he was replacing in the middle of term.

The guy folded his arms over his chest, totally at ease, as if he were modelling for a photo shoot. Then he turned his eyes upon me and everyone else vanished. I tried desperately to drag my gaze away.

Mrs. Livermore's voice cut loudly through my mind. "Pete Loewen. Finally. You're late. Not a good start, young man. Take a seat."

Oh my God. He was a *student*. No way was he sixteen. The rest of us looked like kids compared to him.

"Morning," he said. "My alarm didn't go off."

"That is not *my* fault," she squawked. "Sit down, just there." She signalled to a desk a couple of rows to the left of me. I watched him walk across the room, an inner pinching deep in my gut.

He sat, shrugging his bag to the floor.

I thought how amazing it was that this gorgeous guy was sitting so close to me. If I cranked my neck around, I had a great view of the side of his head. Hmm. Even the side of his head looked good. He turned to the right and caught me gawking at him. Caught me out a second time. He leaned back in his seat and winked at me. Winked! Like we were in some cheesy movie. I sat up straight and tried to listen what Mrs. Livermore was saying, ignoring the new guy completely. Sort of.

AT LUNCH, CLEO AND I HUNG AROUND IN AN EMPTY CLASSROOM. SHE leaned her hip against a desk, her black hair straightened and sleek. She wore a denim shirt-dress and black leggings with knee-high boots, making her look skinny and pretty. As always.

She said, "Your hair isn't enjoying the weather."

I thought of the time I'd spent straightening it. Time when I could have been studying. My unruly blonde curls were the bane of my life. "Stupid hair."

She said, "All the work is worth it. It still looks good."

"Sure." I ran my hand over my head, feeling how the moisture in the air was making me frizzier by the minute.

"That guy is hot," she said.

"Who?" I pretended I had no idea who she was talking about. I didn't want her to know I'd been sneaking peeks at him in every class for, like, the whole morning.

"Come on, Bird. You'd have to be blind not to notice."

"The new guy?" I tried to be casual. The image of him winking at me appeared in my head.

Her iPhone vibrated. "You're just so loved up with Griffin you didn't even see him. Hang on." Her big liquid eyes concentrated on reading a text. She said, without looking up, "Hmm, I thought she'd know him. She knows everyone."

"Who? What are you talking about now?"

"Hello, Bird." She rapped me lightly on the head. "The hot new guy. The one who started school with us today: Pete Loewen."

"Oh, him." I tried to be nonchalant by changing the subject. "*Who* knows everyone?"

"Becca." She held up her phone and flicked through Facebook. "She has all the gossip on Pete."

"So what does she say?"

"Read this."

Hey C! Pete Loewen's at your school now? He'll be expelled again, for sure. Goss: Sleeps around. Into drugs, etc. Everybody loooves him. Girls, anyways. When do I get to seee yooouuuu???? Love and super hugs Becca

Cleo said, "I know you don't like Becca that much, but you've gotta admit, she always knows *everything*."

"It's just . . . I'm not sure how being into drugs and getting expelled makes him so fun that everyone *looovvves* him," I said stiffly.

Cleo rattled on. "Anyway, I have Dan and Joe to think about for now. No time for hot new guys just now. So, Miss Take-Control, tell me what to do."

"Shh, don't call me that here."

"No one's listening." She gestured around the deserted room. "I need your advice. Look—" She tapped through to show me two texts. One from Joe Friesen in the year above us and one, almost identical, from Dan Swain in our Computing class.

"Uh, Cleo. They both want to see you on Saturday night. You can't be two places at once, no matter how good you are at dazzling men."

"One for dinner and one later—or is that terrible?"

I giggled. "Definitely terrible."

"Really? *Terrible* terrible? Let's say I do it anyway, what should I wear?"

"For supper or for later? Will you have time to get changed?" She smiled wickedly.

I threw up my hands and said, "That black dress with the long sleeves for Joe. Show off your legs. Levi's and your silky top for Dan. He's more, you know, casual. And what happened to Xavier? Didn't you see him just yesterday?"

It was a moment before she spoke. "Yeah, except he didn't show up."

"You know I hate that guy, right? And the way he makes you feel." I squeezed her arm.

"Anyway, that was all before Dan and Joe texted."

I could tell from her voice that she was more hurt than she wanted to let on.

Griffin came into the room. As usual, we kissed. His mouth was soft and he pulled away quickly, shyly. Not for the first time, I wished he'd be a bit more confident when he showed me physical affection, more certain of what he was doing.

He gave me a look that was hard to read and wandered over to the far side of the room, where he hauled himself up onto a desk. He picked up a pen and tumbled it from one finger to the other so it was in constant movement—a trick his dad taught him when we were young.

Cleo chatted on about something while I watched Griffin. He looked tired and grumpy. And I should know—I knew him better than anyone in the world. I thought about the first time I'd seen him—the day his family moved next door to mine, when a skinny boy appeared at the hole in the fence at the end of my garden. At the time he was a goofy-looking, glasses-wearing kid, with black hair hanging all the way to his shoulders.

"What are you doing?" he asked that first day in an accent I placed immediately.

"Are you American?" I rubbed my dirty hands on my T-shirt and pulled a twig from my crazy, frizzy hair.

He nodded. "I am. From Montana. What've you done to your leg?" He pointed at the plaster wrapped tight around it.

"I flew out of a tree."

He looked at the blue sky. "I don't think I'd like flying very much. Did it hurt?"

But before I could answer, his dad called him away.

Later I'd watched from my window as Griffin's father scooped up the skinny boy in a side hold, swinging him round with a meaty laugh.

Griffin's dad died three years ago of a heart attack. Life sucks like that sometimes.

Cleo interrupted my nostalgia by asking, "So do you two want to go get lunch?"

Griffin said, "From the cafeteria?"

"Gross," I said. "But it's raining, so there's no choice."

Griffin and Cleo carried on discussing it, and I thought about the day Griffin and I kissed for the first time. We'd been sitting in his room, studying, and suddenly his hand covered mine on the carpeted floor. I felt him leaning closer.

He said, "Would it be weird if we . . . ?"

I knew exactly what he meant.

Everyone already thought we were dating because we spent so much time together, and kissing him seemed like it would make sense. At sixteen I had never kissed a boy before, which was starting to worry me. I knew loads of girls my age had boyfriends, but with Griffin as my best friend, there'd never really been time for any other boys in my life.

Sitting on his bedroom floor, I felt like I was watching myself as Griffin tipped his face so his mouth landed on mine. I remember thinking, *He tastes exactly like I thought he would.* The idea was comforting, so I experimented by kissing him a little harder.

He pulled away and smiled his goofy grin at me. "You're perfect," he said, and the compliment made me feel a bit tingly.

Okay, so I didn't have the rush that Cleo talked about when she described kissing guys, but I wasn't anything like Cleo. And Griffin wasn't anything like the guys she dated.

Griffin stared glumly at me now, so I gave him a small smile, feeling bad about our almost-argument. Maybe my tummy didn't flip-flop when I looked at him, but we were so . . . right together. His fingers touched his neck.

Neen Patel had come in and was loudly gabbing with Cleo, who was still leaning against the desk next to me. "I heard his father was in prison," Neen said.

"Who?" I asked, suddenly interested.

"Pete Loewen. He's in foster care, apparently."

"How do you know?"

Neen said, "His mum left him—she just walked out on the family. Can you imagine your mum just leaving? His dad was bad news, apparently, and Pete's the same according to everything everyone's been saying. He's just got trouble written all over him. Can't you tell?" Her tongue rested between her teeth. "Super sexy. I'm going to ask him out."

Cleo said, "I'm definitely going to ask him first. You can have him when I'm done."

My phone buzzed and I turned to it. It was Griffin texting me from the other side of the room.

Sorry that things are weird.

I smiled over at him. Cleo and Neen were still chatting. I texted him without them noticing.

Me too. We cn b more spontaneous if u like. What do u want us 2 do?

Another text popped into my phone.

No, I get it—we'll stick w the plan. 1 month and counting ;-)

He was being so patient. He flashed a smile at me. It seemed everything was fixed, so I should feel better. But I didn't. I looked at his text again. *1 month and counting.*

All of a sudden I had a bad taste in my mouth.

CHAPTER 3

Sat 16 Oct

Dear Miss Take-Control-of-Your-Life,

My life's totally out of control . . . how do u keep it together?

MetalGirl

Dear MetalGirl,

<u>Tips to Take Back Control</u>

Take a deep breath when you're feeling like you're not in control.

Write a list of all the things you need to do.

Stay on top of your homework and try to keep your work-space tidy—it helps keep your mind tidy.

Meditation, Pilates or yoga can help reduce your blood pressure and calm you down, and you'll find some great classes online which you can watch.

Talk to your friends and family about your feelings.

Remember, you *are* in control, always.

From one teen to another . . .

Miss Take-Control-of-Your-Life

I smiled as I reread my answer to MetalGirl, and then sorted through some of the other emails in my inbox before adding to the new Top Tips section.

TOP TIP 2: DO WHAT YOU LOVE

I'd finished all my homework the night before, so Saturday called out to me like an invitation. I closed up the site and pulled out my new, fantastic Canon Rebel XTi. When my grandmother died, she left me some money and left my mum the house we now lived in. I used some of the inheritance to buy myself the camera—Mum said the money was for me to invest in something I loved. I wandered downstairs and snapped some shots of my dad absorbed with typing furiously on his laptop, his cup of coffee congealing next to him. He didn't even notice me crouched on the carpet trying to get a good angle. Dad is a gigantic man and I wanted to represent how big he was, how he filled any space, not just physically but with his ideas and excitement. Mum passed by in the corridor carrying laundry, which I offered to help her with, but she didn't reply. Shortly after, the laundry gone, she reappeared with a pen and a pad of paper in her hands.

She said, "I have the schedule for the week written out here and I'm just wondering if there's anything we need to add before I post it on the fridge. Any meetings or anything that I should know about?"

Dad told her about a Tuesday evening meeting he'd forgotten to mention earlier, and Mum scribbled down the details.

She glanced at my dad. "Okay, tonight we have you making your Saturday spaghetti with tomato sauce"—she turned to me—"and you, Bird, are doing the salad. Everything's laid out in the fridge where it should be. All set?"

We both nodded. "Sounds good, Mum."

My phone rang. It was Griffin. I headed out the room as I answered.

"Want to hang out?" Griffin asked.

"Come over. I'm taking photos. I could take some of you."

"You know how I feel about photos."

"I'll make you coffee."

I met him on my front step and passed him a steaming cup of coffee. He kissed me lightly on both cheeks, then softly on the mouth.

"Morning," I said. "I know it's cold, but could I take a couple pictures of you out here?"

He growled with displeasure but leaned obediently against the house and I snapped a series of shots.

"Are you okay, G? You seem tired."

"Just a bit worried about Mom."

"How's she doing?"

"You know—the same. Worse."

I lowered the camera and smiled sympathetically at him. "Anything I can do?"

He shook his head.

I said, as flirtatiously as I could, "Would it make you feel better if we talked instead about—you know—the night of my birthday?"

"What's wrong *now*? You know, Bird, for someone who lives by her plans, you sure keep trying to change this one."

Shocked, I said, "I didn't mean I was backing out, Griffin. I'm not backing out. I just wanted to—"

"What is there to say? Look, I can't stay long. Mom needs me around today."

"I'm sorry." I went over and gave him a hug.

He leaned his chin on my shoulder, flopping his weight on me, tangling his hands up in my hair. "Thanks for the coffee," he murmured, then slid away and picked up the empty cup he'd placed on the step. "I didn't mean to get so— Things at home are kind of . . ."

"No, you're right. I've been acting like I don't want us to go through with this. It's my fault. I guess it feels like a big deal. Maybe I'm a little scared. I don't know. Everything just feels a bit weird. Don't you feel it too? Like, we're friends but now there's all this other stuff to deal with."

He frowned down at me. "Why would you be scared with me?"

I didn't answer. He wasn't really getting what I was trying to say. I wasn't even sure what I was trying to say. I changed the subject. "Why don't I come over and help you out?"

He wrinkled his nose. "Today's not a good day. You know how she is."

I did know. And I knew he wanted to deal with it all by himself. Secretly I was worried that the situation with his mum was much worse than he let on, but no matter how much I tried to ask, he kept stubbornly silent.

"We'll talk later." He kissed me on the top of my head and headed out the gate, turned onto the path leading to his house and, with a final wave, disappeared. I let out all the air I'd been holding.

Wandering away from the house, I began to photograph my street. I loved getting shots of empty streets—completely the

f my love of taking photos of people. The absence
ade the photographs intriguing. I tried to catch
gnt filtering through the tree branches, and then I
stood on a wall and pointed my camera down at the line of the
deserted road.

All of a sudden, the image of the new guy floated like a life-
boat into my mind. Pete Loewen. That strong, toned body. That
mussed-up hair. That penetrating stare. He was so grown up
and so . . . so . . . so . . . *sexy* . . .

I realized I was biting my bottom lip.

I WAS UP IN MY ROOM THAT EVENING WORKING THROUGH SOME EXTRA
reading for Spanish when Dad knocked on the door.

"Can I come in, little Bird?"

He burst in before I even had time to answer. He patted his
big gut, saying, "Should be eating less. Those stairs wear me
out." He sat heavily on the bed and took a few ragged breaths.

I asked, "Didn't you study Spanish once? Do you know anything about the subjunctive voice? I just can't figure out why
the writer's using it in this sentence."

He frowned and scratched his chin. "That was your mother—
she's still pretty fluent. Uh, subjunctive: something to do with
the future."

"Yeah, I know that much."

He flipped up both palms. "You know more than I do, then."

"Never mind. How was work today?" He didn't have a con-
ventional job; instead he worked in his office downstairs, often

trying to secure funding for one of his business plans. I loved that he was an entrepreneur—it made him seem exciting and dynamic, although I wasn't sure my mum saw it the same way.

He said, "Ah, well, you see, I wanted to talk to you about this new idea I have. What do you think: instead of solar-powered panels, solar-powered bricks? I've been doing the research and it seems to me this country's crying out for a way to get energy through the walls."

I loved Dad and his big ideas. "Huh, might be brilliant."

"See, that's what I think. But your mother doesn't want to invest in it. Thinks it's risky."

I wheeled my desk chair closer to him. "I guess a little research couldn't hurt."

His eyes sparkled. "Exactly. And research is the expensive part. I knew you'd be on my side."

"That's not what I was saying—"

"That's my girl." He hauled himself up from the bed and kissed me on the top of my hair.

"No, Dad, that's not what I meant."

"Anyway, I shouldn't interrupt you working. How are you going to get to Oxford University if I keep stopping you from studying?"

Oxford University. Just the words conjured up spires and bicycles and long afternoons of fascinating conversations in cluttered cafés. I imagined myself wearing a cool vintage outfit I'd just picked up from a little boutique shop, carrying my camera and photographing my fellow students. The plan was that Griffin and I would go together when we finished school in a year and a half.

Dad was admiring the corkboard next to my desk. I followed his gaze to a printout of the homepage of the Oxford website. Around that, I had pinned inspirational quotations and things I'd found online to help me with the Top Tips section on my website. One of my favourite quotations read:

It is possible to fail in many ways . . . while to succeed is possible only in one way.
Aristotle

Out loud, Dad read the two quotations underneath it:

I wasted time, and now doth time waste me.
William Shakespeare

There is no greater guilt than discontentment.
Lao-tzu, *The Way of Lao-tzu*

"Very profound. And that's a good photo." Pinned to the far left was a photograph I'd taken three months ago. It was a self-portrait. In it I was sitting on the bench in the park opposite my school. I'd used the self-timer and framed myself entirely against the sky so neither the bench nor the park trees could be seen at all. My hair was straightened, blonde against the blue. My mouth was firmly set. Looking at the shot, I wondered why I looked so grimly determined.

Dad said, "It's well composed. 'Nicely framed,' as your mother would say. Only it doesn't look like you."

I frowned at it, surprised. "What do you mean?"

He put a hand on my shoulder. "I suppose it does. But you look all grown-up. Not like my little Bird, ready to take a risk and fly out a tree."

"I broke my leg when I did that." I forced a laugh.

He peered down at me. "Are you okay, Bird?"

"I just have a lot of work to do. Big year."

"I should let you get on." He squeezed my shoulder.

"Okay, well, good luck with persuading Mum about the bricks."

His phone rang and he answered it on his way out the room. I heard him chatting excitedly about solar power as he headed downstairs.

My phone buzzed and it was Griffin.

Mom fine. Gd 2 C U earlier.

I replied.

All okay? Want me 2 come over?

His reply popped into my phone.

All fine. Love U. Maybe 2moro. xxx

I replied.

Love U xxxx

He texted back.

2 ½ weeks and counting. xxxxx

OVER THE NEXT FEW DAYS, I STUDIED HARD AND CONCENTRATED ON staying ahead in my classes. Occasionally I'd look up and spot Pete Loewen. As soon as I caught myself staring, I'd stop, but as the week went on I found myself thinking about him more and more often. I tried to pay attention to my teachers, even to Mrs. Livermore when she ranted on.

"You might think you're all very mature," she droned one day, "but this is a huge year for you, one in which you become adults. Don't throw your chances away." She shot a glance at Pete, which made me look around at him too. *God. Look away, look away.* Her voice was like the buzzing of bees. "If you fail you'll end up going nowhere . . ."

But I wasn't listening anymore. I half twisted in my seat and bent down, pretending to be getting something out of my bag. Covertly, I studied Pete's trainers . . . his jeans-clad legs . . . his tight black jacket . . . the side of his head. His sandy hair looked soft, touchable. His chin jutted out like he was mad about something; maybe he was clenching his teeth. Hmm, perfect cheekbones, full mouth. I'd have bet the rest of the room could just disappear and he'd still sit there, jaw clenched, staring off into the distance. I couldn't help but be reminded of the rumour I'd heard from Becca. Expelled. Into drugs. He was so blatantly *not* my type.

I was gazing up at him, so when his grey eyes flicked to rest on mine, amusement danced over his lips. I must have looked so *stupid* all twisted up in my seat, my empty hand resting on top of my bag while I goggled at him. As the blush heated my cheeks, I stared back and I was pretty sure he'd seen right through me. This had to stop. I tried to think about the advice I'd given that twelve-year-old girl Mercedes on my website recently. I was acting just like her. But sitting there, chewing on my pen, I couldn't even remember the things Cleo said were ways to forget a crush. A *crush*.

Mrs. Livermore beamed in my direction, oblivious to the fact my heart was beating three times faster than it should. Even though I found her so boring, she clearly favoured me—probably because I always got such good grades. "Yes, those exams are very important. As we all know, don't we, Bird?"

I glanced at Cleo, who rolled her chocolate-brown eyes at me and stuck her tongue out. Thank God for Cleo. I grinned at her quickly and then I said, "Yes, Mrs. Livermore," as I was expected to.

CHAPTER 4

Wed 20 Oct

Dear Miss Take-Control-of-Your-Life,

I bet you get questions like this from girls all the time. My girl-friend wants us to have sex and you'd think I'd be happy about it. I do want to have sex. Thing is, I'm a virgin and like only 60% sure that she would be cool with that. I'm running out of excuses. I'm not gay but she might think I am if we don't have sex soon. And how do I know she's the right girl?

Adam99, 16

Adam99 sounded great. I wished Griffin could be more like him.

As soon as the thought crossed my mind, I regretted it. Griffin wasn't pressuring me: what he wanted was *normal*. I paused before answering Adam99, pulled out a sheet of paper and began to write a list.

Pros of having sex with Griffin:

- First time is a big deal and it will be with someone I trust and know well.
- I'm not shy with him.
- He loves me.
- It will be a good step for us as a couple.
- He's my best friend (apart from Cleo!).
- I've known him forever. We'll be friends forever— together forever.
- We will be careful and safe.

Cons of having sex with Griffin:

- I am feeling pressured. Not sure why. Not sure I should have sex just because I feel pressured to. Maybe I'm feeling worried because it's my first time. Will it hurt?
- He's my best friend. Okay, this is a pro too, but sometimes it seems like a con.
- Although I'm not shy with him, maybe I will be if we're not wearing clothes. Might be weird.
- Is he the one? I know he is and we have a great future planned, but sometimes he's just so . . . so him. I wish he could be more confident and more mysterious—maybe I just know him too well.
- I keep thinking about Pete Loewen. The idea of being with him doesn't make me feel anything except excited. Maybe this is a pro reason for having sex with G . . . Would it get me back in the right headspace?

Seeing the words I'd written led me to doodle a frustrated series of angry lines and squares under the list. This was getting me nowhere. I scrumpled up the page and chucked it away, returning my attention to Adam99.

Dear Adam99,

I bet a lot of girls would love dating a guy like you: one who isn't putting pressure on them. I get the feeling that you and your girlfriend don't know each other that well—you don't seem very sure about what she thinks of you.

Tips to Take Back Control

You should be more confident that lots of girls would be happy with a boyfriend like you.

If she's the right girl, you'll feel comfortable with her. She should be honoured to be your first, not judging you. And she should respect your decision to wait if that's what you want to do.

Get to know her better, take a little time, and when she brings it up, tell her what you want.

From one teen to another . . .

Miss Take-Control-of-Your-Life

CLEO CAUGHT UP WITH ME BY THE LOCKERS ONE AFTERNOON AFTER the final bell.

"What's up with you?"

"Nothing. Everything's good." Rain began to spatter against the opposite window. "I guess I'm stressed about school."

I thought back to when Cleo and I met. We were eleven and were attending a photography class that Mum got for me as a gift. I noticed Cleo right away. She had streaks of purple in her black hair. I'd never seen anyone my age with purple in their hair.

She stood in the middle of the room, her fancy camera looped round her wrist on a pretty chain, and said to the teacher, "I don't really like taking photos."

I envied her camera, I envied her purple streaks and I envied her for being cool. Pure hatred quickened in my blood. I decided that the way she'd spoken to the teacher was the rudest thing I'd ever heard, so I was furious when we were paired up to work together.

The girl hooked her arm through mine as if we'd been friends forever and said, "So how are we going to make the time go faster?"

"I like taking photographs. I *want* to be here," I replied.

She started laughing.

"What? What's so funny?"

"You are. You're so cross and stiff, like a cardboard cut-out. You need to relax."

"You need to realize you're not the centre of the universe."

She laughed harder. "You're hilarious," she said. "I think I love you."

"I'm not being funny. Let go of my arm." I put my hand up and said to the teacher, "Please can I be paired with someone else?"

The teacher sighed. "Come on, girls. Let's get on, shall we?"

"But she doesn't even *want* to be here."

Cleo said, "Because it's a *Saturday*. Who wants to be on a course on a Saturday?"

"Why did you come, then?" I spat.

She shrugged. "My dad bought it for me as a Christmas present."

"My mum got it for *me* as a Christmas present and I'm *happy* about it. I want to learn about photography."

She smiled broadly, her braces showing fully in her mouth. "Okay, well, let's learn about photography. At least I've got you as my partner. That should make things better. What's your name?"

Even though I didn't like her, I couldn't help but warm to her smile. She was what my dad would call a live wire. "Bird," I said. "It's my nickname. My real name's Amy Finch."

"Don't be mad at me, Bird."

"Can we just get on with this?"

"You've forgiven me?"

The rest of the day was great, but afterward I figured I'd never see her again. However, we started at the same new school in September of that year, and we both grinned like idiots when we recognized each other.

Now Cleo said, "Uh, helllooo, Bird, I'm still here. Sure you're all right?" She slung an arm over my shoulder. "Come on, 'fess up. Is the idea of having sex freaking you out?"

I turned away from the window. "How do you know what's going on in my head?"

"Your first time, it's a big deal . . ."

"But it's me and Griffin, remember? It's so obviously the next step for us."

"It'll be over before you know it. Then you won't have to worry."

"Yeah. I guess so. Can we talk about something else?"

"You know, you don't always have to be the one giving advice. I can listen too."

"I know, I know. Maybe you're right and I should just get the whole sex thing over with. It's just Griffin, right?" I said it again. "Right?"

"Well, you know him better than anyone. He's been kind of like your brother forever."

"Oh my God, that's disgusting."

"I don't mean it like that. It's just, you were best friends for so long that the thought of having sex with him might be weird."

I wondered if I should tell her about my crush on Pete—perhaps she could help me figure it out. I was just about to try to bring it up when she spoke.

"So I tried to ask the hot guy out. Pete."

Jealousy flared through me. Pete Loewen was *nothing* to me, so I shouldn't care. Oh God. I was going to have to watch Pete and Cleo together the *whole* time.

"Huh. So, um, when are you seeing him?" I asked, trying not to sound like I felt.

"Mr. Sleeps-Around turned me down. Me?" Her eyes widened. "I told him I'd heard he wasn't the type to turn women down and he laughed. He's going to have to do the running around when he realizes what he's missing." She pulled her music-playing phone out of her bag. "Oooh, gotta take this. It's Joe—I think things might work out with him."

"Joe Friesen?"

She nodded.

"See you later," I said. I leaned against my locker and took a breath. Thank God Pete had turned Cleo down, although I couldn't understand why he'd done it. She had boys after her all the time. He was probably playing hard to get. I slammed my hand against the cool metal door. I hated that I was thinking about him again.

I pushed off from my locker and jogged down the corridor, suddenly keen to get out of school, glad classes were over for the day. I shoved open the main door and stepped out, rain dampening my hair and clothes. I should have gone back, but instead I hurried out the front entrance, my shoes splashing up water. Ruined. I was being an idiot. I stopped under a clump of trees in the small park opposite the school, feeling weirdly free. The rain eased off a little and I smoothed my hair behind my ears, wiping my face on my sleeve. The wet and the cold felt bracing, and my skin tingled. When a hand touched my upper arm I almost jumped out of my soaking clothes.

I spun round and was practically in Pete Loewen's arms. I could see dewy drops of rain on his cheeks and I could smell the cigarette he must have just smoked. I'd imagined being close to him more times than I cared to admit, but it was even better in real life. The rain slowed to a light drizzle.

"So," he said, his mouth easing into a smile.

"I, uh, what, um." Not cool.

"I wondered if I'd be able to get anywhere near you," he said.

My heart was slamming, my skin on fire. I figured steam was probably rising from me, considering the heat generated between us. I should have stepped back but I couldn't stop looking in his eyes. They were the colour of flint.

As I stared at him, I figured something out. He *wanted* me. I could *tell*. No, I was being ridiculous. He could have his pick of any girl in the school—he'd just turned Cleo down. I was way too ordinary for a guy like him. A girl like Cleo was tall, slim, gorgeous, whereas I was just . . . just okay.

"I, uh, should go," I stammered. My body was humming. This close I could see a tiny scar cutting up from his top lip. Silvery. I wanted to touch it.

"So, Amy," he said. His voice was low and steady. "Finally we get to talk. It seems like you've been wanting to talk to me."

"I, um, I don't know what you mean." *He knew my name!*

"I've seen you staring. You're sweet when you blush."

The blush I'd been trying to stop seared my cheeks. I stood my ground. "I haven't been, um, staring at you," I said, my voice coming out way less confident than I wanted it to.

"I saw you the first day I started at this school. You and your *boyfriend*."

"Huh. I, uh, hadn't noticed."

"If you say so."

He leaned closer, and even though his lips weren't touching mine, I felt the warmth of his breath. His face was damp from the rain.

He murmured, "You're a terrible liar. I know you've been looking at me, because I've been looking at you."

My insides zipped all the way up and I sucked in a breath.

"So what's the deal with you and that guy?"

"Griffin?"

"Him."

"He's my, uh, boyfriend."

"Are you sure?"

I stood with my face upturned, his mouth a heartbeat away from mine. With a fierce jolt, I knew I wanted him to kiss me more than anything.

"This is crazy," I mumbled, mustering all my self-control, but wanting to cover the millimetres between us and taste his lips on mine.

He murmured, "I'm not so bad, you know." His expression was hard to read. He stepped back, leaving me with nothing but cold air on my mouth.

"That's not what everyone says," I managed to whisper.

His eyes narrowed and he gave the smallest of nods, like my words had just confirmed something he didn't want to hear. Just as I was trying to understand what was going on in his head, he turned his back and sauntered across the street to school like nothing had happened.

And nothing had happened. Technically.

AFTER THE NON-INCIDENT (WHICH IS WHAT I WAS CALLING IT) WITH Pete in the park, I forced him from my mind and tried extra hard to be the perfect girlfriend. I kept my head down at school, ignoring Pete Loewen at all times, kept things light with Griffin and tried not to think about the night of my birthday.

But November 3 rolled around faster than I could have imagined. The idea was to have supper first with Cleo, Griffin and my parents. Cleo knew all about the big sex plan, so she kept smirking at me.

Mum ordered in Thai food from the place she always used when we had Thai, and the table in our cozy kitchen was laden with foil boxes full of spicy and steaming delicacies. Everything smelled delicious, but because I knew what was coming later, my gut was knotted like a rope. I wasn't even sure I could eat. I found it hard to look at Griffin. I reassured myself that after this, everything would start to feel normal again.

Dad came to join us at the table and everyone served themselves.

My phone vibrated in my pocket. I pulled it out. A text from a number I didn't recognize. It read:

Bet Ur thinking about me.

Pete? It had to be him.

My heart leaped about like a fish in a net. I swallowed the feeling. "Could someone, uh, pass me the, um, green curry?" I had studiously avoided speaking to Pete since the moment together in the rain. The non-incident—so unimportant I hadn't even told Cleo, so unimportant it was *all* I'd been thinking about—had been interfering with my concentration at school.

Mum handed over a silver box of hot curry. I smiled quickly at her but she didn't smile back. She looked even paler than usual, with dark blue circles under her eyes: I should probably have made time to ask her what was up.

Dad chatted away. "I can't believe you're seventeen, my gorgeous birthday girl. I remember the day you were born. You had this little scrunched-up face and crossed eyes and a little upturned nose and you were the most beautiful baby in the whole world. You used to burp so loudly—"

"*Dad*, stop."

"You were a darling. When you were about four, you came up to me and said, *Can I marry you when I'm older, Dad?*"

"Gross, *stop!*" I cried, giggling. I was enjoying the banter with my dad, while secretly thrilling at the idea that Pete was waiting for me to reply.

Dad said, "You wept when I explained you couldn't ever marry me—"

Mum cut in. "Anyone want any cashew chicken? I got an extra box because I know you like it, Griffin."

Griffin said, "Sure, thanks. Remember when we met, Bird? You were in a clump of bushes. You had a broken leg."

"Could we all *stop* with the nostalgia?" I begged.

"Ah, so modest," Dad said. "But it's your birthday, so we're supposed to talk about you." He started coughing. "Gah, hot chili, sorry."

My phone vibrated again. I slid it out of my pocket to give it a glance.

Am I right? Cos I'm thinking about you. X Pete

Mum's eyes sharpened. "Who's that?"

I hardly heard her. My whole head was full of Pete's intense eyes, his hot, smoky mouth. "Um, someone, uh, wishing me happy birthday. I'll deal with it later." I shouldn't be thinking about Pete with Griffin right here. I shouldn't be thinking about Pete at all. I switched off my phone and shoved it deep into my pocket.

Griffin said, "Did you get the history homework done?" He was wearing a white shirt and his hair looked like he'd just washed it—clean and shiny.

"All done," I said.

Cleo elbowed me. "Of course she did, but do we have to talk about homework now? I'm trying to eat here."

Dad said, "None of that. Did I tell you, Griffin, about my plan for an extension at the back of the house? We're going to use it for company offices."

Mum sighed heavily, and Dad hesitated, clenching his teeth. When she said nothing, he continued talking to Griffin. "The solar bricks are going to take off. You know, no one's ever thought about this before, yet by my calculations they catch twenty-one percent more sunlight than solar panels. I just need some more start-up money and we'll be—"

Mum interrupted with "Okay, time for gifts."

I opened my presents. Here's what I got:

- Cleo—A silver necklace with a twisty pendant.
- Mum and Dad—Money, and a memory card for my camera that can hold way more photos than my old one, and a subscription to a great photography magazine.
- Auntie Mel—Money.
- Uncle Robb—A postcard from some hostel in Tibet. At least he remembered!
- Griffin—A playlist for my iPod. I flicked through the songs. There was the goofy Simon and Garfunkel song we'd kissed to the first time. There was the Minpins song we'd been listening to when he'd told me he loved me. There was the Lhasa album we had on in the background when we studied. And a load of my favourites plus a load of his.

We finished supper. Cleo winked one of her big eyes at me—

knowingly—and then she left. Mum and Dad started to bicker about something, so Griffin and I took the opportunity to slip out.

Griffin took my hand. The plan was unfolding. The stones of his gravel path crunched underfoot. I shivered in the cool night air. As we went inside, I noticed how quiet the house seemed. His mum was out somewhere with a friend, like he'd told me she would be. She rarely went out, and without her there, the house felt lonely. The corridor was too narrow and the book-lined walls closed in. I remembered running in there when I was nine or ten with a cut knee. I was sobbing hysterically and Griffin's mum took me in her arms. I wondered now why I didn't go to my own mother.

Griffin's mum was so different since his dad died. She'd always been a bit . . . eccentric, I guess, but after the death, she wafted about like a ghost. I knew Griffin made her supper most nights, and once, from my window, I saw him supporting her as she stumbled along the corridor to her room. I pretended I hadn't seen anything because it felt like that was what he wanted. Along with my crush on Pete, it was one more thing we didn't talk about.

He stopped at the bottom of the stairs now and leaned forward to kiss me. I kissed him back, telling myself this was what I wanted.

"I love you, Bird." He kissed along my jaw toward my neck, which he knew I liked.

"Mmm," I murmured.

"You're so beautiful." He tugged at my waistband and pulled me against him. I could feel through his jeans that he was hard. He slipped his hand up my top.

I felt myself freeze, but to stop him noticing, I said, "Let's go upstairs." He was being confident and assertive, and I should have been pleased. Instead, it just made me more uncomfortable.

He pulled back, his eyes searching mine, and after a pause, he kissed me on the nose. "I love you."

I didn't feel I could respond to him, but I followed anyway, my heart pounding like it was trying to break out of my body. I told myself I'd made him wait long enough. But everything felt so *wrong*.

"Griffin," I murmured to his back, "wait."

He didn't hear me. He got to the top of the stairs and beckoned me up. I joined him and he wrapped me in a warm hug. He said, "I can't believe we're finally doing this."

When I even *looked* at Pete, my body responded like I was dissolving. A tiny voice called out from deep inside me: *you've never felt anything like that with Griffin.*

Griffin pulled me along, kicking open his door, still holding on to me. We half fell into his room. He'd made the bed with new-smelling maroon sheets and covered the pillows with rose petals and paper cut-out hearts. He was such a . . . such a . . .

"It's, um, perfect," I stammered, trying to be nice.

"You okay?"

I looked at the hearts lying on the pillows. Each one had writing on it. I stepped closer to see more clearly what the words said.

FOR BIRD I LOVE YOU HAPPY BIRTHDAY

"Um, cute," I said. I wanted him to tell me that it was all one big goofy joke, that really we were going to go outside and ride our bikes and hang out like we used to when we were kids, laughing and racing each other from the top of the hill to the lake. When did we stop being kids? When did we stop being *friends*? He began to unbutton my top. Then, with some fiddling, he flipped the clasp of my bra.

He said into my hair, "I have condoms."

"Uh-huh."

His cheek was warm against my ear. Embarrassed? Turned on? He lay back on the bed and pulled me closer. My hands wanted to cover every bit of me.

"I love you, Bird." His pupils widened. He really meant it. He wriggled out of his T-shirt and I kissed his chest. His hand was in my jeans; the buttons had come undone.

He said, "Are you sure?"

"Mm-hmm." I nodded, keeping my gaze from his.

He helped me get my jeans off and took off his own. Now both of us were nearly naked. I curled my legs up but he man-oeuvred them straight with his thighs.

"Don't be nervous," he said. "It's me."

He pulled at my underwear, which I had to kick to get free from my legs. One of his hands cupped my breast. My breath came out faster.

He reached over to his bedside table and, from the drawer, pulled out a condom, tearing the package carefully with his teeth. "Can you put it on?" he murmured. He laid me back on the bed and smoothed my hair from my face.

My hands were clammy, as if I had a fever.

"You're beautiful," Griffin was saying.

Just him telling me I was beautiful made me feel irritated with him—like, couldn't he just stop *talking*?

"Just relax," he suggested.

I twisted awkwardly below him. We were so close to . . . to actually doing it.

I froze.

"Bird, is something wrong?"

It's strange how your body can be one place and your brain somewhere else entirely. Lying there in Griffin's arms, I thought of a third Top Tip for my website.

TOP TIP 3: IT'S CALLED A COMFORT ZONE FOR A REASON

"Griffin, I'm really sorry," I muttered.

He stopped and looked at me.

I held his gaze. "I can't do this," I said. I jumped up off the bed, pulling the sheet with me to cover myself. "I'm sorry, I . . . I'm really sorry," I stammered again. "I just . . ."

He slumped back. "Oh, Bird." He added, "I don't get it."

Suddenly I wanted to be far away, climbing a tree or taking a photograph of an empty street. I found my knickers and slipped them on. I grabbed my bra and shirt. I still hadn't answered him. I said, "I should go."

"What's wrong?" he pleaded.

"Um, Mum and Dad will be wondering where I am."

"We should talk. You've been trying to slow things down. This is my fault." Concern spread like a blush across his face. "You know I love you, right?"

Even though it was me causing all the drama, my skin prickled with annoyance that he wouldn't just let me go. "Everything's fine," I said. I scrambled to get on my jeans. "I just have to go."

"Will you wait for me tomorrow to walk to school?" He sounded like he used to when he was a kid.

I couldn't be cruel to him. I bent forward and kissed him gently.

"Of course," I said. "Sure."

CHAPTER 5

Thurs 4 Nov

Dear Miss Take-Control-of-Your-Life,

I did a stuuupid thing but I thought Id got away with it. I didnt tell anyone not even my closest friends but someone saw me . . . now everyone knows . . . Im in so much trouble.

A Liar

Dear A Liar,

Don't be too hard on yourself. I don't know from your letter what you did, but my imagination is running wild!

<u>Tips to Take Back Control</u>

I could tell you all the things you're probably telling yourself. You know that you should have come clean before you got found out, that you shouldn't have done whatever it was that got you into all this trouble in the first place, etc. But what good would come from me telling you what you already know?

Apologize.

And face up to what's happened. That's all you can do.
From one teen to another . . .

Miss Take-Control-of-Your-Life

After I was done answering A Liar, I wrote a to-do list:

- Bring out winter clothes and pack away summer things—
  it's definitely full-on winter: stop kidding yourself!
- Review website stats—up or down this month?
- Is there time for a job with schoolwork this year? Write
  list of pros and cons.
- Get ahead with reading for English. Books next to bed.

I'd start going through the list as soon as I got home. Right
now, it was time to get on with the day.

On my way out the house, I passed the kitchen and saw
Mum leaning against the counter, her eyes shut. On the fridge
to her right were all her lists for the week. She was dressed
and ready for work in the black suit she always wore (she had
four that were practically the same), but she seemed different somehow. I checked my watch—I didn't have time to talk
to her.

I texted Griffin.

Leaving right now. By any chance, u awake?

He texted straight back.

Slept in. Bad night. Can u wait?

Pulling my front door closed behind me, I glanced over at his
house. The curtains weren't even open. I knew I should wait
for him—I'd said I would—and I should deal with everything

from the night before. My tummy clenched at the thought. I texted back.

Will see you at school. Love u. Am sorry.

I hoped he realized I was apologizing both for not waiting for him *and* for everything else. I shoved my phone in my pocket and hurried down the road, keeping my eyes glued to the ground.

I WAS AT SCHOOL, DRINKING MY LATTE, PUTTING A BOOK AWAY IN MY locker, when Cleo cornered me and said, "If you don't tell me, I'm going to scream."

"Cleo—"

"How was it? You had *sex for the first time* and you haven't called me. What? Am I, like, not your best friend or what?"

"Come on, that's not it."

"You did do it, didn't you? You didn't bail on him, did you, Bird?"

"I wasn't—"

She interrupted, "How was he? What was it like? Was it better than I said it would be, or was it crap?"

"I didn't—"

Kitty Moss, a skinny blonde who always wore too much makeup, came over. "Everyone can hear you guys," she said.

"Leave us alone," Cleo said.

"So you finally did it with Griffin," Kitty said. "About time. Poor guy was probably wondering what was wrong with you."

"Just go away," Cleo said, turning her fiercest glare onto Kitty, whose slow eyebrow raise showed she wasn't bothered at all.

"I'll bet Griffin was glad to be put out of his misery. God knows what he sees in you," Kitty said to me.

"Things are great with Griffin."

"Sure, that's why he looks so puppy dog all the time," Kitty said. "I bet you didn't even do it, Miss Perfect."

"We did," I lied, heat high on my cheeks.

Cleo said, "Come on, Bird." She pulled me away and into the girls' toilets, slamming the door behind us. Then she said, "She's such a bitch."

"She's right. Griffin's unhappy."

Cleo shook her head. "Of course he's not. He loves you."

"Yeah." I clambered up to sit on the table next to the sinks and swung my legs beneath me.

She said, "You know that, right?"

I picked at a split end in my hair. "Course. How are things going with Joe?"

"Joe Friesen? Forget him. So tell me, you think I should ask out Mark? He seems pretty nice and I know you keep saying I should date guys who are nice."

"Did I say that? When?"

"Well, you were right about Xavier. He was *not* a nice guy. Hot, though—shame so many other girls agree." She grinned. "Anyway, that's the end of that. So should I ask Mark to the party? Should I just ask him straight out or be more subtle? Oh, I have to email you the stuff about the caterers so you can help me chose."

Cleo was having a big party—she did it every November, figuring it made the worst month of the year bearable.

"You, *subtle*? Ask him. He'd be crazy to turn you down. Just go for it. I love that you're brave enough to ask a guy out—I would be too scared."

"Don't guys like to take the lead? I read that somewhere. On your website, maybe, in one of your answers to someone?" She gushed, "Miss Take-Control-of-Your-Life, tell me what to do!"

"Um, remember to be casual. Be yourself. And *don't* call me that here. It's a secret, remember?"

She jumped up to sit next to me, precariously. The table groaned in protest. "Casual is *not* a problem for me. It's commitment I find hard. Hang on. How are we talking about me and not you? How do you always manage to do that? Come on. I want to hear all the details about your hot sex life."

The bell rang and a girl burst in, clearly hurrying so as not to be late to class.

"I'll tell you later," I said. "Send me that catering stuff and I'll get back to you."

A Top Tip for my website slid guiltily into my brain, to be typed in when I got home.

TOP TIP 4: SOMETIMES YOU'RE LYING WHEN YOU SAY NOTHING AT ALL

I REALIZED I WAS AVOIDING GRIFFIN WHEN I DUCKED OUT OF SCHOOL at the end of the day without even looking for him. This was ridiculous. He was my *boyfriend*, my best friend, the person I was most intimate with in the world, and I was acting like this. We hadn't spoken *all day*. I crossed into the park opposite the school and slunk to sit shivering on the bench by the lake. The water was calm but reflected the deep grey clouds above. There was a rumour that snow was coming. In London. In November. The weather was going mad. The world was going crazy. I let out a deep sigh just as Pete Loewen appeared in front of me.

He crossed his arms and said, "Look who we've got here."

I stood up, which only made me physically closer to him. I was surprised to find I was furious with him for the way he kept getting into my head. My tone sharp, I said, "What do you want?"

"Now that's not very friendly."

"God, Pete, what are you playing at? What was that text about on my birthday? How did you even get my number?"

"It was your birthday? I didn't know that. Okay, I did. I saw it on Facebook. And I was right, wasn't I? You were thinking about me."

"You're so arrogant. Of course I wasn't. I don't know you or like you or think about you or . . . or anything." *He'd Facebook stalked me!*

He took a step nearer to me. His eyes were open and honest. "You didn't even bother replying to my texts. What's your problem with me, Amy?"

My body fizzed. I said, softening, "I wasn't thinking about you."

He reached a hand up so that one of his fingers rested on my chin. It was the first time he'd touched me and I held my breath.

He said, "You're a terrible liar."

"I . . . I . . . just . . ." Words were failing me. What did I know about this guy? Nothing. What did I like about him? *Every-*

thing. I liked the way my body felt. I liked the way he seemed to see right through me even though he hardly knew me.

I took a tiny step in his direction.

His hand slid to the back of my neck, making all the hairs on my arms and legs stand to shivery attention.

"Can I kiss you?" he said, and the tone of his voice made me feel like he was hopeful, not arrogant at all. Maybe I'd got everything about him wrong. He said, "Amy?"

He said my name like *I* had bewitched *him*.

And the way he said my name made me do it.

I leaned my face up toward him and pressed my lips lightly to his. God, his mouth felt good against mine. I kissed him a little harder, letting my tongue slip to touch his. Then he put his other hand along my back and crushed me against him. My arms were around him, his tongue was in my mouth, my body melted entirely in his embrace and I felt . . . free.

When I was eight years old, I climbed up a tree and told my mum I was a bird. Before she could stop me, I jumped out the branches trying to fly.

I could remember being at the top of the tree, the branches wide around me, the leaves dancing in the breeze. I'd balanced at the edge of one branch and looked into the blue, tempting sky. My mum had screamed at me, "No, Amy, stop."

"I'm a bird," I cried, and flew.

That was how I broke my leg.

Now, in the park, with huge effort, I pushed Pete away. I wiped my mouth. This was too risky. I cried, "What am I doing?"

His grey eyes sparked with frustration.

"I can't, Pete." I took another step back. "I can't believe I did that. Oh my God." I turned away from him and started walking fast. I had to get out of there. I had to get as far away from Pete Loewen as possible.

I spent the rest of the evening ignoring my phone and studying hard. When I went to bed, I couldn't help but notice that Pete hadn't texted. And that Griffin had—three times.

THE NEXT MORNING I SLEPT THROUGH MY ALARM. IMMEDIATELY UPON waking I checked the time, bewildered, and then I thought of Pete, remembering him sliding his hand to the back of my neck, remembering him kissing me. My skin got goosebumpy. For a moment, I felt light and cheerful. Weird that I could be happy when I should be feeling like the worst person on earth. My joyful mood dissolved like sugar in hot water. I'd *cheated* on Griffin. Cheating was the sort of thing other people did. Not *me*.

My phone beeped. It was Griffin. Guilt seeped through my veins.

Am outside. U up? We really need to talk xxx

I stuck my head up to look out the window. I'd forgotten to shut the curtains the night before. The sky was full of white flurries. It was snowing! I sat up properly and looked down to the road. The whole of the street was blanketed in white. A car was trying to weave along the road, headlights on. And there was Griffin, waiting by my front gate.

He waved. I waved back and sent him a text. Going through the motions.

Give me 5 mins.

Outside, my boots sank in the thick snow blanketing the front steps. The cold sneaked up the sleeves of my jacket and twisted round my arms. Brrr. Griffin stood looking the other way. He wore a black coat and striped red-and-navy scarf. He swivelled his head and a smile lit up his face. He looked good. Bright blue eyes, big smile. My camera was slung round my neck. I lifted it and clicked. In the digital screen, I could see it was a good photo. A perfect image of a perfect moment in a teen girl's life: cute, loving boyfriend framed by the snowy street. I felt suddenly tired and worn out. I had to tell him what I'd done. Oh my God, what had I done? Telling him would ruin everything.

He threw a snowball at me and it hit me lightly on my jacket, bursting into powdery flakes. "Hey, Bird," he said, "you look pretty in the snow."

TOP TIP 5: SNOW SUCKS

"It looked good from the window," I said, wondering guiltily if *Pete* found me pretty. "But it's so cold," I added.

"I didn't know we even had snow like this in England," Griffin said. He was so oblivious of what was going on inside my head, so oblivious of what a lying, cheating, horrible girl I really was.

I smiled at him, trudged down the path and kissed him lightly on his cold lips as he was expecting. "It's November. It's crazy. I'll have to buy proper boots."

"Even with the wrong boots, you do look really pretty."

"Griffin—"

"Come on, Bird, lighten up. Let's not talk about the other night right now."

I remembered the last time I'd seen Griffin as I rushed out of his room.

Later, I told myself, *I'll tell him later.* The argument began in my head. I had to tell him about kissing Pete, I had to deal with it, I had to fix what I'd done.

Or I could break up with him. I could tell Griffin it was over and, I dunno, start dating Pete.

Just the idea made my brain whirl. I could never actually *do* something like that, could I? It would be so . . . so . . . I imagined telling Cleo that I'd dumped Griffin to be with a guy who *everyone* knew was no good. I just wasn't the sort of girl who fell in love with a bad boy and started breaking all the rules. *Drugs? Expelled?* Those were the words that came to mind when I thought about Pete. Plus, I couldn't be sure he even really liked me. He was the kind of guy I warned Cleo about all the time, the kind *she* adored. Sure, Pete seemed to have a soft, sweet side when he spoke to me, but he was probably like that with all the girls. Even thinking about Pete made me all confused and crazy. There was no way I could date him.

I looked at Griffin standing there, as excited by the snow as a lovable puppy. With Griffin, I knew exactly where I was and where we were going. I plastered on a smile and slipped my camera from my neck to place it safely in my bag.

"You have to catch me first."

I started running but the slippery blanket under my feet made me tumble. Griffin grabbed me before I fell, which made both of us collapse onto the snowy ground.

"You want to take the day off with me?" he said, pinning me down. Snow slithered down my neck.

"What are you talking about?"

"No school. Don't you check your email?"

Good. No school. No Pete. Although half of me wanted to see him, half of me was dreading it. "I only just got up."

"You got up late? What's wrong with you?"

"I guess I just—"

He flopped down next to me and we lay cuddled in the cold, nose to nose. "I'm worried about Mom," he said.

I waited for him to say more. It was rare that he wanted to share his worries. His breath came out in steamy clouds that puffed over my cheeks.

"How's she doing?" I prompted.

"Not great. I don't know. She left the oven on last night."

I put my hand up to his chest. My fingers were so cold I could hardly feel the wool of his sweater.

He continued, "I don't know what to do."

"You can't deal with this on your own, Griffin."

He said quietly, "I know. But I don't want anyone else involved."

"Surely they have someone in Social Services or something— someone who could give you some support."

He glared at me. "This isn't anyone's business but mine. She just hasn't got over Dad yet."

"Let me help, then."

"I shouldn't have said anything. It'll be fine. I don't need any help."

Bile rose in my mouth—I was disgusted with myself. Griffin needed me. I pulled him closer.

He kissed me. His mouth was warm. Familiar. Nice. And completely different from Pete's mouth.

I mumbled, "I'm sorry, G. I just have to tell you—"

"You have nothing to be sorry for. It's me who's been pressuring you. I get it."

"That's not true. It's normal to want— It's not you. You're great."

He turned so his face was in profile. "I just wish it was easier right now. I wish Mom would just, I dunno, just get back to her old self."

I was selfish and horrible and awful to even think about ending things when he was going through such a hard time. He needed reassurance. He needed a proper *girlfriend*.

I forced thoughts of Pete and what had happened from my mind, and I said, "No school, hmm?"

His eyebrows lifted. My back was freezing. The ground was very hard. He kissed me on the neck.

"What do you want to do?" His voice was low, his breath close to my ear.

I was about to answer when a white car skidded round the corner and swerved to a stop near a tree. We both sat up as the horn beeped into the still air.

"Who *is* that?" Griffin said, pushing his hair back off his face.

It was such a familiar gesture and it drove me crazy, but not in a good way. I reminded myself that he was just being *himself*. It was me who had to get my head in the right place.

The window opened and Cleo stuck out her head. Her dark brown skin and big dark eyes contrasted with the white of her car and the white of the snow around her. She wore a cute sky-blue woolly hat and white scarf. Movie star. She puffed words into the frigid air: "Come on, lovebirds, get up and get a room. Check out my dad's car!"

"You nearly crashed," I yelled.

"Yeah, yeah."

"You haven't passed your driving test yet!" I was giggling.

Griffin's eyes narrowed. He jumped up and pulled me after him, then dusted the snow off us both in swift, light slaps. We stumbled over to her. I grabbed my camera from my bag and took a few photos of her posing out through her car window.

"Make sure you get me at my best, darling," she cried. She had the hugest smile on her face. She said, "Mum and Dad are away. The car was sitting there, like, calling me to drive it. *Cleo,* it said. *Cleo, come and drive me.* Too tempting. *No school,* it said—"

"You're crazy," I cut in.

"Come on, where shall we go?" she asked

"How about . . . um, I don't know," I said.

She said to Griffin, "I'm almost qualified. Don't look at me like that."

Griffin's blue eyes deepened to indigo. "We're supposed to spend the day, the two of us, together," he muttered so Cleo wouldn't hear.

"I know," I whispered back.

Cleo honked the horn. "Enough secret talk. Get in."

I shook my head. "You can't drive. You haven't passed your test."

"Bird, live a little, would you? Come on, Griffin."

"I'm staying right where Bird is."

I looked at him. I looked at Cleo in the car. My blood quickened. I imagined us driving somewhere we'd never been before, the snowy road like a blank page waiting for us to write a new story on it.

I said, full of enthusiasm, "Should we, Griffin? It might be fun."

He shrugged. "If you say so."

I leaned in her window. "Okay, then, where do you want to go?"

She said, "Anywhere."

Griffin said, "Bird, are you sure?"

Cleo said, "I won't kill us. I got here, didn't I?"

"She did," I said, then wished I hadn't contradicted him, because he turned away.

He started walking back toward his house. It seemed like lately one of us was always walking away from the other. My heart squeezed to see him trudging through the snow.

I turned to my friend. "I can't, Cleo."

TOP TIP 6: YOU *CAN* REGRET WHAT YOU HAVEN'T DONE

She wrinkled her nose. "Yeah, yeah. I knew it. You're way too, you know, sensible," she said. She wasn't being mean, but the words crawled like wasps under my jacket and stung me hard. She chattered on. "Calm that lovely boy of yours down. I'll leave the car here and we can hang out. Unless you guys want to, you know, spend some quality time together?"

"No," I said, a little too abruptly. "It's fine," I added. "Give me five minutes. By the way, that hat is very cute."

She looked sorrowfully at the car as she got out. "It could have been so fun," she said.

"Look, go over to my house and see what we have for breakfast," I said to her. "Here's the key. Mum's at work. And you know what Dad's like; he won't mind. I'll come back in a few minutes. Let me just go get Griffin and we'll all eat together."

I jogged up to Griffin's house, my shoes sliding on the ice. The air hung empty and crisp. I pushed open his front door and called to him, "Griffin, don't be angry."

He appeared in the corridor, definitely angry. "I just don't get you. It's like you're, I dunno, just different today."

"No, I'm not. I'm sorry."

He pushed the hair from his eyes. "I just don't . . . I don't understand."

"I guess we should probably talk."

"Right." He leaned against one of the bookshelves that lined the corridor wall. "Okay, what?"

"I've, um, I have to tell you something . . ." My voice trailed off and I grasped for the right words.

His mum burst onto the upstairs landing. She flung her arms wide. "Bird, little Bird, you're so big now. My Griffin loves you, dearest Birdy." She danced out of sight.

"Mom," Griffin called, pushing away from the bookshelves. He said to me, "Sorry. I'll come over to your place in a while. Go hang with Cleo."

"Do you want me to stay?" I added, "Can I help? Griffin?"

"No, just go. She's not herself."

I said, "Cleo and I are making breakfast next door. Come over when you're ready."

He replied quickly, "Yeah, okay, whatever. I'll see where things are at."

"Really, I can stay."

He shook his head. He was already halfway up the stairs. "It's okay, Mom."

She yelled, "Can I get a biscuit? I want a biscuit."

I felt tears pricking my eyes: Griffin's mum frightened me— I'd never seen her so childish. Griffin shouldn't be handling all this on his own. He needed help, but I was the only one who knew what was going on and he wouldn't even let *me* help. If I called someone in, he'd be furious.

I hesitated, not sure what to do, then I opened the door quietly and headed into the chilly morning.

CHAPTER 6

Thurs 11 Nov

Dear Miss Take-Control-of-Your-Life,

I have never written for advice before and you'll probably think this is nothing. Well, we were all at this party. It was Jamie's birthday. I have never had a girlfriend and I have been friends with Jamie since we were really young. He's always the life and soul of the party, and he's got a beautiful girl. Anyway, it was getting late and his girlfriend and me were in the kitchen just chatting. Well, on some weird impulse I kissed her on the mouth, and she kissed me back. We didn't say much and went back to the others. I can't get her out of my mind. I don't know what to do.

CyberG, 15

I was the worst teenage advice columnist ever. I couldn't figure out how other people made it look so easy to give advice when I was so clueless. I typed out a lame answer and deleted it, retyped it, deleted it again. I needed to find my confident Miss Take-Control self. Everything going on in my own life was getting in the way of me being able to deal with CyberG's question, and I was sick of being so overwhelmed with my own drama: Griffin, his mum, Pete. Okay . . . kissing the wrong person—with my own recent experience, I should be able to figure out the right thing to say.

I read the question over, then began to type.

Dear CyberG,

Your friend Jamie probably doesn't realize that you are a bit jealous of him and his life. It doesn't seem to me that you really like this girl, even though you're thinking about her now you've kissed her—that's normal. Earlier you describe her by saying, "He's got a beautiful girl." It makes me think you want her because she's *his* girlfriend.

Tips to Take Back Control

I think you need to realize that if a guy like Jamie is friends with you, you probably have a lot to offer.

Don't betray Jamie again.

Try to find confidence in yourself without taking what he has.

Forget about the girl. Your friendship is worth more than that.

From one teen to another . . .

Miss Take-Control-of-Your-Life

Pete appeared in my mind—I could feel his skin against mine, his lips on my mouth. Thinking about him made me wince. Lying to Griffin and to everyone about Pete had turned me into . . . into someone I didn't recognize.

At least now I knew it had meant nothing to him. A week had gone by but Pete hadn't spoken to me or even looked in my direction; he hadn't texted, hadn't called. My secret played large in my head. Cleo had no idea, and I couldn't figure out how to tell her—she was my best friend, but the thought of voicing what I'd done made me feel more guilty.

Griffin met me at school every day and neither of us mentioned the sex thing, even though the whole issue stood between us like a giant. Or maybe the real issue was that *I'd kissed someone else.*

I focused on being Miss Take-Control-of-Your-Life as I flicked through the pages of my site. I landed on the Top Tips section and typed in:

TOP TIP 7: SECRETS BREED LIES

Mum came into the room and, automatically, I minimized the screen.

"What are you doing?"

"Homework. You know."

She nodded but didn't seem to be listening.

"You should knock," I said.

"Yeah. And you should keep it clean in here."

She was distracted, not even looking at me. For weeks she'd been grumpy and unpredictable; hormones and menopause or whatever.

Her pale eyes darted left and right, clearly surveying the mess. She snapped, "Bird, I mean it. Tidy up."

"Okay, relax."

"When did you get so slovenly? You're as tidy as I am, normally." She picked up a couple of books and put them next to me on the desk.

"Mum, I'll clean it up, all right? I've just got a lot on. I don't know, it just got away from me. It's like the first time ever. I promise it'll be tidy by the end of the day."

She stopped and gave me a quizzical look, her fair eyebrows furrowing together. "You have no idea, do you?"

"What?"

My phone beeped on the desk. A text flashed up.

Thinking about me? Pete

Mum leaned forward, blatantly looking at the lit-up screen of my phone. "Who's Pete?"

I spun round in my chair. "God, Mum, don't read my texts."

"I'm not."

"Yes, you are. Anyway, he's no one. Just someone who I'm doing a project with. Look, do you want something?" Pete's text felt like a code for the fact *he* was thinking about *me*. Which made no sense—he hadn't *spoken* to me all week.

She blinked a couple of times. "You know, I spent so long wishing for another baby that I wonder if I did a good enough job of being your mum. Did I?"

I concentrated on what she was saying. "What are you talking about?"

She spoke softly. "You should have another quotation on your board: *Happiness is when what you think, what you say, and what you do are in harmony.* Mahatma Gandhi."

"Mum, what do you mean about the baby? What's going on?"

Her eyes moistened. She kissed me on the top of my head.

"Don't worry about it now, darling. Just get back to work. Perhaps when you've got some time, I could take some photos of you, like we used to."

"Sure. Is everything okay?"

But she was already on her way out the room and she didn't reply.

IT WAS LIKE MY ROOM WAS A STATION THAT EVENING AND MY PARENTS had trains to catch. After Mum left, Dad wandered in.

"Hey, Birdy," he said.

"What is this? Parents-Gone-Mad Day?"

"Just seeing how my sweet Bird is."

"Uh, trying to do homework."

"Right. I'm going for a run."

I burst out laughing. "What sort of run?"

"I want to do an Iron Man. It's not funny."

Wow. He was being serious. I thought, *Why don't you try running to the end of the road first?* But I didn't say anything. He was so busy chatting about the distance he needed to complete that he wouldn't have heard me anyway.

"Sounds good, Dad. Look, is Mum all right?"

He paced across the room and sat on the bed, resting his hands on his knees. "Ah, little Birdy, I don't know."

"She was a bit—"

"Don't worry yourself. It'll all fall into place. The solar bricks are such a good idea. I can just feel it."

"Right."

"I'll let you get back to work, then," he said, standing abruptly.

"Did you, you know, want something?"

He jogged on the spot. "Got to get training," he said, and puffed out the room like an elephant.

It would have been funny if everything hadn't felt so weird.

Finally alone, I uploaded some photos onto my computer. I'd started work on a photography project on the theme of colour. I looked for groups of the same colour and photographed them—a white building against a milky sky; a purple flower in an oily puddle next to an indigo boot; a green umbrella resting on the grass. Then I uploaded some neat images of a discarded newspaper caught in a breeze, which I took on the afternoon of the snow day. The white-and-black pages against the white of the snow looked cool. Next were the photos of Cleo in her car. I emailed them to her. For a while, I'd been toying with the idea of getting a job at a photographer's studio—extra money wouldn't hurt and it would be interesting work. I wasn't sure it would help with applying for Oxford, though—perhaps I should try to do something that might lead to a job later on. Temping in a lawyer's office or something. Although I didn't think I wanted to be a lawyer, it sounded good on paper.

The photograph of Griffin standing in the snow came up on the screen. Automatically, I glanced out my window. He was sitting at his desk, probably playing a computer game. I watched him. I was just about to text him to look up when my phone rang. It was Pete.

I answered, knowing I shouldn't. "What do you want?"

He said softly, "What do *you* want?"

"Pete, stop. You've ignored me all week. I don't want to play your games."

"*You* haven't even looked at *me* all week," he said. "I miss your little glances my way."

My tummy flipped. Griffin leaned back in his desk chair, saw me through the window and smiled.

I said, far more firmly than I felt, "Don't think you can just text me and call me whenever you want. I've got a boyfriend. Look, I'm sorry, but we should just forget it. It shouldn't have happened."

He said, "Call me when you know that's not true."

The silence on the end of the line told me he'd ended the call and the conversation. For the moment.

CHAPTER 7

Mon 15 Nov

Dear Miss Take-Control-of-Your-Life,

My friend is super angry with me becoz i keep buying the same clothes as her and copying what she says. she yelled at me that i need to get my own Life. Im scared everyone hates me . . . I hate my life . . . its ordinary and pathetic. My friend has an Awesome life and Awesome parents. Theyre so much better than mine . . . my dads an alcoholic and my mum tells me shes leaving him but never does . . . I want to be someone else . . . famous, rich and gorgeous . . . I read celebrity magazines all the time and dream. My life is terrible and i feel like crap from morning until when i go to sleep.

Copycat, 14

Dear Copycat,

You *know* you need to stop copying your friend. You could tell her that you're only trying to flatter her, but she knows you actually want to *be* her, and that totally creeps her out. And take a break from reading celeb mags. They're making you feel worse. (I know, totally addictive, but in your case BAD NEWS.)

Tips to Take Back Control

Tell your best friend what's happening at home. You're dealing with a load of stuff with your family, and your friend—if she's any sort of friend—will probably be more understanding if she knows that. Your home life sounds like a nightmare and it's maybe giving you low self-esteem.

Remember, although I'm sure it's hard, alcoholism is a disease. Your father isn't doing this to hurt you; he just can't stop himself. You might want to look at the support group for families of alcoholics I found for you: click here.

From one teen to another . . .

Miss Take-Control-of-Your-Life

Griffin texted just as I logged off.

Up early—want to walk in together?

I grabbed my bag and texted him on the way down the stairs.

Meet u outside in 2 mins.

The snow had vanished in the rain of the last week and the world outside looked only mildly wintery. Wrapping my arms around myself, I waited for Griffin to join me. I looked up at his window and he waved down. I gestured at my watch and he nodded, disappearing from the frame.

He bounded along the path. "Wow, it's pretty good getting up early."

I laughed. "I've been telling you that for years."

"Mom woke me wanting something—she's fine—but then I couldn't get back to sleep." He yawned, then leaned in to kiss me.

I kissed him lightly, pulled back and said, "Let's get to school."

We walked for a while, an awkward silence booming between us. We got to Coffee Grounds and I ordered my coffee. The bustle in the café eased the weird quiet between us, and Griffin said, "You excited about Cleo's party?"

"I haven't done anything to help."

"She doesn't need help. She always has everything sorted for these things. I don't know how she gets it all together when she seems like the most disorganized person ever."

I put the lid on my coffee cup and we headed back outside, walking through the park to get ourselves to school. As we crossed the spot where I kissed Pete, I felt like I could see my past self in his embrace. Griffin was asking me a question but I didn't hear what he said.

"Are you even listening?" he interrupted.

"Sorry, I'm just, you know, there's a lot of— I guess I'm stressed about how much homework we have."

"You'll be fine, Bird. You've got it all under control. So I was saying, we should plan something fun for the two of us—no schoolwork, no stress. Why don't we go out somewhere?"

"What about Cleo's party? That'd be a good place for us to have fun. I, uh, don't know if I should take any other nights off—with all the schoolwork we have, I mean."

He draped an arm around me. "Sounds good. But I actually meant a date where just the two of us do date stuff—we haven't really ever been on a date. We could get milkshakes or something. A real American 1950s-style date."

I giggled. "I wouldn't have any idea where we could get a milkshake," I said. "But okay, you're right. We should do that. It'd be good for us."

"Surely there's a perfect date place somewhere nearby—I'll figure something out." He squeezed me against him.

Suddenly, I felt like I couldn't breathe. I tucked my head under his chin and tried to get my emotions under control.

I GOT A B IN MY ENGLISH ESSAY, AND I NORMALLY NEVER, *EVER* GOT lower than an A-minus. Then Mr. Hopkins yelled at me for not listening in class and Ms. Devlin criticized my lame attempt at a reply in spoken Spanish. Cleo was busy all day hanging out with Xavier—I saw them arguing in the corridor and then in deep discussion against the lockers. Things seemed to be back on with Xavier—yuck. I was just passing Cleo when Griffin came over. He tried to kiss me, but I ducked my head.

Cleo pulled a face, grabbed Xavier's hand and said, "We're leaving you lovebirds to it." They headed off.

I caught sight of Pete. He was leaning against his locker and staring over at me and Griffin. He held my gaze, making my body quiver, then gave me a slow smile. I could tell he'd seen me avoiding kissing Griffin and I felt in that moment that he could see everything about me. It was a feeling I'd had with Pete before. It was a feeling I enjoyed. I liked how I seemed to Pete—a little wild, a little free. I bit my lip. He stared at me for a second too long, then turned and walked away.

GRIFFIN HAD TO STAY AFTER SCHOOL FOR A GROUP PROJECT MEETING,
so I walked home alone, my mind spinning with the image of
Pete staring at me, of the way I shuddered when Griffin kissed
me and of the way everything in my classes was suddenly going
so wrong.

I arrived home and I could hear Mum's voice spiking the
cool air as I opened the front door.

"What do you expect? What do you honestly expect? We
can't go on like this."

"It's only one more loan." That was my father. "It's brilliant.
Support this, darling."

"Will you stop? Please? I just can't—"

"I'm only doing it for you and Bird."

"For me? For us?"

"Yes, who the bloody hell else?"

She yelled, "The bank called. You tried to get a mortgage on
our house. *My* house. You wanted to put it up as collateral for
your stupid—"

"Oh, it's stupid now, is it?"

"For God's sake."

There was a pause, then Dad said, "You weren't supposed to
know."

"My house," she yelled. "My inheritance from my mother.
The only stable thing in our lives. I can't live with this. With
what you've done."

"We'll be rich, darling. This is going to work. I can feel it.
Support me."

"Support you? How much more can I support you? You're
never going to change," she cried. "I can't believe how much of

my life I've wasted. Can't you see how miserable I am? I don't want—"

I couldn't listen anymore. I headed back out again.

I WALKED FOR A LONG TIME, THINKING ABOUT GRIFFIN, ABOUT MUM and Dad, about Pete, about my life, about what I wanted, whatever that was. The streets were slick with winter night. I was starting to feel like night was sinking all the way through me, that's the sort of mood I was in, when I realized I'd walked nearly all the way back to school. I was at the edge of the little lake in the park opposite the front entrance of the school gates when I heard voices. Three or four guys were laughing, and from the whoops and the shattering of glass, it sounded like they were throwing bottles at trees. Early to be drunk, I thought. And then I felt a little scared: I was all by myself. That's when one of them noticed me as I stood there like an idiot.

"All right, darlin'?" he yelled, walking toward me.

My breath caught. It was Pete.

At exactly that moment, he said, "It's you. Good."

His mouth curled in that smile that made me sick. Sick. With. Wanting. Him.

I looked at his lips and thought about the way he tasted. Smoky and hot.

His friends—none of whom I recognized from school—yelled out that they were leaving, one of them snickering loudly. But I hardly noticed. Pete stepped closer. My heart beat faster, taking on a rhythm all its own. In the orange glow of a streetlight, I could see through the opening in his jacket how his muscles looked under his T-shirt. Hard. Taut.

"Do you want a drink?" He handed me a bottle of beer, the cap already off. I took it wordlessly. "You okay?"

A sigh escaped me.

"Come and sit down. Tell me about it."

He came closer and my body—stupid body—felt like it was melting.

He lightly placed a hand on my arm and guided me to a bench, where we sat. I could feel where his hand had touched me even after he'd taken it away.

I blurted out, "It might not have been a big deal to you, but I hate what I've done to Griffin."

He leaned his elbows on his knees. I tipped the bottle to my mouth and tasted the warm beer. I liked that he'd just been drinking from the same bottle.

He said, "I don't want to make things difficult for you. I really don't. And it seems like you've got a good thing going with Griffin. I can't make any promises, right?"

I tensed.

He turned and put his hand up to my face. Every pore of my skin opened.

"Hey, Amy."

"Don't . . ."

"Come here."

I shifted away. "Really, I don't want this. I don't want something that doesn't have any guarantees."

"I guess that's what I like about you."

I couldn't look at him. I leaned against the cool, hard bench.

I said, "Okay, so we're clear? We can just forget about what happened?"

"If that's what you want."

I drank again. I said, "I don't normally walk about in the park on my own late at night."

He let out a short laugh. "Good."

"I just had to get out the house."

He was quiet. He seemed to understand my need to get away from my family without me having to explain it.

I said, wanting to explain anyway, "My parents were fighting. Again. They seem to be fighting all the time. I had to get out of there." I continued, "Things seem, I dunno, they just seem to be going through something. If I think about it, they've been at each other for months. Mum is . . . God, I don't know why I'm even telling you."

"My parents used to fight all the time. I was much younger but I remember standing upstairs, face pressed against the banister, desperate for them to stop yelling. I can still feel the wood of the banister. It was an old house. It was almost like I enjoyed the feel of that splintery wood against my face."

"I heard that your mum walked out."

His jaw clenched. "That's the simple way of looking at it, I guess."

I sipped again from the beer. I said, "It's probably no big deal with my mum and dad. They go through patches where they don't get on and then things are fine. It's just . . . well, my mum's so distant right now."

"Do you get on with her?"

"I don't know. Not really—well, we don't really talk or anything.

We're not close." I drank again, flat beer spilling from my lips in a tiny trickle, which I wiped away with the back of my hand.

Pete reached out and I passed the bottle to him. He drank. Watching him, I wanted to shake off everything in my life. I knew, suddenly, exactly what I was going to do.

"Pete, would you mind . . ." I said, the words feeling naked in the fresh night, "would you mind if I kissed you?"

He turned, arching an eyebrow in surprise.

My heart was the bird now and I was just Amy. I faced him, sliding closer on the bench. And then my lips were on his. He tasted of smoke and cider and nothing that should taste good, but my mouth was responding, my body was curling like paper in the heat of a fire.

"Follow me," he whispered, and pulled me up to standing.

I tried to say something, but the words dissolved in my throat.

His eyes glittered and he grabbed one of my hands. "Follow me," he said again.

I let him lead me, my fingers entwined in his, the calluses of his palms rough against my skin.

TOP TIP 8: TEMPTATION IS JUST TOO TEMPTING

He pulled me down to the ground, on grass that was rough and soft at the same time. I was kissing him as if I would break in two if I stopped. He yanked up my top. I wriggled out of my jeans.

His hands were warm; the air was cold, but not so cold I couldn't bear it, and tiny twigs scratched against my bare skin.

I didn't care. I laughed and tipped my head back. He kissed my neck, my collarbone, trailed his lips lower. My body shivered and pressed against him as if it were not under my control.

Stopping, he looked at me. "Amy?" he said, his eyes question marks.

I nodded. I pulled him closer.

I couldn't stop.

I didn't want to.

Afterward, we lay next to each other on the grass, the night heavy on us.

I kissed him on the mouth, whispered goodbye, leaving him lying there, his hands folded behind his head.

Walking home, I replayed every minute.

As I collapsed into bed, I smiled. Then I wrapped myself up in my duvet and sat on my bed, fully dressed.

My phone vibrated in my pocket. A text from Griffin. I slid the phone onto my desk, leaving his message unread.

I burst into tears.

CHAPTER 8

WHEN I WOKE UP, I STARED AT THE CEILING, MY TONGUE THICK IN MY mouth, my guts churning. I'd been so careless, so carefree. We hadn't even thought about using protection until it was too late. The whole time, I hadn't worried about a thing, and the moments when it hurt had melted away in the heat of what came next. Thank God he stopped himself just before he . . .

I sat up and pushed my hair back from my face. My clothes were in a heap on the floor where I'd left them; my school bag lay open and unpacked. I grabbed my phone. There were two text messages.

Both from Griffin.

A pang of loss went through me: it was over now between Griffin and me.

I pressed in Pete's number. He answered on the third ring.

"Hey," I said. "I was thinking about you."

There was silence on the end of the line.

Eventually he said, "How's it going?" Formal. Cold.

My heart dropped like an egg rolling from the kitchen counter, smashing on the ground.

"Pete, it's Amy," I said, hating how I sounded.

"Yeah," he said. "I know. Look, I can't talk now. I'm really sorry."

"What do you mean you can't talk now?"

"I just . . . I can't make any promises—you know that, right?"

It was my turn to be silent. Oh my God. Without saying another word, I hung up the phone.

A text buzzed into it immediately.

For about a second, I thought everything was going to be okay. Pete had written. That horrible conversation hadn't just happened.

But it was Griffin.

Cleo and I r waiting outside—walk with us?

The last two people I wanted to see. I texted back:

Will be down in 5.

I threw on the first thing I could find, grabbed my disorderly school bag and a couple of textbooks, and hurtled out the door. The day greeted me with cold sunshine and the smiling faces of my two best friends.

After the conversation with Pete, I already knew what I had to do for now. I was going to act like nothing had happened. Like nothing had changed.

I hugged Cleo and kissed Griffin lightly on the mouth. See, all fine. I could do this. Avoiding their eyes, I said, all cheeriness and light, "Come on, we should hurry. We don't want to be late."

OH GOD. ONE DAY WENT BY, THEN TWO. PETE DIDN'T TEXT ME OR EVEN *look* at me at school, and my shame—if it was ever that—began to turn to anger. I'd gone all the way with a guy who didn't care about me at all. I couldn't gather my feelings together properly to begin to process what I'd done—I didn't even recognize the girl I had become. So I studied hard, trying to stop myself constantly checking my phone for word from Pete. I avoided hanging out with Cleo and Griffin at school, and I hardly spoke to my parents.

The second evening, I was mournfully checking through my Miss Take-Control inbox when a new message arrived.

Thanks so much 4 ur amzing helpful advice on getting over a crush!!!! i can't believe I even ever thought about that guy like I did . . . everythings great now and ur advice was really really really great.

Luv and hugs 4EVER,

Mercedes, 12

With a sharp jab of the delete key, her email was gone.

TWO DAYS BECAME THREE WITH NO WORD FROM PETE, NO SIGN OF what had happened between us, nothing . . . and then the Friday of Cleo's party dawned.

I was putting some stuff in my locker when Griffin grabbed me round the waist.

"Hey, gorgeous. You've been so busy this week, I've hardly

seen you. All recovered from the B grade? All your homework ahead of schedule? Ready for the party tonight?"

I turned so I was looking up at him. I had been an idiot to take Griffin for granted.

Just behind him, I saw Pete. After days of acting like we were strangers, he was now looking at me with a curious expression on his face, one I couldn't read at all.

Griffin bent down, so I tilted my face up to receive his kiss. If Pete Loewen thought it was okay to do what we'd done and then just ignore me all week, if he wanted to treat me like one of the girls in his long line of conquests, then I'd show him I wasn't hanging around waiting for him to—

I pulled away from Griffin. Pete's expression had changed. He looked like . . . looked like he wasn't surprised, like I'd gone and disappointed him, like *I'd* just done something wrong. He shook his head slightly, clenched his jaw and spun away from me.

CLEO'S HOUSE LOOKED NORMAL FROM THE FRONT BUT HER MUM HAD designed it so the back was all made of glass. I loved loved loved it. My mum wouldn't have done anything so audacious and beautiful with our old, boring house. Not that we ever had enough money for anything like that—it was just like it had been when Granny gave it to Mum. Full of old relics and antiques that weren't worth anything.

Because Cleo's mum and dad were so successful (she was an architect, he was a lawyer), Cleo pretty much got whatever she wanted, so along with holidays in Jamaica every summer to visit her gran, she had these fantastic parties every November. Everyone at school wanted to come.

She'd invited over a hundred people. Her mum had caterers in, so the room overlooking the gardens was groaning with food. The other guests hadn't even arrived and I was already gobbling down a fifth mini-sausage-roll.

"This is going to be great," I said.

Cleo wore a short sea-blue wrap-dress, which made her limbs look even longer than usual. She grinned at me, her white teeth perfectly straight, and hugged herself with obvious glee.

"Everything's falling into place. The caterers have got it all organized. You know what Mum's like."

"Want to trade parents?"

"What I want is to be in love like you are. I know I'm always saying it's fun to date different boys, but I'd love to meet someone I really like."

"Where did that come from? What's going on with you and Xavier? Or did you ask Mark to come in the end?"

She blew me a kiss. "Not my type. Plus, Xavier said he might be coming tonight, so I just . . . You know, it would be so much easier if I was with someone like Griffin."

"You don't even like Griffin very much."

"That's not true." She touched her earlobes lightly. "Oh, I forgot my earrings. Come with me."

I followed her up the sweeping stairs to her bedroom. It was twice the size of mine and decorated with lavish soft curtains and a four-poster bed. When we were younger, when I stayed at her house, I imagined I was a princess. I'd never told her that because she didn't even notice her lovely room. Sometimes I wished I lived at her place instead of mine.

She had loads of pictures of us on the wall over her desk. We were laughing in nearly all of them. My favourite was one where we stood back to back with our faces slightly upturned. The low sunlight softened us, blurring the contrasting lines between my skin and Cleo's. My mum had taken the perfectly composed shot, making it look like Cleo and I were two halves of the same person—it was a photograph about friendship.

Cleo was digging around in her massive jewellery box. She said, "You know, I'm still annoyed that Pete Loewen turned me down. What's wrong with him? Apparently he's said no to every girl who's asked."

I felt a flush of pleasure, quickly replaced by guilt. Now was a perfect time to tell her what I'd done with Pete.

She said, "He's not coming tonight. I didn't ask him."

Good. That was good. Okay. It was now or never. I tried to get the words out.

But Cleo was already talking about something else. "Do you want to come to Jamaica with me this summer to meet my family?"

It took a second to process what she was saying. I shrieked, "What? Are you kidding? You bet I do! Wow, I'm totally going to apply for a job with a photographer and start saving. Like, now."

"Really? Excellent. Every year I go and think, *Why isn't Bird here to enjoy this?* Are you sure you can bear to be away from Griffin for all that time?"

I lay on her bed, propping myself up on one elbow. Jamaica

or not, I *had* to tell her about Pete. "Things aren't that great between—"

The doorbell rang. She slipped in a pair of dangly earrings. "Come on. They're arriving," she said. She stopped in the doorway. "Bird, is everything okay? I mean, are you all right? Are things with Griffin all right?"

I couldn't find the words. The party was about to begin. I said, "Nothing's wrong. Just, there'll be no sausage rolls left if you let me near the food," I said.

She grabbed me and laughed. "Let's go."

TOP TIP 9: EVEN THE BEST PARTIES AREN'T ALWAYS FUN

By the time the moon came up and the stars were jiggling in the sky, Cleo's house was bursting with people. As usual, more people came than she'd invited, but she never turned gate-crashers away, especially if they were good-looking. She stood, laughing and gesturing, with an admiring group of guys. Griffin went to play on the computer in the den with some other guys, after kissing me all over my face and promising to come back soon. I was absently picking at the food.

I felt someone's hand on my shoulder, so I turned, expecting to see Griffin. My heart raced. It was Pete, wearing his usual black T-shirt and jeans. He was staring down at me and his brooding eyes were the colour of slate in the evening light. Intense.

"What are you doing here?" I said as nonchalantly as I could with my insides in knots.

"My date brought me." He gestured over at one of the girls dancing.

"You came with Kitty Moss?" Oh my God. He was at the party with *Kitty Moss*. Total bitch. Total slut. I was so *stupid*. I said, "I should have listened to what people were saying."

Rage flickered in his eyes. "What were they saying?"

"That you're . . ."

"What? I'm what?"

I couldn't help a scornful smile, and at the same time my stomach felt like someone was wringing it out to dry. I said, with more confidence than I felt, "I guess for you it . . . it was just what always happens with girls. Well, I fell for it."

"I just needed a bit of time to work out what was going on in my own head. The phone thing was a mistake. I was . . . I dunno."

"And you thought you'd just ignore me all week too? After . . . after what happened? Was that just a *mistake* too? I don't understand what you want from me. You can't just wander in and make my head all crazy and act like that's no big deal."

"It's not like you were waiting around."

"What's that supposed to mean?" I snapped.

"So I should have been . . . different . . . afterward. Just like Griffin would have been. That's what you're saying? I'm not him, Amy."

"Think about what you *said* to me on the phone the morning after. How do you expect me to feel? You want me to walk away from Griffin after you've treated me like that? He's worth a hundred of you."

He continued, "So I did what I've always done in the past, but you have to believe I got it wrong. I freaked out, okay? I just couldn't handle it."

I wanted to believe him, but I wasn't going to make that mistake. I said, "You're just like everyone said. Arrogant, full of it."

"No. I've changed."

"That's exactly what Xavier tells Cleo all the time. You don't get it, Pete. I'm happy with how I'm running my life. I like how everything is. I like being with Griffin."

"Why would you settle just for something you *like*?"

Just then, Kitty prowled across the room and leaned up to kiss Pete on the cheek. She gave me a savage glare and said, "Honey, wanna dance?"

I bit my lower lip. Pete whispered something into Kitty's ear, and with another nasty scowl at me, she sloped off.

Kitty Moss. He was here with Kitty Moss. So what if he seemed to be saying he liked me, and the way he was on the phone had been a mistake. So what if he was saying he'd changed.

I mumbled, "I was kidding myself."

"You don't know anything about me."

I said, "You've been messing with my head and I just want to get on with my life. Anyway, you've got Kitty now: I wasn't the only one not waiting around."

"You jealous of Kitty, Amy? Is that what this is about? You're here with Griffin, remember?"

"I don't even know you," I said. I could make out his muscles under his T-shirt.

"If you say so," he said, coming suddenly close to me. I felt his smoky breath on my cheek and it tickled down my jawline, along my neck and down my spine.

"Don't even think about it," I said. My eyes flicked over the busy room.

Griffin came in, saw me and waved, a slight frown creasing his face.

"Oh, I think about it," Pete said. His look was tender, his voice serious.

My stomach jumped. I gritted my teeth, fighting it. I couldn't trust him at all: he was way too big of a risk. "You're better off with Kitty. She's your type," I muttered. Then more firmly, "Back off."

Griffin appeared at my side. "Everything okay?"

I smiled over at him. "Everything's fine. Pete was just asking me about some Spanish homework we had to do."

"Didn't know you did homework, Pete," Griffin said.

"I don't," Pete replied, glowering at me. Before any of us could say anything else, he spun away. He went over and grabbed Kitty round the waist. She squealed.

Who even had a name like Kitty?

Griffin leaned over and kissed me hard on the mouth. "What was that about? Everyone knows Pete's a waste of time."

I felt a flush of irritation.

He said, "You let me know if he bothers you again. He's a loser."

"Why are you being so judgmental?"

"I heard he's been in trouble with drugs."

"Where did you hear that?" It was true, then. My skin prickled. I was being blinded by my feelings. Everyone kept saying he was trouble. And *trouble* didn't really fit with my plan for the future. I shouldn't even be thinking about the future when thinking about Pete Loewen. He was here with Kitty Moss. He'd treated me horribly.

"Do you want to go upstairs?" Griffin mumbled.

His words didn't make me tingle anywhere. I made myself smile up at him. "Here?"

"We don't have to, you know, but I thought we could just hang out."

Cleo yelled over at us, "Okay, lovebirds, I know you can't keep your hands off each other but"—she stuck her tongue out at me—"we're having a party here."

I tugged a reluctant Griffin over to the crowd. I heard him sigh. I squeezed his hand. Cleo slung her arm over my shoulder. I smiled at her, grateful that she'd rescued me even though she had no idea I'd needed rescuing.

TOP TIP 10: SWIM OR SINK

The moon was vanishing into the dawn. Griffin and I sat cuddled up on a huge leather sofa in the heated summer house, watching the sun rise over the main house opposite. The giant kitchen windows were illuminated, so we could see Pete and Kitty wander in. They were idly chatting, oblivious that they were being observed.

I replayed the earlier conversation with Pete. I replayed the week he'd just put me through. Perhaps he meant it when he said he'd made a mistake. Perhaps I should follow what my heart was telling me to do, which was to walk over to him and ask him if he did really regret the last few days.

I squirmed on the sofa. I was supposed to be getting good grades, getting on with my future, getting into Oxford.

Griffin pulled my head onto his shoulder. He said, "I don't like that guy."

"Hmm," I said, noncommittally.

I tried not to watch Pete and Kitty, but I couldn't help it. My eyes were drawn to his hands, which were now on her waist. I recognized the look on his face.

Then Pete turned and fixed his gaze on me as if he'd known the whole time exactly where I was. My heart practically stopped beating. I swallowed hard. It was a coincidence he was looking in my direction. He couldn't see us nestled away in the summer house.

But it seemed he *could* see us, because he kept staring. He seemed to be challenging me, saying, *Walk away from Griffin and I'll make up for how I treated you last week.* Perhaps I was reading too much into it. Perhaps he felt nothing like I felt. Perhaps he was checking out his own reflection in the kitchen windows. I stared right back at him, just in case. I wasn't going to play his games.

He clenched his jaw and bent to kiss Kitty. I wanted to throw up. He lifted her onto the kitchen counter and she wrapped her legs round him, laughing in his ear. Gross. Anger uncoiled inside me. I'd been a total idiot to go anywhere near Pete Loewen. Everyone said he was bad news, and here was the proof.

Thank God I hadn't told anyone about what I'd done. It would make him easier to forget. It was time to get back to the plan. I turned to Griffin and pulled him to me, kissing him fiercely on the mouth.

He broke the kiss and smiled down at me. "Hey, Bird, where did that come from?"

I mustered up a huge smile. "It's been fun tonight, hanging out. And milkshakes will be good when we get round to it. You know, I've missed you."

From the corner of my eye, I could see Pete had stopped kissing Kitty and was glaring at me. So he could see me after all.

I squeezed Griffin's hand. It was time to get on with my life.

CHAPTER 9

A COUPLE WEEKS AFTER THE PARTY, I CLEARED OUT MY MISS TAKE-
Control inbox and got to answering a question.

Thurs 9 Dec
Dear Miss Take-Control-of-Your-Life,
Christmas is coming and i don't know what to do. whenever
im in the same room as any of my family i feel like screaming.
my mum yells at me when i haven't even done anything. my
dad doesn't know anything about my life. they dont understand me. they tell me what to do. they make decisions for me
like telling me we have to go to Grandma's this year. Grandma
is so strict, i cant do anything i want. No one ever asks me
what i want plus i dont have enough money to buy everyone
presents because my mum cut my allowance because we fight
all the time. i hate them all.

   i need help to make it thru Christmas.

Dreading Turkey, 12

Dear Dreading Turkey,

<u>Tips to Take Back Control</u>

Get out the house as often as you can.

Bite your tongue when your mum starts yelling (I know, not easy).

Call your friends when things get terrible.

What if you offered to help with the cooking? Show them how grown-up you are so they treat you like an adult.

Stay cool and calm.

As for presents, could you make something? Parents always like that sort of thing.

From one teen to another . . .

Miss Take-Control-of-Your-Life

Outside my bedroom window, I could see multicoloured lights hanging from the tree Griffin had put up for his mum in their downstairs front room. It was sweet of him to try to make Christmas special for her. Farther down the street, one set of neighbours had gone completely Christmas-mad with lights everywhere and a giant plastic Santa *Ho-ho-ho*-ing so loudly I could hear it through the glass. Above that, I could hear Mum and Dad arguing about something. To block out them and the Santa, I put on loud music and sat in my bedroom wrapping everyone's Christmas presents. I had out my list, nice paper, tape and fancy tags.

- Bath stuff: *Dear Mum, To give you some time to relax. Love Bird*
- Fancy cheese: *Dearest Daddy, It's meant to be good with red wine! Love you xxx*

I'd been meaning to clean out the spare room as a Christmas gift for them both, but I had way too much homework to undertake such a huge task. I hated that I hadn't got round to doing it.

- Mascara, red lipstick, matching nail varnish: *Cleo—Like always! Loads of love xxx*

We'd been buying each other makeup for Christmas since we first became friends.

- Computer game: *Dear G, Happy Christmas, Love from Bird*

I knew he'd want something more personal, like a photo of us, but I just couldn't. Couldn't.

As I was wrapping Griffin's present, I saw my phone flashing. Pete was texting me for the first time in weeks.

Want 2 meet

I didn't know if it was a question or a statement. I lay back on the bed. Suddenly the night in the park felt like minutes ago. I could still taste him kissing me, hear his voice urgently whispering *Amy*. I groaned. I could feel his mouth hard against mine, feel his hands as they owned my body. I could feel my skin burning where he touched me, and me responding to him, unable to stop myself.

I told myself two words: *Kitty Moss.*

Griffin's half-wrapped computer game lay next to me on the pillow. I pushed it to one side and it fell to the floor. I held my phone and reread Pete's message. I imagined what Miss Take-Control would tell me to do.

I deleted his text.

I lay there studying the ceiling. About a minute went by and then my phone rang. I answered, not recognizing the number.

It was Pete. He said, "What are you thinking about?"

I didn't speak.

"Come on, Amy. This is stupid."

My mouth was dry. I stammered, "W-what are you doing? Where are you calling from? This isn't your number."

"I'm at my dad's girlfriend's house."

"Your dad's in prison. You're in foster care."

"Where did you hear that?"

"Everyone says so."

He laughed. "Everyone says a lot of things." He went quiet. "Amy, I've got a Christmas present for you."

It was my turn to laugh. "What about *Kitty Moss*?"

"I'm serious."

"I didn't know you could be serious."

"Don't be like that."

I said, "What do you want?"

He exhaled loudly. "You know what I want."

I wasn't going to listen. "You said that before, and then you kissed Kitty right in front of me."

"It was stupid with Kitty, okay, but it was nothing. Amy, just give me another chance. Do you know how hard it is to watch you kissing Griffin every day?"

His sentences were like long snakes uncurling. Part of me wanted to hear them, for him to keep talking. The more sensible part of me looked at my corkboard—Griffin, Oxford University, my quotations. I reminded myself that Pete *couldn't make any promises*.

I said, "Please stop. And promise you won't tell anyone what happened. It was a mistake."

"You wanted it as much as I did. I don't see why you're even with Griffin."

"I have to go."

"Amy, wait."

"No, Pete. Really. Griffin and I have a future together." I was more sure of myself now. I was doing the right thing. "I've got to go."

I THREW MYSELF INTO SCHOOLWORK FOR THE FINAL COUPLE OF WEEKS of term. I asked all the teachers if there was extra reading I could do to prepare myself for my Oxford application next October. I told them I wanted a long head-start and so, after a few puzzled looks, they gathered me some reading lists and suggestions. Mr. Bennetts said, "I'm impressed you're planning so far ahead. Even the keenest students normally wait until the summer break." Then he smiled—the first time I'd seen him smile, like, ever. "But I'm not surprised, young lady." I still wasn't sure exactly what course I wanted to take—maybe History and English, or History of Art. Both choices worried me because I wasn't sure what sort of job I could get afterward.

One evening, I was sitting at my desk, reading through some of their other courses online, when Griffin came into my room.

"Hey, baby," he said, kissing me on the top of my head. "What you doing?"

"You know. Trying to figure this stuff out."

He sprawled on my bed, lying back, his legs dangling to the

floor. "Your dad let me in. He seemed upset about something."

I turned from the computer. "Really? What?"

"Not sure. He's gone out now. Told me to behave myself up here."

I came to sit on the bed beside him and put a hand on his knee. "How's your mum?"

He shrugged and briefly closed his eyes. "Same old. I just wish sometimes— Well, doesn't matter."

"What?"

"Just that my dad was around. Christmas, you know, sucks."

"You guys could come over to us for the day." I lay back next to him. He turned to me.

"No. She'll be better off having a quiet day with me at home." He ran a finger along my jawline. "I'm so glad I've got you, Bird."

"Me too." When Griffin was being so sweet and reliable, I knew I'd made the right decision.

"You know," he said, his bright eyes fixed on mine, "I want us to keep the whole sex thing out the picture. You're clearly not ready."

"It's not fair on you," I said quietly, guilt probing my ribs like an accusatory finger.

"Bird, we're going to be together forever. There's no rush. Right?" He climbed on top of me, his body pressing me against the bed. He whispered above my lips, "See, now you don't have to get all tense when I'm doing stuff like this."

He bent to kiss me. I kissed him back, trying to enjoy the feel of his mouth.

Griffin's phone rang in his pocket. He checked. "It's Mom," he said. He looked down at me and asked, "So we're agreed? No rush. We'll just wait until it happens naturally?"

I nodded mutely, biting on my lower lip.

He turned to head out my room, answering his phone on the way. "I'll be there in two minutes. Promise. Yes, I promise."

TERM WRAPPED UP AND I HARDLY SAW PETE LOEWEN. IT WAS LIKE he'd disappeared from my life, and from the school. The Christmas holidays began, and I started on my homework and studies. I browsed through the questions posed to me by readers of my website, but they were all questions I'd answered before, so I worked instead on the HTML coding and did some upgrading to make the site run more smoothly.

I met up with Cleo a couple days before Christmas to help her shop for all the presents she had yet to buy.

She gave me a huge hug as she came into Coffee Grounds. "You look good," she said. "I like your hair curly, you know."

I put a hand up to touch my curls. "Yeah," I said. "I just wanted to see what it was like. Anyway, do you have your Christmas list?"

"Course not. Oh, thanks." She took a hold of the coffee I'd bought her and we headed out together.

We caught the train to London Bridge and dived into the market below the station. It was packed with holiday shoppers and cheerful carol singers, and the thick smell of mulled wine and apple cider permeated the air. On the train we'd worked out what she was going to get everyone and we started with the stall where the guy made his own pasta.

Cleo picked up the first packet she saw. "This'll do for Mum."

"Come on, that's not how to shop. You need to consider everything. Would she like sage-and-pumpkin ravioli or the fettuccini that comes with organic tomato sauce? They're the same price."

"Okay, Bird, you choose. And Dad'll have that herb selection. He's pretty into cooking, when he's not at work or away on work trips."

"I got my dad cheese."

"That would work too." Her phone rang and she went to answer it, stepping away from the stall, but not before handing me her wallet. "You select stuff. It's Xavier."

I picked out the sage-pumpkin pasta coupled with the herb selection for her mum—Cleo had plenty of money—then stepped over to choose a cheeseboard with four cheeses for her dad. Cleo's face twisted up with frustration as she raised her voice into the phone. I tried to listen to what she was saying, but a group of carollers appeared at the corner of the cheese stall and sang "Silent Night" to an appreciative crowd.

I put the things into my bag and went over to wait against an old stone warehouse. I watched Cleo yelling and then her face crumpled. Hordes of busy shoppers passed her by.

Eventually, she shoved her phone in her bag. She wiped her face and hurried over. I gave her a hug, then murmured, "You okay?"

"He's just such— He says we're getting too serious."

I waited.

"You don't have to tell me you told me so."

"I'd never say that."

"I know. It's just, I wish . . . I don't know."

I was so glad of Griffin, of how kind he was, of how I never spent time yelling and crying on the phone to him in public markets. Poor Cleo. I said, "Forget Xavier for the rest of the day. Look." I pointed at a steaming vat perched on the refreshment stall. "That Hot Apple Whatever sounds good right about now."

She smiled at me. "Sounds perfect."

ON CHRISTMAS MORNING, DAD HUFFED INTO MY ROOM LIKE A WALRUS.

"Come on, Bird. Time to get the quiz ready."

"Go away," I groaned.

He shook my leg. "Get up, get up, sleepyhead."

I buried my head under my pillow. "Go away."

"I've got a great idea for this year. Round one: you'll cut and paste some photos of celebrities and then everyone has to guess who they are. Round two: I've already sorted out fifty general knowledge questions—it'll be so fun. Round three: you and I have to put together the treasure hunt for your mother." I felt his weight as he sat at my feet. He sang, *"On Christmas Day in the morning . . ."* When I didn't answer, he yelled, "Get up, get up, sleepy Bird."

I pulled the pillow away and opened my eyes. I was so tired.

He was beaming at me with a hyper-happy smile. "Good morning, darling. Happy Christmas."

I stuffed the pillow back over my head. "Dad, go away," I mumbled, but I was smiling. He was like a big kid.

"Ding dong! merrily on—"

I threw the pillow at him, laughing. "All right, you win. Give me five minutes to have a shower."

He jumped up. "This year, the games are going to be better than ever."

I had a sudden worry that his jollity was forced. "Everything okay, Dad?"

"Of course, little Bird," he said, but he didn't catch my eye as he left the room.

I HAD A SHOWER AND SQUEEZED INTO JEANS AND A VINTAGE MARC

Jacobs top that Cleo had passed on to me. I rubbed my temples to ease a headache. Huh. I never got headaches. My phone beeped. A text:

Happy Xmas Amy

Pete. I hadn't heard from him for ages. The familiar twisting of my tummy started as soon as I thought about him. My phone beeped again immediately, and with relief, I saw it was Cleo.

Hey u, hpy Christmas.

I texted back:

Quiz time. Dad v overexcited.

She replied:

Ah, lucky u. ;-) Did u get anything gd? Shud I txt Xavier????

I called her. *"Happy Christmas to you,"* I sang.

"You're in a good mood."

"Am I? Guess so. My dad got me out of bed to make games. He's making me be all Christmasy."

"If you say so. It's a bit early in the morning for that sort of thing."

"It's kind of sweet how he wants to still do it every year. Mum's probably cooking already. I have a weird feeling, though. Something's wrong with her."

"What?"

"Oh, you know. She's probably fine, stressed with work, whatever. But how are you?"

"We-e-e-llll," she said slowly. "Soooo I got a car."

"Shut *up*! Oh my God. You have to pass your test now. *Have* to."

"Yeah, yeah. Should I text Xavier?"

"You. Got. A. Car!"

"I know. Superb. It's black. Gorgeous. I love it. So should I text him?"

"Who?"

"Xavier," I heard her sigh. "I wish I had someone. You know, for Christmas."

I giggled. "A man is for life, not just for Christmas."

"I mean it. I wish I had someone adorable to drive around in my new car."

"You are so lucky. A *car*. You can drive me around if you like."

She said, "True. A boyfriend would be better, though."

"Where's all this wanting a boyfriend coming from?" I asked. "Xavier isn't really, you know, boyfriend material—especially after your fight at the market. Wait for him to text you."

"You're right. I shouldn't even be thinking about him. Don't even mention his name. I'm just a romantic under this sexy exterior, that's all. Are you seeing Griffin later?"

"Tonight, probably."

"What did you get him?"

I glanced at myself in my mirror. I sucked in my belly; I was looking bloated. "A computer game. I definitely need to go on a diet after today." My camera rested on my desk. I scooped it up with one hand, resting the phone between my ear and my cheek, and took a couple of shots of my body in the mirror, cutting off my head. I tended to avoid looking at myself too much in the mirror, finding that if I did I noticed all the things I'd like to work on—like tightening my abs, or doing more squats to tone up.

"Uh, hello, Bird, you still there?"

"Sorry, yes. I was just figuring out a photo I might want to take." I put the camera down.

"So I met this guy yesterday—Ben."

"Ben? Okay."

"He's a friend of Becca's. He seemed interested."

"Is he cute? How's Becca?"

"He is cute, and don't pretend you care about her." She continued, "Yeah, he's cute. Maybe I should text him instead."

"Texting the next day . . . well, it seems a bit, you know, eager. 'Specially on Christmas Day. Maybe stop thinking about boys to text. Have a fun day with your *new car*. Do you want to hang out tomorrow?"

"We could start diets together."

"Like you need to diet, Cleo."

"Did anyone write to your website today?"

"I haven't checked yet. Probably. Lots of fights. Stress. Christmas. I won't have time to answer, though—not with Dad and all his plans."

"You haven't been updating it at all recently. Your fans *need* you."

I giggled. "You're right. I've been neglecting the site. I'll get back to it, I promise."

"Okay, I should go. Mum wants to test-drive the car with me. I can't believe I have to drive with her until I *pass*; it's like they don't trust me to be a superb driver."

I remembered the day she drove over in the snow, and laughed.

She said, "Why don't you come over here tomorrow?"

"A *car*. You lucky cow. Happy Christmas."

I WANDERED ALONG DOWNSTAIRS, MY SLIPPERS PADDING ON THE carpeted floor of the hallway. As I got closer to the living room, I overheard Dad say, "Do we have to talk about this now?"

Mum replied in a strained voice, "You haven't helped with any of lunch. You worked until two in the morning and now you get to play Super Dad while I slave away. I'm sick of being in the background of your crazy life."

"Don't do this."

She said, "You wanted me to stay for Christmas. So I am. Like you asked."

TOP TIP 11: LIFE IS NOT FAIR

Ice slid down my spine. What was *that* supposed to mean?

I tiptoed in, my cheeks flushed. She was on the loveseat, he was on the sofa and I was by the door. My dad broke the silence.

"Shall we get on with planning the game, Bird?"

"What do you mean *stay for Christmas*, Mum?" I asked.

Mum's eyes glistened. "You shouldn't have heard that," she said.

"What's going on?"

Her voice cracked and she dipped her head forward, speaking to her hands. "I can't live like this. Not anymore." Then she whispered, as if talking to herself, "We should tell her."

I felt suddenly sick. "Tell me what?"

Dad stood. "Not now."

"Yes now," she said, leaning back on the seat, her face grey.

"What?" I repeated.

"Your mother is leaving me," Dad said to me, then he turned to her. "There, happy?"

She shook her head. "You want to blame me, blame me."

The floor felt like it was spinning. I put a hand out to balance myself. I wanted to throw up. "You're leaving us? Why?"

"It's Christmas Day," Dad said.

"It's too late," Mum replied, closing her eyes.

"I don't want this, Bird," he said. "I can't persuade her to stay. The business is nearly there, just another few months."

"If I hear another word about your business," burst out Mum, "I'll go insane."

He thundered past me, but he didn't get out the room quick enough because I heard him choke on a sob.

"What are you doing, Mum?" I cried. "You *love* Dad."

Her eyes were still closed, her head back on the couch. "I'm sorry, Bird."

I stared at her, not understanding. Not wanting to understand.

She said, "Your dad will stay here—he can't afford anything else and I'm not going to be cruel. But you—I want you to come with me." She opened her eyes. "I've found a hotel for now—there's a room for you, if you want, just until I get a place. Please."

"It's Christmas Day," I said, echoing Dad.

She said, "I can't pretend anymore. I've been pretending for so long."

"Pretending what? Oh God, I can't believe it. I think—" I put my hand up to my mouth to quell the rising nausea. "God, really, I'm going to be sick." I ran to the toilet, pushed open the lid and fell on my knees, retching.

Mum came in and smoothed back my hair. "I'm sorry, Bird." She sounded like she was crying.

"It's just, I don't know, I don't understand." I heaved again. "What about Dad? He can't live without you."

"He doesn't even notice me. Neither of you does."

I pushed her away, wiping my mouth with the back of my other hand. "Just leave me alone, would you? Give me some privacy." As she got up to go, I regretted saying it. Because she was leaving. Leaving me and Dad. "No," I said. "D-don't go," I stammered. "Please, Mum."

She stood in the bathroom doorway. Tears dripped down her cheeks. With sudden clarity, I knew as I watched her standing there framed by the light behind that I was going to remember the moment forever: I could feel the image being etched into my aching head. I willed her to change her mind. Begged her with my eyes.

She said, "I want you to understand. I'm sorry. There was never going to be a good time to do this. I have to go."

CHAPTER 10

Sun 26 Dec

Dear Miss Take-Control-of-Your-Life,

I really need ur help. Ive played the guitar since I was 8 and its the most important thing in my life. I'm 14 now and me and my friends have set up a Band and we're nearly good enough to play in public and we practise whenever we can, but my parents always want me to study for school when I want to be rehearsing and I dont know how to persuade them to let me play my music. My friends depend on me and I cant bear the thought of not being part of the Band but the fights with my parents are getting pretty bad.

Rockstar

Dear Rockstar,

Your band is the most important thing in your world, but your parents probably don't realize how much it means to you. By fighting with them, you might be making things worse.

Tips to Take Back Control

Could you show them how good your band is—perhaps play them something you've been working on?

Can you negotiate with them to let you play if you do your school stuff first?

If you don't treat them like the enemy, they'll respect your choices more.

Rock on. ;-)

From one teen to another . . .

Miss Take-Control-of-Your-Life

Answering questions like this made me feel as if the world made sense. Easy answers. Quick solutions. I posted my reply.

I looked out my window and Griffin was opening his curtains. I waved over, gesturing for him to come visit, and shut down the website. He arrived within ten minutes and I went downstairs to answer the door. The house was quiet, no coffee brewing, no radio playing in the kitchen. I noticed an empty space where Mum's camera normally sat on the shelf by the cookbooks, and I shuddered.

Griffin came in and scooped me into a comfortable hug. I clung to him and took several shuddering breaths.

He said, "How's your dad? How are you? I wish you'd let me come over yesterday."

I mumbled into his chest, "I'm in shock. Mum was packing, everyone was crying. I don't even want to think about it."

He led me through to the kitchen and started fiddling with the coffee maker, replacing the filter and filling the machine with water. He said, "I can't believe it. I can't believe she's really gone."

I watched him and replayed the terrible Christmas we'd had—my aunt showed up, and my mum left with her, despite my dad's pleas. Once they'd gone, he went after them, vanishing for hours, leaving me worried sick, watching the clock, and wanting to curl up and die. When he got home, he staggered straight up to bed. God.

Eventually, I said, "How's *your* mum? I didn't even ask."

"She was good yesterday. Pretty good. Have you seen your dad yet today?" The coffee burbled and hissed as it filtered through the machine.

I said, "I hope he's sleeping." Just then, I heard a clattering on the stairs. Dad stumbled into the corridor, pausing to stare at us.

He said, "I wondered who was here. Has she called?" He wore an ancient tracksuit, the legs baggy and ill-fitting. Stubble had sprouted on his chin and his eyes were bloodshot.

I said, "Uh, we're making coffee. Come and have some breakfast."

"She hasn't called, has she?"

I shook my head. "You need to eat, Dad."

It was his turn to shake his head. "I'm, uh, I'm going back upstairs." He held on to the banister. "If she calls, you come and get me." With that he was gone.

Griffin wordlessly poured us coffees and stirred in milk. I cupped the mug in my hands and sat at the counter, unable to drink, unable to speak.

MUM TRIED TO PHONE ME EVERY DAY THAT WEEK, BUT I WOULDN'T take her calls. Dad, on the other hand, only got off the couch to answer her. Most nights, I could hear him pleading with her to return. Cleo, who'd called me every day and been round a couple of times to cheer me up, wanted me to come to her house for New Year's Eve, but so did Griffin. In the end, the three of us went to her house for a quiet night in.

I was so glad they weren't making me do anything loud or busy. Kitty Moss was having a party, but Cleo swore she didn't want to go—I knew she was only saying it because she figured I was too wiped out with looking after Dad to want to go myself.

We sat around in Cleo's bedroom, watched a couple of movies and at ten seconds to twelve began the countdown.

Griffin squeezed my hand and kissed me full on the mouth as it turned midnight.

Cleo said, "Okay, that was the worst New Year ever. Next year, we're going to be somewhere really good—promise?"

I said, "Like where?"

She grinned. "We'll figure something out. How's it sound? Jamaica this summer, then a great New Year—that'll make up for exams and all the stuff with your parents."

Griffin frowned. "What do you mean about Jamaica?"

I said, "Cleo and I were thinking of going this summer. I, uh, just didn't tell you yet."

He gave me a look but didn't say anything else.

Cleo, perhaps sensing something was up, said, "Let's just enjoy the first minutes of this year. It's all bright and shiny and new—full of possibility."

I said, "I'm sorry I'm so miserable, guys. This has really hit me. I think I just want to go home."

Cleo brightened. "If you're going home, I'm going out. No offence, Bird, but the night is young and Xavier will be at Kitty's, perhaps."

"Are you guys on or off? I can't keep up."

"We don't have a name for it," she said. I thought I saw a flicker of misery in her eyes, but it was quickly gone. "That's what we both want." She turned to Griffin. "Want to come to Kitty's?"

He said, "I'll go home, get Bird back safely. Have fun."

Cleo giggled. "I knew you'd say no."

Griffin was quiet in the taxi back. I knew he was thinking about Jamaica and the fact I hadn't told him, but I was too exhausted to talk about it. We kissed an awkward goodbye and I tiptoed into my house.

The bright, shiny new year was already going badly.

I WOKE UP ON NEW YEAR'S DAY AND FELT LIKE GOING BACK TO SLEEP. I didn't know how my life had become such a mess. I forced myself out of bed and went downstairs. Dad was slumped on the couch.

"I don't feel good," he mumbled.

When I kissed his cheek, the sharp smell of whisky was on his breath. A glass on the table next to him was sticky with alcohol. He must have drunk it as soon as he woke up—if he even went to bed.

"Let's go out for breakfast," I said. "You need to eat."

He didn't answer.

I made him a cup of coffee, setting it next to the whisky glass, but he didn't even seem to see it.

"I love you, Dad. I won't be long."

THE SMALL CAFÉ—LYDIA'S—AT THE END OF MY ROAD BUZZED CHEER-fully inside. The smell of coffee and fat frying greeted me like an old friend. I ordered bacon, eggs, sausages, tomatoes, toast and a latte. A couple of strangers said "Happy New Year" as I went past on my way to sit down by a window. When my breakfast arrived, I had a nasty taste in my mouth and didn't have the appetite I'd thought I had, so I left the food congealing to one side and turned my attention to my napkin, wielding my pen, ready for my yearly ritual of writing my New Year's resolutions.

Bird's New Year's resolutions:
- To get fit. Go jogging.
- Eat five portions of fruit and veg a day.
- Avoid Pete.
- Do well in my exams.
- Work on the photo project Empty Streets.
- Look after poor Dad.
- Make my website even better.
- Get a job to earn some extra money. Jamaica, YAY! (Look round photography studios and see if anyone is hiring— perhaps I could help a photographer or something.)

I hovered the pen over the page, struggling to come up with anything more inspiring.

- I want to go in a hot air balloon and watch the birds go by. I wish flying could be a resolution . . .

I left the café and meandered homeward. As I passed Griffin's house, he came out the door wearing jeans and a white polo shirt, and smiled at me. If he was still annoyed about Jamaica, he didn't say so.

We were watching a movie at his house, my legs over his lap and the remote in his hand, when there was a sudden crash upstairs. We both jumped, and then Griffin leaped up, pushing my legs out the way.

"Mom?" he yelled.

Her voice came floating down the stairs. "The bed got jumpy." A giggle like that of a small girl followed.

"I'm coming." He shot a look at me, his blue eyes bright with worry. "I have to—"

"Do you want me to help?"

"No, I'll call you later."

"Griffin—let me help. I really don't think you should be handling this on your own."

He looked at me sharply. "It's fine. I'll call you later. Do *not* tell anyone. We're fine. She's much better than this most of the time. I promise."

There was no way to help him if he wouldn't let me. "Okay, okay. I won't say anything. But if it gets worse, you should let someone know."

As I left the house, my chest hurt with the guilt of what I'd done to poor Griffin, but it was a new year and time for a fresh start. I pushed the feeling aside and resolved to let the past stay where it belonged.

I decided to go for a jog, following my first resolution for the year. I started out okay but soon had to stop and bend over double because I was out of breath. Nausea rose right up and, suddenly, I vomited in the road.

SITTING IN THE LIVING ROOM WITH DAD A COUPLE DAYS LATER, I heard the click of a key twisting in the lock of the front door. Mum. She came in, wearing black trousers and a knitted green top. Her curly hair was in a messy bun. Her eyes were puffy and I wondered if she'd been crying.

"Hi, Bird," she said.

Dad leapt off the sofa like he'd been electrocuted and said, "You're back." Then, "Thank God." In the quiet, he added, "I love you."

She shook her head almost imperceptibly, looked at him and said, "Are you okay?"

TOP TIP 12: SOMETIMES WHEN NOTHING SEEMS TO HAVE CHANGED, EVERYTHING HAS

I answered for him, "What do you think?"

"You don't look well either, Bird."

"I'm fine, just tired. Looking after Dad is tiring."

"Why won't you take my calls?" she asked.

I stayed silent.

"I need to talk to you about all this. I'm your mother." Her bottom lip shuddered.

I said, "There's nothing to talk about."

There we were, the three of us in the living room, just as we had been on Christmas Day. Nothing had changed. Except this time, I walked out first.

CHAPTER 11

Tues 18 Jan

Hey Miss Take-Control-of-Your-Life,

So I broke up with my boyfriend and got together with a new guy. The other day my ex and I ran into each other and he was all over me and I ended up realizing I still love him. My ex is being really distant right now but two nights ago he called me and said he wanted to come over, then he never showed up, then he called the next day telling me he wanted me back. I figure if I break up with my boyfriend things with my ex will be good again. He's so hot and cold it makes me confused but I know I love him. How do I break up with my new boyfriend without hurting his feelings?

QueenTeen, 16

It was difficult to know what QueenTeen should do. I wished everyone's problems could be tidied up and put into neat boxes or filing cabinets, with solutions available in alphabetical order. I chewed my lip, trying to figure out how to answer.

Hi QueenTeen,

Maybe your ex wants what he can't have. Is he blowing hot and cold because you're now in a new relationship? Or is he genuinely realizing he still has feelings for you?

<u>Tips to Take Back Control</u>

Tell him his games make it hard for you to know what he wants.

Set some boundaries so he doesn't leave you hanging.

Remember, you deserve a guy who treats you with respect.

If you're sure the feelings for your ex are real (and remember why you broke up with him and started seeing your new boyfriend in the first place), then breaking up with the new guy is top of your list. You probably will hurt him, but if you're clear and straight with him, it'll be easier. Take responsibility and he'll thank you for it one day.

From one teen to another . . .

Miss Take-Control-of-Your-Life

ONE JANUARY MORNING IN SPANISH CLASS, MS. DEVLIN WAS CHAT-ting about our long-planned March trip to Barcelona. When I was little, I'd been to Spain and France on trips with my mum and dad, but it had been several years since we'd been able to go away—Dad was always too busy. The last holiday we'd taken had been with Griffin and his family before Griffin's dad died. The holiday to Barcelona was going to be exactly what I needed. I could hardly wait.

The Spanish trip was supposed to help us get ready for our speaking exam—although they speak Catalan in Barcelona and not Spanish, so it didn't make much sense to go there. I figured we were going because Ms. Devlin loved Barcelona and not to help us with our exams at all. I remembered when they'd given us the forms to fill in and Mum had sighed at the cost, but she'd found the money somehow. Then I thought of all the cooking I'd be doing for Dad and all the cleaning up: Mum had been in charge of everything to do with running the house (except for Saturday suppers), and she'd been working full time to pay for trips like the one to Spain. For me. I forced the image of my mum's face from my brain, only to find it replaced with an image of Pete. He was going to Barcelona too. But not Kitty. Or Griffin. Neither of them took Spanish.

Ms. Devlin chattered on, but all my senses were suddenly atuned to Pete sitting behind me. I sat stiff-backed because I could feel him there, his every movement, his breath. Then he tapped me on the shoulder. My whole body burned but I refused to turn round. I remembered when Neen Patel gossiped that Pete's mum had left his family. Thinking about his mum leaving, I felt my connection with him deepen; a thin, silvery line joining us.

Still, I faced the front. I was not going there again. Ever.

AFTER SPANISH WAS ENGLISH. MR. BENNETTS THOUGHT DICTATION was fun and had never heard of blogging or websites, which said a lot about him and our lame English classes.

He was muttering away at the front about feminist interpretations of *Wuthering Heights* when Cleo texted me.

Bored. Want 2 get out?

I caught her eye.

She winked. Suddenly she was coughing so hard I thought she might choke. Mr. Bennetts came to a stop and turned like a turtle to look at her. "Ms. Teague, is there a problem?"

She stood up, coughing more dramatically.

"Sir," I said, "I, uh, think I should take her to the nurse."

He swivelled his beady eyes over to me. The pause was very long while he weighed me up. Most teachers would never fall for it, but Mr. Bennetts lived on a different planet from the rest of them and I could see he was being persuaded. He just wanted Cleo out of there. Cleo coughed louder.

"I really think she needs to see the nurse," I prompted.

"Yes, Ms. Finch. Off you go. Take her."

We were hardly out the classroom when Cleo started laughing. "Sir," she mimicked.

I thinned my eyes at her. "I thought I did a good job—Oscar-worthy.

She laughed.

I said, "What do you want to do?"

"I don't know. Anything? Not go to the nurse."

We wandered comfortably together along the empty corridors, the sound of our shoes clicking on the shiny floors.

"English was so boring," I said.

We were both quiet.

She asked, "So what's up with you?" We headed down the back stairs, keeping our ears open for roaming teachers.

"What do you mean?"

"Are you annoyed about me and Xavier? I know I've been wrapped up with him, like, all month while you've been dealing with all that stuff with your parents. *And* I know you don't like him . . ."

"It's none of my business."

"I knew you were annoyed. You shouldn't give advice to people if you're not okay with them ignoring it."

I faced her. "Honest to God, Cleo, I haven't even thought about you and Xavier. I'm happy you're happy."

"Well, something's up. This thing with your parents . . ."

I muttered, "I don't want to talk about them."

"Okay, well, how are things with Griffin? You haven't even told me about you guys. I know it's my fault and I'm really sorry I've been so . . . busy." A little smile danced over her face. "So tell me about *it*. Have you guys been like rabbits since the first time?"

I pushed open the door to outside. A fresh breeze filled my lungs, cold and tasting of winter. "No," I said quietly.

She grabbed my shoulder. "*No*? Why not? Come on, Bird, 'fess up. Was it terrible?" she said.

I shook my head. "Nothing like that."

God, I wished I'd told her about Pete. There was no way to explain what was going on with Griffin without being honest about that.

She assessed me with her bright eyes and smiled. "You're just scared probably. You think he doesn't love you? He adores you, Bird."

"God, Cleo, would you just *listen*. I've been . . . I've done something—" I suddenly thought about her reaction if I actually told her about Pete. *Pete*. She'd be so mad I hadn't already told her. And then so judgmental about him. Plus, it was weeks ago. I licked my dry lips. I said, "Nothing. No, you're right."

"You don't have to stress about anything, Bird. You have your website, you have me, you have your boyfriend, who is gorgeous and who loves you, you get top marks in everything, you can do whatever you want."

"I want to fly," I mumbled.

She burst out laughing. "Oh, Bird, you're so *you*. Do it again with him. It'll get better every time—and then you'll be sure he loves you, if that's what you need. You're just stressed about your crazy parents."

"Maybe. I feel like everything's falling apart."

"Really? Your life is so normal. Except for your parents, everything about you is, I don't know, predictable. Without you being like that, where would the rest of us be?"

That word again. Griffin had said it as well. "Predictable?"

She shook her head. "I don't mean predictable like *boring* predictable, I mean like I know where you are. You're the girl who keeps the rest of us together. Think of your website."

A cold wind blew. I could see the school building through the fluttering leaves of low-hanging branches. "I suppose so."

"You give great advice, and you're steady as a rock."

"What if I don't want to be steady anymore?"

She snorted with laughter. "You? Seriously, Bird, I think all this is because of what's going on with your parents," she said gently. "I'm sorry I haven't been there for you properly. You're shaken up, that's all. Do it again with Griffin. Poor guy is probably wondering what's wrong."

"You sound like me," I said. "Giving advice."

She smiled. "I do, don't I? Well, I've learned from the best."

I looked at her, all elegant and long-limbed like a deer. She was right. That's who I was: stable, organized, *predictable* Bird. I said, faintly, "I can't believe what's happened to Mum and Dad."

She put an arm around my shoulder. "I can't believe it either. If anyone was more predictable than you, it was your mum."

AT HOME ONE EVENING AT THE END OF THE MONTH, I WAS WORKING IN my room. I fiddled round with some updates for the website, looking at the piles of questions people had written in to me that I hadn't yet got round to answering, and then I wasted a chunk of time looking at Pete's Facebook page, wishing he didn't keep sneaking into my head.

I thought back to mid-November, the rain, the tension building. I remembered him kissing me, the way he'd taken off my jeans so expertly. Expertly—sure, that was the type of guy he was. I could remember the taste of him as if he'd just kissed me five minutes before.

I looked at an online calendar. Ten weeks had gone by since we had sex and he was in my thoughts all the time. This was ridiculous. I *wanted* both of us to act like nothing had happened. But it was just so hard to forget.

I made myself click over to Oxford University's website, where I read student testimonials saying why it was the best university in the world. I imagined how good it would be to be able to tell people I went to Oxford. How impressive it sounded. Huh, that didn't seem like the best reason to go.

I imagined myself going to the college I wanted to apply to—Pembroke College, small, intimate, friendly. I pictured the life I had planned, trying to feel good, but deep inside I had an uncomfortable feeling like heartburn. I turned back to my website.

TOP TIP 13: YOU DON'T ALWAYS KNOW YOURSELF AS WELL AS YOU THINK YOU DO

I finished up with my homework and lay on my bed. I tried to read, but I couldn't concentrate on the T.S. Eliot poem assigned to us. I lay awake watching the moonlight falling like feathers into my room, and eventually I drifted into a drowsy, uncomfortable sleep. Images of Pete pulling me to the ground flashed through complicated dreams of Griffin yelling at me, his mother pressed against a window, screaming.

Suddenly, I *knew*.

I woke up in a cold sweat.

I couldn't believe I hadn't realized.

With everything going on, I hadn't noticed.

It was no excuse.

I'd been so stupid.

But it couldn't be true; it couldn't have happened, not to me.

Not. To. Me.

TOP TIP 14: THE TRUTH COMES OUT IN THE MIDDLE OF THE NIGHT

PART
TWO

PART
TWO

CHAPTER 12

Thurs 27 Jan

Miss Take-Control-of-Your-Life,

Im pregnant and I can't tell the father because he never wants to see me again and I can't tell my parents because they'll kill me. Im terrified. What do I do?

Desperate, 16

Dear Desperate,

You tell *me*.

Miss Take—

I deleted the words. The computer screen felt too bright. I hadn't slept. I called up Cleo. She answered on the tenth ring.

"Uh, Bird, it's, like, stupidly early."

"I have to talk to you."

She mumbled, clearly still half asleep, "Do you want a ride to school? Mum's coming so I can test-drive—"

"Oh God."

"What? I drive superbly." She yawned.

"Can you come over?"

"What, now? Bird, what time is it? Oh my God, it's, like, six-thirty in the morning."

"I'm going crazy."

She became attentive. "Are you okay?"

"Just come over. Now. We have to miss school."

"You're freaking me out. What's wrong?"

TOP TIP 15: SOME SECRETS ARE TOO HARD TO KEEP

I spoke really fast. "Oh God, Cleo. I can't tell Mum and Dad, and I can't tell Griffin." I couldn't even bring myself to think about Pete.

"What, Bird? What is it? You're scaring me."

"I can't even *say* it."

"What?"

It came out as a whisper. "I'm . . . oh God . . . I think I'm pregnant."

I heard her sharp intake of breath. I waited for her to comment, but for the first time ever, she was actually speechless.

"Cleo, come over. No, don't. Meet me at Coffee Grounds. I'm going to buy a test and do it there. I have to get out the house. Oh God, I'm not even thinking straight."

"I'll meet you there in half an hour."

I HURRIED TO THE ALL-NIGHT SUPERMARKET AND STAGGERED ALONG

the empty aisles as if I were in a dream. The pregnancy tests sat neatly under the condoms. Condoms. I was so *stupid*. Stopping before . . . God, that clearly didn't work as contraception. I pulled off a pregnancy test that said it was over 99 percent accurate from the day of your missed period. It had two white sticks in the box. With a shudder I tried to remember when my period last came. I was never very regular and I'd been so stressed. But I was sure it was *ages* ago.

I shoved the money over to the cashier, huddling myself deep into my hooded coat so she couldn't see my burning face. Then I stumbled into Coffee Grounds, paid for a cup of tea and, without waiting for it to arrive, rushed into the bathroom.

With shaking hands, I pulled out the instructions for the test. Following them, I peed on the first white stick. Then I waited.

I texted Cleo:

Am here.

She texted back:

B there in 5 mins.

I WAS SITTING AT A TABLE NEAR THE WINDOW WHEN SHE ARRIVED. I

saw her through the glass before she saw me, so I left my un-drunk tea and hurried to meet her outside in the freezing morning. She wore a Burberry red coat, a white scarf and an expression of utter concern. She grabbed me into a hug and I breathed in her newest perfume.

I pulled back, shivering. "Oh, Cleo."

"Are you sure?" she asked, the words popping like bubbles of gum out of her mouth.

Tucking my arm through hers, I pulled her away from the café. The sky was damp and grey, the tarmac beneath our feet wet from an earlier drizzle, although the rain was holding back. Heavy, dark clouds stacked up to the far left. The air smelt faintly of rotten wood.

I said, "What am I going to do?"

"I thought you only did it, like, once. Didn't you use a condom?"

I pulled the pregnancy test out of my pocket. She took the white stick from me and held it up. It was a shiny plastic thing, smooth and flat against the ominous sky. "Oh, Bird. There are two lines here. Doesn't that mean . . ."

"I know."

"But these things aren't always accurate," she said.

I pulled out the second one. Gave it to her.

"Oh, boy."

"Cleo, I'm, like, going crazy—I can't deal with this," I said.

"What are you going to do?"

"I'm freaking out. How could this be happening to *me*? I tried writing a to-do list early this morning but my brain was like a cloud, full of air and no thoughts. I just called my doctor's office. They must have thought I was insane—I could hardly string words together—but they had a last-minute cancellation, with a different doctor from the one I normally go to."

Words stopped pouring out. We were both silent. Then I muttered, "Nine a.m. We have to get there at nine a.m."

"Okay. Okay. Wow. Trust you to be able to get your head together enough to even think of calling the doctor. So nine this morning, that's good. That's, like, two hours from now. We'll miss school. Good idea. Of course. How pregnant are you? You had sex with Griffin how long ago? Ages ago, way before Christmas, right? Like November sometime? Or have you guys been doing it since then? This doesn't make any sense— Griffin's, like, a careful person. And you . . ." She babbled on, but I wasn't listening.

I thought about the night with Pete in the park, the way we'd fallen to the ground together. I'd honestly thought we'd been careful enough by stopping. I cut into Cleo's monologue. "I can't believe I didn't realize my period hadn't come. It's all the crap happening at home."

I looked at the cars driving by, the rumble of their engines the birdsong of the street. I wasn't going to cry.

"God, Bird. How do you feel?"

"I've been okay. I guess if I think about it I was sick a few times. I threw up when Mum left, but I thought I was just being dramatic. Whatever. Then I vomited once when I went jogging. I figured I was just out of shape. I wasn't hungry for my New Year's breakfast. Stuff like that. I was a bit tired. Bloated. But nothing, nothing, *nothing* that would have told me I was having a *baby*. It's inside me, Cleo. I can't even . . . Oh God, and I don't even love Griffin, but I was going to make it work because of how things are with his mum and . . . and I was going to fix everything."

"You're really stressed out. You do love Griffin. Course you do."

I turned to her, my cheeks hot. "Listen to me. I'm *not* in love with Griffin. I don't think I ever have been. Not like *that*. How can I make *him* believe me if *you* don't?"

"Okay," she said. "Okay, I believe you. Let's go get breakfast somewhere—eggs and bacon and things, not here. We've got a while to wait—is there a place near the clinic? Do you want to get the bus?"

I said, "Let's walk for a while. I need the air. I feel like I can't breathe."

AFTER A STROLL AND A LONG BREAKFAST IN A CAFÉ, DURING WHICH neither of us ate anything, we went to the doctor. I was numb as I entered the office. The damp air had seeped into my bones. I took off my coat and went over to Reception while Cleo went to sit down. The room smelt of antiseptic and it was library quiet.

I pressed the bell on the desk and was startled by the shrill sound. A smiley woman with round glasses came out and took my details even though I could hardly get words out of my mouth.

When we were done with the forms, she said, speaking as if I were a small child, "Doctor will see you in a bit, take a seat." She smiled and gestured to the chairs lining the walls, so I went numbly to sit down next to Cleo, who put her hand on my knee. Her nails were painted with a silver stripe along the middle.

Two elderly people sat opposite us. The walls behind them were covered with pamphlets and posters. My eyes picked out certain words.

BE ON TIME FOR YOUR APPOINTMENT.

BREASTFEEDING IS BEST.

ABORTION COUNSELLING. CALL US.

"Have you spoken to Griffin?" Cleo asked. "You need to tell him."

"Don't start, Cleo," I snapped. "Sorry, I'm in total shock," I said. "I'm sorry."

She put her hand back on my knee.

When my name was called out, my throat clamped. Cleo nudged me.

"Wait here, okay?" I said.

I went into the doctor's tiny room. He was a huge man who dwarfed his swivel chair. He wore a checkered shirt that strained around his bulging middle with jeans tucked under his belly. He had grey hair but was balding in the middle. He reminded me of my dad, which was totally awkward.

The doctor adjusted his glasses as I sat, and said, "How can I help you?"

"I, um, I . . ." I fell silent. I couldn't get my words out.

"Go on."

"I think I'm—"

"Yes?" He leaned forward. The room was stifling.

"Pregnant." I said it so quietly the doctor had to lean even closer.

He sat back. "Right."

Out the room's small window I saw it had started to rain. My life was punctuated with rain.

"And why do you think so?" he asked.

"I've done two pregnancy tests."

"Aha."

"And they both say I'm pregnant. But they're not always accurate, right?"

"Two home-test positives would mean you're pregnant."

Desperation swelled in me. I took a second to speak. "Just like that?" I said. "Really?"

He leaned his chin on two chubby fingers.

"Don't you need to do some other sort of test here to confirm it?" I begged, feeling like I was being washed away.

"Not anymore. The home-tests are accurate predictors nowadays. Is this good news?" He hesitated. "I have to ask."

I shook my head.

"What was the date of your last period?"

My face scrunched up as I tried to remember. "The beginning of November . . . just after my birthday . . . I guess, the fourth."

"So"—he looked at his computer and then typed in something—"you're twelve weeks pregnant."

"What do you mean?" My voice dropped to a whisper. "I had, um, sex ten weeks ago. I *can't* be twelve weeks along."

"We count the weeks of the pregnancy from the date you last had a period. The baby will have been conceived after the end of the second week—at the beginning or the end of the third week, depending on your cycle."

I thought of Pete in the park that night. I said, "Twelve *weeks*? How could I not have known? Surely being pregnant is like, I don't know, obvious?"

"Are your periods regular?"

"No. Not always. But twelve *weeks*? I mean, I can't believe I didn't realize. I'm normally so . . . so *organized*."

"It happens like that more often than you think. Especially for, um, younger women. Sometimes because you don't expect it and because you don't know what to look for . . ."

I'd never been called a woman before, not by someone as old as him. I swallowed. Hard. "Can I still have an abortion?" I asked.

He blinked owlishly behind his glasses. "It's a big decision. You need to have a scan as soon as possible. Normally women have their scan at thirteen weeks. We'll book you in as quickly as we can—early next week, probably."

I swallowed. In the face of his efficiency I could hardly breathe. "Can't I just have an abortion? Like, now?"

"We need to have the scan to check your dates are right, then we can determine what type of abortion is possible. We'll book a separate appointment after the scan, if that's what you decide to do."

My hands rested on my stomach. I was firm. "I don't have any other option."

He tapped his pen on the desk and said, "You'll make the decision that's right for you. We offer counselling to help. Perhaps it would be a good idea. Now, we ask all pregnant women this: have you been taking folic acid? Do you know what it is?"

I shook my head. "Oh, but I take a multivitamin."

"Good, that's good. Check it has folic acid, just in case. So now, I need to ask you a series of questions and we need to fill in this form and book you an appointment with a counsellor. We'll have to move quickly."

I nodded, suddenly as unable to speak as a stone.

CHAPTER 13

Tues 1 Feb

Dear Miss Take-Control-of-Your-Life,

I dont know how it happened but my dad is having an affair with the school secretary . . . i found out and accidentally blurted it to my best friend . . . she promised she wouldnt tell anyone but the next day i got to school and everyone was pointing at me and laughing . . . we live in a small village and I go to the local school in the town about 5 mins away, so then mum found out . . . shes messed up and dad is acting like hes forgotten all about us, and Im soooooo mad at my best friend that i wont speak to her, so Im all alone dealing with this hell . . . my best friend keeps saying she's sorry, blah, blah, blah.

i always thought Mum and Dad were so happy together. Im feeling so ashamed and desperate and cant really ask Mum what to do as she's stressed out and crying. Its my fault she found out.

Gina, 15

I wanted to make things better for Gina so badly. God, parents were always making life more complicated than it was already. At least by answering Gina, I could forget the nightmare that was my own life. Sort of.

Dear Gina,

Your trust has been betrayed on so many levels all at the same time that you're feeling hurt and lonely right now. Your father has deceived both you and your mum, and now your best friend has let you down. It sounds like she regrets it; people do stupid things sometimes.

<u>Tips to Take Back Control</u>

You might want to hear her out and let her explain what led her to spill your secret. You need the support right now, and if you can forgive her, I bet she'll be there for you.

See if there's a school counsellor you can talk to.

What's happening at home is incredibly distressing. Your dad is acting like he's the only one who matters in the world, and that's very difficult. You're probably being a great listener for your mum, but she needs to know how you feel as well. Together you and she will come out of this horrible experience.

And remember, none of this is your fault. Your mum would have found out one way or another. Try to ignore the gossips at school. They'll move on to gossiping about someone else soon.

From one teen to another . . .

Miss Take-Control-of-Your-Life

MY GUTS WERE TWISTED UP WITH EITHER MORNING SICKNESS OR anxiety, it was hard to tell, and I hadn't spoken through the bus ride or during the walk past rows of terraced houses to get to the main doors of the hospital. I looked at Cleo and her face was set in a grim smile.

She said, "You okay?"

I thought about the weekend waiting for this scan. I'd been paralyzed. I thought about Griffin. He and I had watched a movie together the night before, me unable to tell him—everything the same, everything changed.

As we walked into the hospital, I said to Cleo, "I just want this over with." The only thing I could be glad of was that the February break had started Friday and would run until Wednesday, so we didn't have school. It meant that I hadn't had to face anyone, and that Cleo could be with me for this appointment.

The corridor at Mayday Hospital in Croydon was the longest I'd ever seen. Cleo and I walked down it together, her arm linked through mine. I could smell her expensive face cream and perfume over and above the sterile stench of bleach that permeated the grey walls. We had to get to an area called the Yellow Zone. Hurrying by a room full of old people looking sad, I saw that Maternity was just ahead. I averted my eyes to avoid seeing women cuddling babies or proud dads kissing newborns. God.

She said, "I still think you should have told your mum. Or Griffin."

"Cleo, don't," I croaked, then my voice gave out. We arrived at the Yellow Zone. Suddenly the long corridor seemed too short.

I pushed open the heavy door and we followed signs to the reception. Women round with pregnancy huddled close to their husbands, smiling, the two of them looking at baby magazines. A warm blush crept onto my cheeks. I was so totally embarrassed. I felt young, and really stupid. At the reception an overweight nurse with a huge smile greeted me.

"Amy Finch," I whispered to her.

"Do you have your chart?" she asked.

I pulled out the stuff the doctor had given me the week before and handed it to her. She read it through and indicated I should sit down. Cleo ushered me over to a chair by the window and I gazed out at an empty cement parking area. Nausea rose through my entire body. My boobs hurt and they pushed against my bra, squeezed in. My belly was bloated, my mouth dry and I needed to pee, so I got up to go to the bathroom, but a woman with grey hair and wearing a white coat came out of a room to call my name.

I grabbed Cleo's hand. "You're coming with me."

She gripped my fingers. "It'll be okay, Bird."

We followed the grey-haired woman into a small, dark room. I said, "Is it okay if my friend's here?"

She said, "Is anyone else with you?"

I *knew* she was wondering where the father of the baby was, and was judging me and weighing up my age. I cast my eyes down.

"Lie here and pull up your top. No need to take off your jeans. I'm going to put a gel on here, a cold gel."

"I'm going to have an . . . abortion," I said, struggling suddenly with the word.

"We just have to see how far along you are. Are you comfortable?"

"I don't want a baby. I haven't even finished school."

"Just try to relax. Is that too cold?"

I studied the white ceiling. "I don't want to see the baby. I just want all of this to be over."

"That's fine. I'm just having a look now."

Cleo, who was sitting to my right, gasped. The "Oh!" was loud in the small room. She said, "Wow, look! No, don't look. Oh—"

I didn't mean to, but it was too late. My eyes lifted and I saw the screen, and there before me was a wriggly *baby* with a big head and little kicking legs.

The frizzy-haired woman said softly, "That's the heartbeat."

Cleo pointed. "The flashing bit? I had no idea. Wow."

"I thought," I said, "it would look like a bean."

"Baby did a few weeks ago, but you're twelve weeks, five days along. These are the hands, can you see?" She pointed.

I gazed at the kicking green shape as the technician slid the scanner over my skin. I said, "It's moving so much."

"That's good. There's your placenta. And there's the umbilical cord. The fetus looks fine to me. A good heartbeat. I'll measure the nuchal fold and take another couple of measurements and then we're done."

I wanted to lie there forever. There was a pull through my heart that I'd never felt before, a really weird feeling. "Oh, Cleo," I murmured. "What am I going to do?"

She turned to me with her big chocolate eyes. Her lips moved but she didn't say anything.

I looked again at the image of the kicking baby. The technician pulled the scanner away, and with a blink the baby was gone.

I WAS IN A HAZE AND SO I FOLLOWED CLEO TO THE ROOM I'D BEEN told to go to and listened while the doctor explained I'd have the abortion two days later. He gave me details of the type of procedure—and options for counselling, which I refused.

Cleo nudged me. "It might be a good idea," she whispered.

I realized she was holding my hand.

The doctor gave me the number to call if I changed my mind.

"I just want to go home," I said.

We left the doctor's office and somehow I got home and to my room. Cleo wanted to come in, but I told her I needed some time alone.

I pushed the door shut and collapsed on the bed, my head hurting and my eyes moist. I slept fitfully for hours.

THE MORNING AFTER THE SCAN, I LAY IN BED TRYING TO FIGURE OUT what I was supposed to do about Griffin. An awful thought sneaked into my head: after the abortion, I could perhaps get away with never telling him about the baby, carry on like nothing had happened. But I couldn't do that. It would be so *wrong*. With shaking hands, I called Griffin to let him know I was coming over. His phone was off. I dressed quickly and walked up the path to his house with my insides as tight as a blown-up balloon. I tried not to puke as I knocked. When no one answered, I pushed open the door. They always left it open, as if they still lived in some tiny town in the States rather than London, and they'd never been burgled—amazing.

Griffin's mum stood in the corridor, the features of her face all blurred. I guess *blurred* was the word. Or smeared, as if she was confused.

"Bird?" she said.

"Are you, um, okay?" I asked. The world felt full of grown-up problems, bursting at the seams with things I didn't want to deal with.

She frowned and fumbled with the pockets of her dressing gown. "Bird, Bird, the sun fell into the lining and I can't get it out."

"Is Griffin here?"

"I put it in my pocket for safekeeping, but it slipped like water and was gone."

"Um, uh, maybe it's in the living room. Why don't we, uh, go and sit down in there?"

"Oh, no," she said, her speech suddenly clear, "I know where it is." She hurried down the carpeted corridor into the kitchen and I heard her cry out with delight. "I can see it in the stove."

I followed her. She was crouched on the floor, switching the oven light on and off, crowing with pleasure. "See, darling, there it is."

"Why don't we, um, get you upstairs and away from the oven? Come on with me, that's right." I helped her up. She was frail and light. She let me lead her like she was a toddler and I an adult. We climbed the stairs. The smell of lavender wafted from the bathroom.

"It smells so good," she cried. "Like childhood." She stopped and her face transformed into her normal features. She said, "What's happening to me? It's all so strange. I don't know how everything became so— I just don't feel like myself right now." She admired both her hands. "I don't want this," she said. She raised her gaze to me and I could see from her glazed eyes that her moment of lucidity was gone.

"Come on, follow me." I took her to her room.

"*There* it is," she cried. "*Outside.*"

The sun hung low in the sky, rising over London.

Sitting on the bed, she started humming, gazing enraptured out the window.

God. Poor Griffin. I kissed her on the cheek, feeling her papery skin, and she curled up on the bed. "I'm so tired, little Birdy. Fly with me," she murmured.

I sat with her for a long time, waiting for her to fall asleep, then tiptoed out and went down the corridor to G's room. His door creaked, but the noise didn't distract him. He was sitting at his computer, headphones on, frowning just like his mum had been, his tongue poking out from between his lips. He wore his favourite khaki-green T-shirt and jeans. His feet were bare. He must have sensed movement, because he turned to me, his whole face lighting up.

"Bird," he cried.

"You're up early," I said. "I wasn't sure you'd even be awake yet."

"I'm just watching some guys fighting in Tokyo on the Internet. It's dumb."

I said, "Your mum seemed pretty out of it."

He froze. "Was she okay?"

"It's okay, G. You should let me help. Have you thought about, you know, other help?"

He stayed silent.

"You're taking on too much here."

He said, "No one else knows, Bird. And you have to trust me—most of the time she's fine. She just has these periods when . . . She's going to get better, I just know it."

"It seems like the last few times I've been round, it's worse. Have you taken her to the doctor? They'll be able to help."

"Bird, she's all I've got."

"Okay," I said. "Forget I mentioned anything," I added.

I sat gingerly on his bed. He came over and sat next to me. I had the sudden urge to cry, but I managed to stammer, "I'm s-sorry I've been so distant." No matter what was going on with his mum, I *had* to do this.

"You've had a lot happening with your family."

"That's not it," I said.

"No? What?" His handsome face filled with questions.

I didn't know where to start. But I *had* to say something. It wasn't fair on him—none of this was his fault. I pushed aside thoughts of his mum, swallowed hard and managed to say, "Griffin, I can't, um, do this anymore."

"Do what?"

"Oh God, I don't know how to say this."

His tone brimmed with concern. "What's wrong? Is your dad okay?"

Trust him to be so thoughtful. I squeezed the bridge of my nose. With a burst of clarity, I saw exactly what to say.

"Nothing's changed with my parents. It's, um, us. I mean me. And you. Me and you. It's like since we became a couple, we're not friends anymore—we don't, uh, talk."

"Is this because of the sex thing? I'm being patient, right?"

"No," I said, too sharply.

He was silent. Who knew silence was so loud?

"I mean, y-yes, you're being patient, but that's not it. I don't know how I— God, if I'm honest, I don't know how I . . . feel anymore. I'm sorry, Griffin. It's, um, not you," I said lamely into the thick heat of the room. When had it got so hot?

"I don't understand," he came out with eventually, and the words cut through me.

I remembered once, after his father died, Griffin came over to my house and we sat together in my garden, our legs buried in the long grass that my dad had failed to cut all summer. Griffin hadn't said much about his father since the funeral, which had been the saddest day ever. He looked up at the sky that day as we sat together in my garden and his Adam's apple bobbed. He said to the blue emptiness above, "I don't understand."

In the room, facing me now, he said it again. The same words. "I don't . . ." he said. "I don't understand."

I was sick at myself.

He pleaded, "Don't you love me? Look, I know you probably think I'm, I dunno, but I'm trying to be patient with you and not . . . I sound pathetic. I hate this. I hate what you're saying right now."

"Griffin, please."

"You're having a hard time with your parents but don't ruin

what we've got here—it's a good thing." The words left him looking empty.

"It's not that. Oh, Griffin, everything's so out of control."

"What, Bird?"

"I do love you. I do. But I think I love you like, I don't know, a friend. Like a brother."

He got up from the bed and swept his hand through his hair. His T-shirt rose, exposing an inch of his pale skin. "What does *that* mean?" he asked.

I couldn't speak.

The room filled with silence and I studied the carpet, the tiny hills of woven fabric. I imagined what it would be like to be minuscule, crawling amid the weave of the carpet, exploring the floor as if it were a mountain range. I heard him let out a slow breath, and if anything, the room got even hotter.

"Bird," he said, "you don't mean this. You're my best friend. My girlfriend. You're the only thing in this crazy world that keeps me going. You can't do this to us. Think of everything we've been through. It's just things with your parents. You'll feel better if you just give everything a bit of time. We'll take everything more slowly."

The room veered off its axis. The conversation was all wrong.

He gazed down at me. "I hate that I rushed you and screwed it all up. I'll wait, you know. Let's just think about this. We're together forever. Remember?"

My heart crashed against my ribs. It physically hurt. I had the bizarre image of a mirror smashing into thousands of pieces. I had to tell him about the baby, about the abortion I was planning. About Pete. But there he was looking at me, love filling his face. Love and confusion. And then there was everything going on with his mum.

"Oh, Griffin," I murmured. And then—it must have been the heat—I fainted.

I WOKE UP STARING AT A DARK BLUE CEILING, MY HEAD SPINNING.

Griffin's room. I was in Griffin's room, lying on his bed.

As soon as I stirred, he said, "Hey, you okay?"

"I don't feel well." I sat, woozily, and looked at him.

"We'll figure it all out. Let's get you home so you can get some rest."

By the time we'd got me back to my room, I was feeling even worse. I croaked, "I think I must have flu."

He lay me down and tucked me in, kissing me on the forehead. "I'll make you some soup or something."

I couldn't figure out why he was kissing me—I thought I'd broken up with him; I thought I'd made it clear. "I'm just going to sleep. See you tomorrow at school."

Even as he said goodbye, I knew I wasn't going to go to school the next day. I just couldn't face any of it anymore.

CHAPTER 14

Thurs 3 Feb

Dear Miss Take-Control-of-Your-Life,

My girlfriend's parents have split up and she's pretty stressed. She's the perfect girlfriend and she's my best friend too. I know she loves me—I love her too—but things are weird between us and I don't really know why. What should I do?

Did you guess, Bird? Don't be annoyed with Cleo—she didn't mean to tell. But now I know about your site, I figured I'd just write to you and see: what's your advice on making things better between you and me?

Love you,

Griffin

I read Griffin's words in my Miss Take-Control-of-Your-Life inbox and I wanted to throw up. Today was the day of the abortion. I minimized his message and was faced with the reminder in my inbox. *Appointment Thursday: 11 a.m.* Today. Nausea rushed up into my throat.

I had to keep the appointment and get the abortion.

I had to tell Pete. It was his *right* to know. It was *his* baby.

And I had to break up with Griffin properly.

I read a quotation on my corkboard:

> *It is easy to be brave from a safe distance.*
>
> Aesop

I clambered from my desk to lie on my bed.

I put the pillow over my head and lay cocooned in the soft dark.

I flung the pillow from me and texted Griffin:

I'll call you later, Bird.

A text came straight back:

LU ;-) Computing VERY boring today. Why aren't you at school? 2 days off? You must be REALLY sick?!! Can bring you soup later if you like. See you later xxxxx

He was still acting like our breakup conversation hadn't happened. Like everything was the same. But my life would never be the same after today. It never could.

I watched the clock . . . I watched the clock as the seconds turned to minutes. The minutes turned the digital face to *10:29*.

I couldn't move.

10:30

10:31

10:32

TOP TIP 16: TRUST YOUR INSTINCTS, EVEN IF THEY MAKE NO SENSE

I groaned again. I had to get up. I had to *leave.*

10:36

10:39

I lay on the bed, taking long, slow breaths.

10:41

My phone rang, startling me out of my inertia. Cleo laid into me with a loud "What's going on? I'm at the clinic. Where are you?"

"I'm . . ."

"Where? What's going on?"

"I just can't get off the bed. I can't do this."

"This is crazy, Bird. I'm coming over."

TOP TIP 17: YOU HAVE TO MAKE YOUR OWN DECISIONS

"The baby." I tested out the words. "I keep thinking about the baby." I stood up.

I put my hand on my stomach, which was thicker than it used to be. "I'm already showing a little," I said, pulling up my shirt and looking in the mirror at the softening of my waist above my jeans. "I can't help feeling a bit happy about that. I know it's ridiculous."

"Hang on, let me just go outside. I don't want everyone in the waiting room listening to this."

I could hear a door swing open and then slam.

She said, "This is crazy. You're not thinking properly. It's your hormones. You're acting like a baby isn't a big deal. You should have gone to see the counsellor they booked for you."

"I just, uh, can't get the image of the wriggly baby on the scan out of my mind."

"It's not a cute, fuzzy pet. You're screwing up your whole life."

"I already screwed it up."

"What about Griffin? It's *his* child. Have you told your dad or your mum?"

I sighed and dropped my top back down. I felt like a five-year-old.

She carried on. "Bird, it's like I don't know you. Even if you think you want to keep it, or whatever's going on in your screwed-up head right now, you can't actually keep a *baby*. It's going to take over your whole entire *world*. You'll have to drop out of school. We won't be able to go to Jamaica."

I whispered, "But I want to. I want to keep it."

TOP TIP 18: WHEN YOU MAKE A DECISION, SAY IT OUT LOUD

My voice grew stronger. "I want you to stop talking about me getting rid of it. I know you think I'm insane. You don't approve. Whatever. I wish I wanted an abortion. It would be much easier, but now I've seen the scan I don't think I can do it. Okay?"

"Okay," she said finally. "I'll make you a deal. I'll be okay with all this and an even-better-than-best-friend friend and I'll even hang out with you and the baby sometimes, but you *have* to tell Griffin. If you plan on keeping this thing, he's going to find out anyway, right?"

"Cleo, I have something to tell you."

TOP TIP 19: BE HONEST WITH YOUR BEST FRIEND

I said, "Griffin's, um, not the father."

I studied the ceiling of my room. The silence echoed between us. I pressed the phone closer to my ear.

"Okay," I whispered, "you can speak now, Cleo."

"I don't get it."

"I, um, didn't do it with him."

"You *told* me you did."

"No, technically, I didn't tell you anything. I just didn't *say* anything."

"So let me get this right: you *didn't* have sex with him."

She seemed to have missed the point of what I was saying, but I answered her anyway. "I just couldn't go through with it. I tried to break up with him yesterday, but things with his mum are pretty bad. I just . . . I know I have to deal with this but I don't know how."

"You tried to *break up* with him? *What*?" she screeched.

"Cleo—"

"Hang on. *Hang on*. If Griffin's not the father, then *who* is? Is this like the Immaculate Conception? I don't get it. *Who* did you have sex with? You'd better tell me *right* now."

"You're going to pass out."

"Is it someone I know?"

I nodded.

Even though she couldn't see me, she squealed. "It *is*! Let me guess. Is it Alec Jones?"

"No. Disgusting. God."

"Henry Morris?"

"Stop it. Really." I added, "We did it *once*. It was nothing."

"Once is not nothing! Was it one of the teachers? Mr. Smith?"

"Shut up, Cleo. Seriously."

"Then who?"

I spoke really quietly. "Pete." In the silence that followed I imagined her standing outside the clinic. She'd probably dropped the phone in shock. "Cleo?"

"*Pete Loewen*? Hot, sexy player *Pete* who would screw anything?"

"I just couldn't stop thinking about him. We kissed one time . . . then I ran into him at the park . . ." I put my hand to my lips.

"You did it at the *park*?"

I muttered through my fingers, "Uh-huh."

"What, like, in the bushes? I can't get *over* this. Do you still *like* Pete?"

"I don't know. Even if I did like him, he's *Pete*. Nothing's going to happen. I told him that."

"Sounds like it already happened," she said.

"Ha ha, very funny."

"I can't believe you slept with Pete. And now you're having his baby."

"Okay, Cleo."

"This whole situation is crazy. You have to tell your parents."

"About Pete?" I said.

"About the *baby*." She paused. "Tell your mum. It's not like you can hide stuff from her, anyway. She's got mum-detector sensors."

I giggled. "You're not mad at me for not telling you?"

"Of course I'm mad. But I'll get over it."

"You're the best friend ever."

"That's your sentimental hormones speaking. Don't think you can butter me up and change the topic like that. Break up with Griffin. Tell your parents."

"I have to tell Pete too—keeping the baby tangles me up with him forever," I said. "I will tell them all. I promise." I clicked shut my phone.

I DIDN'T GO IN TO SCHOOL FOR THE REST OF THAT DAY OR THE NEXT, which felt strange—taking any time off school was something I'd never done in my whole entire life.

On the second day I was sitting in my room, idly looking at the Oxford University website, when the landline rang. I picked it up mainly to quiet its insistent ringtone (Dad had set it to Pachelbel's Canon). Immediately, I regretted doing so.

"Honey, it's you." My mum's voice came over the line, sounding relieved. "You never answer your phone."

When I finally spoke, the words were stiff and awkward. "I'm, uh, busy right now." I wondered if she could tell that my whole life had changed just from my voice.

She said, "What are you doing?"

"I don't think I want to talk to you," I said.

"Listen, Bird, come and meet me. Anytime. I've been staying not far away—in a small hotel. I've been calling you and calling you."

I thought about my promise to Cleo. Oh God. I *couldn't* tell my parents. Dad would freak. Mum would . . . I had no idea what she would do.

"Bird? Are you still there?"

I made a noncommittal harumphing sound.

"Please come and see me," she begged. "Anytime. It's been weeks since I saw you. I can't bear it. My leaving isn't about you and me."

"Of course it is—" I cut myself off before my voice broke.

"When can we meet?"

I couldn't face her.

"Bird, please."

There was no point putting her off. I said quietly, "Okay, tomorrow?"

"Thank you, honey." She sounded like she was having trouble holding back her emotions.

"I'll meet you in Coffee Grounds at eleven-thirty." I said goodbye and dropped the phone back on the cradle. I pulled out a sheet of paper and made a to-do list.

- Find a job, earn money.
- Tell Griffin.
- Tell Pete.
- Homework piled up—see list in day planner.
- Read a book about pregnancy and one about looking after a baby.

I felt sick. Looking after a baby—a real human being. This was insane. I spent the next couple of hours looking up possible jobs on the Internet, and found a studio nearby that wanted a photographer's assistant. That would be perfect.

spotted Dad sitting in the living room with his laptop open, the wire curling across the floor. At full volume, a soprano voice soared from the CD player.

"You busy?" I yelled.

"I want to learn about opera," he said. "This is Lucia di Lammermoor singing her final song before she collapses into a prolonged death from grief."

"It's very, um, loud," I said. The secret I was keeping from him slithered through my mind—it seemed impossible that I was walking around with *a baby* inside me yet Dad had no idea.

He said, "Beautiful. Beautiful. Like your mother. What am I going to do without her, Bird?"

I looked at him in his tracksuit, stubble thick under his chin.

I raised my voice to be heard over the opera singers. "I don't know, Dad." My fingers splayed like starfish on my belly. I still hadn't told him—there never seemed to be the right time. God. And now I was going to go and tell Mum. Perhaps she would tell Dad for me. My head began to hurt. I considered cancelling, then remembered my promise to Cleo.

Dad tapped on the keyboard. "According to the Internet there's a whole world of opera aficionados out there," he boomed. "I never knew. I wonder if I could start a company that mailed out information to opera fans . . ."

"I've got to go, Dad."

"You're seeing your mother. Do you think I can come?"

I shook my head. The soprano hit an incredibly high note and my throat tightened. I wasn't going to cry. I hurried out the room.

I OPENED THE DOOR OF THE CAFÉ AND WAS HIT WITH THE BITTER smell of roasting coffee and the noise and bustle of customers. It took a moment to locate Mum. Then I saw her sitting stiffly in her wooden seat. Her hair was pulled back into a tight ponytail that emphasized her narrow cheekbones and bow mouth. She looked pretty, her pale skin almost rosy. She had already seen me and was just lifting a hand to wave at me when her eyes narrowed and roamed over my body. The funky salsa that was playing seemed to stop, as did all the conversation in the room.

I mooched toward her, squeezing past a woman rising from her seat.

Mum's eyes scanned my body. She met my gaze but paused as if she saw me as a completely different person—a stranger. Her voice was a sigh. "Oh, Bird. What have you done?"

"What?" I said, trying to be nonchalant, desperately hoping she wasn't talking about the pregnancy, but already understanding that she *could tell*.

TOP TIP 20: MUMS CAN ALWAYS TELL WHEN YOU'RE LYING

"Bird," she whispered, "I'm your mother. I haven't seen you for weeks. Did you think I wouldn't notice?"

My mouth was dry. I mumbled, "I'm not showing. How do you *know*?"

"I'm your *mother* . . ." she repeated. "Just look at you. You're . . . it's so *obvious*."

"No one else noticed. It's not even a bit obvious to the rest of the world."

"Your face is the spitting image of mine when I was . . . pregnant with you. Of course I'd notice. But none of this is the point."

Over her head the café was crowded, the baristas whirring up espressos, the staff edging round tables to get everyone served. I shrugged. "At least I don't have to work out how to tell you."

"You think this is some sort of joke?"

"I don't want to talk about it." I sat heavily opposite her. Maybe I was showing more than I thought. I felt paranoia trickle through me—would everyone at school know? Could they tell? No. No one had said a word.

"I'll have a decaf latte," I told the waitress who appeared at my shoulder.

"Anything else?"

I wanted to ask for a whole new life, a whole new set of parents, a whole new personality. I shook my head and the waitress darted away.

Mum whispered urgently, her pale eyes huge, "Bird, this is serious."

I wanted to curl up on her lap and cry like a little girl. But I was too angry with her to admit that. I said stiffly, "You left. It's my problem."

"What are you going to do?" She dropped her head into her hands. "I can't believe I'm having this conversation with you. You've always been so sensible. Well, at least as you got older."

"It's all under control."

She looked up at me, her eyebrows lifted. "You're having an abortion?"

"I can't think about that now."

"How far along are you?"

The space between us over the table stretched wide as an ocean. I muttered, "Thirteen or so weeks."

"Oh, Bird. Is this because of me and your father?" she said.

"It's just something that happened. Dad's fine, by the way."

"Something that happened? How could you and Griffin be so careless?"

"I don't need a lecture from you."

"A *baby*. Oh, Bird, I can't begin—" She broke off and stared vacantly into a space I could not see.

I was reminded of how sad she used to be when I was young. It hit me. In every memory I had of her she was *always* sad. Her bottom lip trembled slightly now and I wanted to reach out and hug her. The waitress arrived and put a large yellow mug on the table before me.

When the waitress left, Mum turned her gaze on me and said sternly, "You're a child."

"Don't patronize me. I'm seventeen. I can cope on my own." Even as I said it, panic flooded my head. I didn't have a plan, and every word Mum said made me feel more anxious.

"Exactly, you're seventeen. You can't cope on your own."

As she said this, my anxiety switched to fury. "You should have figured that out before you left."

"How did we get to be strangers?"

"We?"

"Bird—"

"You walked out on Dad. You broke his heart."

She sighed and then said quietly, "You have no idea what my life has been like. Working for that crappy company just to pay the bills so your father could follow his dreams. You know I quit, right? I've found a new job already, working as an assistant to a wedding photographer, so I'm making some money, although nowhere near as much. I have some savings and the experience is what I need right now. Maybe one day I'll be able to, I don't know, set up my own photography business. And I've found a small place to live. It's much nicer than the little hotel I was staying in, and it's really close. You'd like it." As she spoke her cheeks got pinker. She sounded excited. Girlish. The job she'd just described sounded exactly like the sort of thing I wanted to do—maybe we were more similar than I wanted to believe.

I swallowed. "I don't want to know."

"All his dreams, all his plans, and they came to nothing, absolutely nothing, every time. There was never any money; there's never anything left over for me, for you. And my dreams were . . . well, crushed."

"He has plenty left over for me. He's a great father."

"He is. That's true."

"So why did you leave——?" My voice broke.

"I had to." She turned away and gazed across the café. "Bird, you're seventeen. You're throwing away your life. You have such a great future ahead of you."

"Doing what?" My voice was louder than I'd thought it would be. A couple of people turned around to look at us.

"You were going to apply to Oxford University and then you were going to get a great job, be stable, be happy, not living hand to mouth like Dad and I have been. I know you don't love Griffin, not the way you wish you did. And if you keep this baby you'll be tied to him forever. You're clipping your own wings—that stupid broken leg from jumping out of the tree made you scared of the world, my darling. I should have been braver myself, shown you it's okay to get hurt along the way. Now look what's happened."

This was too hard. I tried to get the conversation back in control, saying, "I *am* happy." The words were muddy and untrue.

"When did you start lying to yourself? I know you, Bird."

"When did I start lying to *myself*? When did *you* start lying to me? Why didn't you tell me how unhappy you were?" I blinked back tears. The hormones raging round my body surged up and frustration took the place of sadness. "You don't know me or what I want or anything. I'm going to keep this baby. It's the right thing." Everyone was looking at us.

"Right thing?" she said softly.

I didn't say anything. It seemed the room was still, eyes fixed upon us, even the whirr of the coffee machine had gone quiet. I slumped. "It probably makes no sense to you, and I know Cleo doesn't understand, and Dad won't either—"

"You haven't told him?"

"I didn't want to tell you." I paused, refusing to cry.

"A child," she whispered.

"I'm going to get a job, earn some money. I'll make it all work out."

"Bird, you need to listen to me. You're not thinking. I'm your mother. You're a child yourself. You're being utterly naive. You need to think about all of this; you need to let me help you."

It would be so easy to let her fix everything.

I thought of Dad sitting on the sofa, listening to opera and crying. Mum had left me to deal with him, along with every-thing else.

I didn't need any help from anyone.

This time rage surged up so swiftly I couldn't stop myself. I jumped out of my seat. "Just leave me alone. And leave Dad alone too." I pushed my cup away, not caring that people's conversations had completely stopped around us. "I don't want this coffee and I don't want to see you again." I put my hand to my chest. "I'm sick of the sight of you."

These last words shocked us both, but I was so wound up it didn't stop me from adding one final thing. "I'm going to be a better mother than you ever were."

And with that, I turned on the wave of anger in my body and surfed out of the café blinded by fury, disappointment and the knowledge that I'd never be able to take back what I'd just said.

CHAPTER 15

Sun 13 Feb

Dear AllTheAnswers,

Like you, I'm an advice columnist on the Internet. But this time I'm the one who needs advice. I don't know what I'm doing or where I'm going or what to do or anything. Because I'm pregnant. Pregnant. I decided not to have an abortion. I just couldn't. But I don't know what to do with a baby. A real baby. I. Can't. Believe. I'm. Pregnant.

A

Hi A,

The shock of this situation is weighing on you. Your hormones are making it harder for you to decide what to do. Are you sure keeping the baby is the right choice? Have you been to see a counsellor? I hope you have friends and family to talk to—you need support. Make them listen to you. Don't rush the decision.

AllTheAnswers

Griffin came into my room just as I finished reading the reply from AllTheAnswers, so I minimized the page.

He massaged my shoulders and asked, "What are you doing?"

"Oh, you know me, just working. Um, the essay for English." The last few days at school had been a blur—the only relief was that Pete wasn't there.

He leaned over and kissed me on the side of my neck. He whispered, "You're lying."

My whole body ran cold. He'd seen what I'd written. Oh God. Then a surprising shiver of relief went up my spine. Griffin *knew*. I didn't have to tell him anymore.

I managed to croak, "What?"

"You were working on your website. I saw it before you closed the page."

I spun round to face him, meaning he had to take half a step back. I said, cautiously, "You read what I was writing?"

"Wow, relax, Bird. I didn't read it. I could just tell. You've gone all red."

"God, sorry. I just . . ." So he *didn't* know about the baby. He didn't know anything about all the lies I'd been telling him.

He said, "I know it's private and it's important to you. Whatever. I promise I didn't read a thing." He sat on the bed. "I don't even understand why you kept the whole thing a secret anyway. I had to find out from Cleo that you are this Internet advice columnist and you've been doing it for ages. I thought we were, you know, friends as well as you being my girlfriend. But then you don't . . . well, talk to me anymore."

"I do. I'm sorry." I stood up and went over to him. "I haven't had breakfast yet. Let's eat. Let's hang out. We can talk." Time to tell him. Time to break up with him. Time for me to take control.

Downstairs in the kitchen we ate toast and eggs together. He wrapped his arms round me as I was doing the washing up. I stiffened, wondering if he noticed my extra weight.

I slipped free of his embrace, feeling confused and worn out. I just couldn't find the right words for now. I said, "Dad wanted to go over my CV for that job at the photography studio one last time. I've been working on it for days. All I need after that is to choose three photographs. It'd be fun being a photographer's assistant."

"I should go home anyway. Have my coffee."

"Thanks," I said. "I'm not, um, drinking coffee right now."

He raised an eyebrow.

"Detox," I muttered lamely as we left the kitchen.

He kissed me long and hard as we said goodbye at the front door. I kissed him back, trying to enjoy the feel of him holding me, knowing it couldn't last.

He said, just as I pulled away, "So will you be my Valentine tomorrow?"

I touched his cheek, feeling suddenly sad. "Of course. Sure, thanks."

DAD HAD HIS LAPTOP ON THE SOFA WITH HIM, BUT HE WAS STARING AT a photograph I'd taken of my mother, which hung on the wall. In it, her curly hair blew around her face and her sad eyes seemed luminous against the grey sky. I nudged him.

"I'm job hunting," I said. "Remember, you told me you'd help with the last draft of my CV."

"I wonder whether I could stop those geodesic domes from leaking if I redesigned them."

"What?"

"Because that's the problem. They leak and they've never been able to stop water getting in along the lines of the connections. It's because the roofs of domes are *curved*. But if that could be fixed, if I could fix it, I could make a lot of money."

"We don't need a lot of money," I said. "We just need enough to get by."

He looked over at me with his hazel eyes and pity crossed his face. Then he laughed. "Get by? That's not what I want for you, Bird," he said.

"Anyway, could you look at this?" My pregnancy felt like a red balloon floating over my head—surely he could see it. I gave him a copy of the CV I'd printed out. He took it from me and read it through.

"Well, what do you think?" I asked.

"It could do with being a bit shorter. Tighter here. You need an Experience section. How about when you worked for the newspaper?"

"That wasn't anything, Dad. It was a week of making coffee that I did only because school made us do a placement."

"Bird, if I've learned anything in life, it's to accentuate the positive. Make the most of yourself. Surely there's a quotation about that somewhere, something like: No one else is going to love you if you don't love yourself." For the first time in weeks, he smiled.

NAME: Amy Bird

ADDRESS: 203 Warmingtan Road, South Norwood, London, SE23 4RE
Contact: birdamyfinch@yahoo.co.uk
07777- 888776

EDUCATION
First year of sixth form, studying for AS levels in Art, Spanish, History, IT, English (in order to complete full A levels next year)
GCSEs from Harton's High School, Forest Hill, London, SE19 3FJ, in Maths, Chemistry, Physics, Biology, Double English, Spanish, History, IT, Art; 9 As, 1 A*

EXPERIENCE
Baby Sitting—gave me experience of looking after others and tending to their needs, and experience of organizing finances
Work Experience through school—one week at the *Croydon Advertiser* working in the photography department

WHAT I BRING TO THE JOB
Enthusiasm, willingness to learn, good attention to detail and a love of photography

REFERENCES
Mrs. Teague, Architect at Teague Architecture
Mrs. Livermore, Head Teacher at Harton's High School

I pulled out a selection of my photographs. My favourite was of my street in the snow. I'd staged Cleo's white scarf on the snowy ground and I loved the way it showed that the colour white was really made up of pale blues and pinks and yellows— the scarf and the snow were laced with shapes and shadows. I chose a photo of Griffin I'd taken six months ago. His face filled the frame, his blue eyes brimming with love. I studied them. I realized that behind the love was a look of disquiet. Huh. The next photo was of Mum sitting with both elbows on the table, her head resting in her hands. She had a faraway gaze, looking off into the shadows of the kitchen, her blonde hair catching the gloomy light. I felt a pang. Suddenly I wanted to cry—my photos showed me more about my own world than I'd been able to see with my eyes. I scooped up the three images and slid them into a black file ready for my application.

AS I WALKED TO THE PHOTOGRAPHY STUDIO, EACH STEP DRUMMED with the realization I wasn't going to be saving for a holiday to Jamaica with Cleo anymore. I was saving up for the *baby*. It made me dizzy trying to comprehend what I was doing. After dropping off my CV, I slowed to a stop. I noticed the cobweb of winter branches the trees made, catching the sky in their spidery grasp. What was I *doing*? I felt like I'd spent the last couple of weeks in suspended animation. I. Was. Pregnant. Was I making a huge mistake? Keeping a baby? A *baby*? A plane cut across the sky. I averted my eyes and was faced with the long, empty street ahead.

When I got home, my head was spinning. I *couldn't* be a mother. I *couldn't* look after a baby or give it the life it deserved.

What, I was going to work part time in a photography studio, probably making tea, and give up school to look after some screaming child? I wandered about the house in a fog, clouds of misery obscuring everything except my nightmare. And then I sat at the computer and slowly typed in

Adoption

One of the first pages I read told me to remember that adoption was permanent. With a weight in my tummy, I read the reasons a woman (a *woman!* I found it so hard to think of myself as a woman) gave up a child.

- Lack of money
- Lack of a partner
- Lack of experience—being too young
- Lack of family support

All those reasons applied to me.

I flicked from page to page. I read through forums and noticed that another girl, Angela, in the same position as me, seventeen and pregnant, said:

> I thnk it ws the best decision for my baby girl. I thnk about her every day, every night, and I cry myself to sleep sometimes, but thn I thnk of her w/ the parents I chose and I know I made the right step for her future.

I clicked to another forum.

Mya: I waited & waited 2 know what to do but then I took Rio home. 1 day became 2 days then 2 days became 6 wks. Ive made up my mind.

Steph: I wanted to write and thank Emmy for giving me my son. All of you wondering if adoption is the way to go, remember there are loving families out there like mine that would never get the chance to parent if it weren't for you.

I looked at photos of people waiting to be parents in California on a friendly U.S. site that made it all sound really easy. I looked at another forum, my heart jumping around inside me and my head spinning. One girl had written that it was a good idea to look at YouTube to see adoptive parent profiles. And there they were: Jane and Jake cuddling each other and smiling. Her doing yoga. Him at a baseball game. But all these families were in America, and when I tried to find a U.K. couple, nothing came up. I flicked over to a U.K. site for parents looking for babies and it all sounded really formal and scary. The legal stuff made me feel nauseous. After that, I read stories by people who had been adopted. Good stories and bad. I thought of Jake and Jane in the photos. I thought of Steph and Emmy on the forums. And of Mya and Rio, one day becoming two, two days becoming six weeks . . .

I had to give up this baby. If I didn't, I might never:

- do my exams
- go to university
- travel the world

- fall in love
- have sex again
- finish my photography project
- be successful in a career
- skydive
- go in a hot air balloon

I had to give it up. *Had* to.

I held my hand to my stomach. It had popped a little more, but not enough for anyone at school to know yet that there was something inside me, growing.

I finger-combed my wild hair and slipped on a jacket. I had to get out the house again. I wandered without thinking about where I was going. I ended up in the park opposite the school. I sat on a bench and let my thoughts whizz around while I watched the ducks on the lake. It had become one of those February days when shafts of sunlight probe their way through the clouds to point down at the earth. My mind wouldn't settle. I was thinking of Pete and of Griffin, of Cleo, of my mum and dad. Suddenly, I realized all I was doing was thinking about other people, not about myself. Not about the baby. Thinking about the baby, imagining it, reminded me I couldn't give a child a good life, because I was too young. It would be better off with another family.

But maybe I was wrong. Maybe I could look after a baby—

My phone rang. It was Pete's number on the screen. I waited a second, not sure what to do.

I answered.

"It's me," the voice said.

"What do you want?" I said.

"Where are you?"

I looked at the park, my eyes not able to avoid the leafy area where he and I had last kissed. "What does it matter?"

"I want to see you."

"It's not a good idea. I thought I'd, you know, made that clear."

"I want to see you," he said again. "And even if you don't want to see me, I'm right here." He started laughing.

As I heard him laughing over the phone, I heard him laughing in real life, the sound bouncing along the path and into my ears. He was walking straight toward me. His lean body, his sensual mouth, his gritty, unnerving gaze.

"Someone's in a bad mood today," he said, then the phone call was cut off as he put his phone in his pocket and sauntered over to me, smiling in that way he had.

"It's not a good time," I repeated.

He sat on the bench. "Fancy meeting you here," he said, and as if nothing had happened, as if we were a *couple*, he slid an arm around me.

I found myself leaning into him slightly. My skin prickled under my clothes.

I said, "Why haven't you been at school? I haven't seen you around for ages."

He shrugged. "I guess I'm not the school type."

"But you said you were starting over."

"So you *were* listening?"

"School's important, Pete. It gives you a future."

"And I've never heard that before," he said sarcastically.

"Okay, okay. It's none of my business."

"What if I want it to be your business?"

"You don't."

He tightened his arm around my body and brought his face close to mine. He said, "Don't I? Have you not forgiven me yet?"

"Pete," I found myself saying. Heat crept up my spine.

He tipped my face up to his.

I was on fire.

He said, "I can't read you at all. That's what I like about you."

"Pete, you have no idea."

"Well, tell me, then." He leaned in to kiss me and I almost let him, but then I held a hand up to his lips. He needed to know about the baby.

I said, "You don't get it, do you?"

He sighed. "God, do we have to be so intense?"

My eyes narrowed and I shoved him off. "This is too intense for you, Pete? You stroll over here, put your arm round me like . . . like things are fine. I haven't seen you for ages; we don't even *know* each other. And you sit down and tell me you want to be my business. That's your problem—you can't be what you say you want to be. You make out you're into me, then when I call you, you can't commit to anything. You come and sit here, trying to kiss me like you own me, but when I try to talk to you, you think I'm being too intense. Well, get this, Pete Loewen, maybe I am intense. Maybe that's what I'm *like*. If you want someone different, there's always Kitty."

"It was a joke," he said. "Relax."

"It's all a joke to you, Pete." The air was cool and the shafts of sunlight I'd seen before were gone. "Well, I'm not laughing. None of it's funny to me."

His eyes became flinty. He clenched his jaw.

I let the words spill from my lips. "I'm pregnant, Pete. Hilarious. Ha. Ha. Ha. Right. Now who's laughing? Not so funny anymore, is it?"

His face went blank.

I continued, "And I'm not having an abortion and I was going to keep it, but then I freaked out and I've been looking at adoption sites on the Internet, but part of me still thinks I should just have the stupid abortion, but then I *can't* and I just . . . I just don't know why. It's a nightmare. I don't know what I'm doing or why I'm doing it and I have no one to talk to because Cleo doesn't know anything about this stuff either and I don't want to talk to a counsellor because I just don't and my parents have split up and they're the last people I could talk about this with and then you come over and make jokes and act like you always do and mess with my head and make me crazy and then everything's supposed to be funny and it's not funny. And my head is just . . . is just spinning because I don't know if I want to give the baby away and I don't even know how to decide something like that."

"A baby?" he said slowly.

Pete. The troublemaker. The guy who was going nowhere with his life. The guy whose dad was in prison. The guy who would sleep with any girl who was stupid enough to fall into his arms, including Kitty Moss. The guy who'd just asked me not to be so intense: *intense*? This baby would tie me to him *forever*.

"It's not yours," I heard myself lie.

His blank face suddenly transformed as it filled with fury, his grey eyes dark. "So why are you telling me?"

179

I pushed my hair out of my face. "You know what? Forget it. Don't come near me. Everything that happened between us was a total mistake. I wish I'd never been so stupid as to go anywhere near a guy like you."

"You're so full of yourself, Amy. You think you know everything about everyone. I've seen your advice column online, Miss Take-Control-of-Your-Life. Huh, you seem to think you know how to tell other people how to live. Let me break it to you: you're the most judgmental person I've ever met. You have no idea how to live your own life, yet you think you can tell everyone else what to do."

"How did you find the site?"

"I saw Cleo checking it out on her phone when I was sitting behind her one day, then heard her call you Miss-Take-Control . . . She's not very discreet, your friend."

"Did you tell anyone?"

He shook his head. "Just our little secret." He smiled briefly, then anger returned to his eyes.

I would have been flattered he'd gone to the trouble of seeking me out online if I wasn't feeling so furious. "People *love* my column."

His voice softened. "Why are you so blind to what you need in your own life when you're so good at telling other people how to live? You're pregnant. What are you doing?"

"I'm thinking of giving the baby away. I have a *plan*. I'm going places. I want to go to Oxford University. And you were just . . . a . . . a crush. You don't care about me."

His voice filled with venom. "You don't know anything. You

never even bothered to get to know me. I hope you and Griffin are very happy together."

"You're the one who started sleeping with Kitty Moss."

"I haven't touched Kitty. We broke up. It was nothing." He rubbed his face. "I only brought her to that stupid party because I was trying to get you to pay some attention to what you were missing."

"Pete, don't give me that. You're a womanizer and a creep."

"You think you're in control of your life? Well, Miss Seventeen-and-Pregnant, you're not. We could have had something really good, Amy."

"No, we couldn't. You're not ready for something good— you're too immature."

My words seemed to strike him hard, because he put his hand against his chest

I said, "Don't. Come. Near. Me."

He slumped on the bench like he'd just been shot. And with that I stood and walked away from him, the sounds of my angry words echoing in the space between us, ricocheting off the walls of my empty heart.

CHAPTER 16

SCHOOL WAS BUSY, WITH MS. DEVLIN IN A FEVER PITCH OF EXCITE-
ment about the upcoming Barcelona trip, so there wasn't much
time to think about stuff, which was good because I didn't want
to think about anything anyway.

As the half-term holidays rolled around, Mum tried to get
in touch with me, leaving messages on my phone saying things
like, *We need to talk,* and *It's not too late. Please, Bird, call me so
we can think about what you're going through together,* and *Have
you told your father yet? You have to tell him.* I deleted every
message and didn't call her back.

Sun 20 Feb
Dear Miss Take-Control-of-Your-Life,
With spring coming, I feel like I should be sorting out my life
but I can't seem to get a grip. Every morning I wake up miserable. I'm swimming under water and I don't know how to get

to the surface. Nothing's wrong but everything is. How can I get out of this funk?

Bellyboo, 17

As I wrote, I wondered briefly if Pete would read my advice, then decided I didn't care if he did or not. Only he, Griffin and Cleo knew my online identity, and that wasn't going to change what I told Bellyboo, or anyone else.

Hey Bellyboo,

You might be depressed. Go and see your doctor for a check-up—depression is a serious issue, and your doctor will be able to advise you (check out the new <u>Other Help</u> section on the site for the number of a support line).

<u>Tips to Take Back Control</u>

Get out of bed when your alarm goes off. Don't lie there feeling worse.

All the usual: exercise, healthy eating, not too much coffee, lots of sleep, blah blah blah . . .

Do one of the things you feel you should be doing every day, but just one thing. Break it down so you don't feel over-whelmed.

Spend time with friends. Take a day off and have fun.

If none of these are working, and you haven't yet been, go and see your doctor.

From one teen to another . . .

Miss Take-Control-of-Your-Life

When I finished my answer, I felt like I was doing a good job. For a few moments, I really was Miss Take-Control-of-Your-Life. I posted my reply, then added a new Other Help section with a list of phone numbers and websites with useful information. I updated some of the coding so the pages looked better. Because even more people were writing in, the whole thing needed a bit of tidying up. By fixing things for everyone else, I felt hopeful I could get back some control in my own life.

Cleo called, interrupting me as I logged off, to ask me what I was packing, and I genuinely didn't know what she was talking about.

"It's half-term . . . remember?"

I flicked through my desk calendar. "Oh my God. We're going to Spain, like, tomorrow!"

"Uh, Ms. Devlin's been handing out checklists constantly. We've been talking about nothing else in Spanish class—hellooooo? And you're supposed to be coming over to stay the night and we're going to the airport together. Remember?"

I ran my pen over the days in my calendar. "I had the dates wrong in my head. God, this is so not like me."

"Pregnancy brain," she said. "I read about it on the Internet on one of those baby websites. You forget stuff all the time because of your hormones."

"Maybe I'm just really stupid."

"Where did that come from?"

I shrugged, not that she could see me. "I just don't know what's going on inside my own head anymore. That ever happen to you?"

"Like, all the time."

"How do you live with it? I can't tell if I'm happy or sad or if I secretly *want* to see Pete every day for a week on this trip or if I hate him."

"I hate him. Can we talk about this later? Like, you have to be here getting ready to go to Spain tomorrow."

"Okay, okay." I glanced round my room and groaned. My clothes were all over the floor—I hated how messy it was, but trying to find clothes that fit took up way too much time every morning for me to be able to clean up after myself. "I have no idea what to bring. My clothes are all too small—I feel like I can't breathe. I'm just huge."

"No one can tell yet. Don't worry. Well, except for your supersonic mum."

She paused and my stomach lurched as I thought about what it was going to be like when everyone found out, when I was showing so much it would be obvious to the rest of the world. I was still in suspended animation.

She said, breaking my thoughts, "My mum has some stuff."

Normally I wouldn't wear anyone's mum's clothes, but Cleo's mum dressed only in designer outfits and always looked great. Way better than I ever did. I didn't hesitate. "Yes. Good. Thank God."

"I'll pull out some of her stuff. You go and find your brain."

"Thanks for looking at baby websites for me. I'll come over."

I grabbed some underwear from the laundry basket and folded up a few things I could bring for myself. I checked the weather in Barcelona on the Internet—warmer than normal for this time of year, but cool in the evenings—and wrote a list of all the last-minute details:

- Passport
- Check-in online (instructions from Ms. Devlin in Spanish folder)
- Money—ask Dad? Bring bank card (does it work in Spain? Take money out before; otherwise, find out online?)
- Warm clothes—wool dress could go over C's mum's leggings, maybe . . . check with Cleo
- Bathroom things—in main bag, can't bring them through Security
- Call Griffin to say goodbye
- Reading for English—bring *Adventures in the Skin Trade*

I gathered everything into a suitcase and called Griffin. He wasn't answering his phone, so I left a message asking him to give me a call later. I did one last visual sweep of my room and headed downstairs to talk to Dad.

I found him asleep on the sofa. He jerked awake and muttered, "What time is it? I should be working."

As I did every time I saw him, I studied his face to see if he knew. I tried to work out if Mum had told him. He rubbed his tongue under his cheeks and coughed heavily. I didn't recognize this man as my father—the cheerful, ambitious, oblivious, loving man he used to be was gone.

I said, "It's Sunday morning, Dad. Like, 11:45. Look, you remember the school trip to Spain that Mum . . . I mean, that you and Mum paid for in September?"

He rubbed his eyes. "I suspect your mother sorted that all out. Was it expensive? When is it? I don't have any money right now for a school trip."

"No, Dad, it's all sorted. It wasn't expensive because a big group of us are going and it's with one of those cheap airlines, and Mum said it was all okay."

"So what do you need?"

"Well, I'm staying the night at Cleo's and we're leaving tomorrow. We're back next Sunday morning."

He grunted.

"Dad, is that okay? Will you be okay?"

"Huh?" he said. "Yeah." He fished in his pocket and pulled out a twenty-pound note. "That should keep you going," he said.

I sat next to him. He smelled a little sour. "Dad, I don't have to go."

"Course you'll go. I'm fine. I'd drive you over to Cleo's but the car isn't working well. I should have taken it in this week."

"No problem. I'll get myself there. Or she can give me a ride. Sure you're okay?"

"Don't worry your little Birdy head over it. Have you spoken to your mother? She won't answer my calls."

That meant Mum hadn't told him about the baby. Thank God. I was pretty sure he wouldn't be able to cope with any more bad news right now, although the state he was in, maybe he wouldn't even register the information.

I said, "I haven't been replying to her. I don't want to talk to her right now."

"Come here," he said, smothering me in a big, stinky hug.

"Thanks, Dad, for the money," I said, pulling away from the smell as quickly as I could.

"I'll bet rain could be turned into an energy source," he said.

I put the money in my pocket, glad I had some left over in my account from my birthday. Dad hadn't given me any money since Mum left, and twenty pounds wouldn't get me very far anywhere, let alone in Spain. I found out online that my bank card would work over there, then I had only a few more bits and pieces to finish off—and I'd be ready.

And so far, I hadn't let the thought that Pete Loewen was going to be on the trip distract me. Well, not too much, anyway.

CLEO AND I LAUGHED TOGETHER LIKE WE HADN'T DONE IN AGES. SHE did my nails and helped me pack her mum's things. We lay around on her bed and chatted, and as I drifted to sleep I felt like the argument with Pete, the tension with Griffin, the pregnancy, all of it was just a dream.

Her dad gave us a ride the next morning, so early that the sun was just breaking into the sky. Everyone from Spanish class was at the airport.

Except Pete.

I waited and waited, pretending to myself the whole time that I wasn't checking around for him. I imagined him loping into the airport, his jacket slung over his shoulder, his eyes fixed on mine. Then I reminded myself that since our fight in the park, we weren't speaking.

Cleo leaned over and whispered, "It's okay to go on a plane when you're pregnant, right?"

"Shh." I put my finger to my lips and looked around at the others from our class, but no one had heard. "I checked on the Internet. It's fine until I'm, like, thirty-five weeks."

Ms. Devlin and the other teacher, Mr. Bartlett, waved everyone into a group, yelling out in Spanish what we were supposed to be doing, chastising a couple of students who hadn't checked themselves in. Ms. Devlin generally managed to be wired, wound-up and smiling all at the same time—she was obviously delighted to be en route.

Pete still wasn't there.

The airport buzzed with the constant chatter of people passing through. Loud announcements boomed about passengers late for flights. Boarding calls and reminders not to leave luggage unattended echoed around the cavernous ceilings. Once we were all through Security—which was a ridiculously complicated drama, what with Ms. D. insisting on only speaking Spanish to us and half the group not understanding anything—Cleo and I wandered round the shops, spraying perfume at each other and trying on face creams. We smelt of musk and roses, of fruity tones and floral hints, our faces plump and smooth, and both of us were heady with the upcoming trip. A holiday from my life was exactly what I needed.

It was only when, with a white-noise roar, the plane took off that I realized Pete really wasn't going to make it. The part of me that was weighed down by the baby was glad. A week without either Pete or Griffin around would probably be the best thing for me, but a small shard inside me missed him, a tiny diamond of longing.

BARCELONA WAS A JEWEL. THE SUN FELL LIKE SOFT FABRIC AS WE arrived, cushioning the higgledy-piggledy buildings, the crowded plazas and the verdant parks. Deep shadows knifed through the glow of afternoon light. The air smelt of churros, sweet and doughnut-like and served on every street corner. Groups of people huddled around, smoking with abandon. The smell of cigarettes made me nauseous but nothing was going to prevent me enjoying the trip, not even pregnancy sickness—I remembered how all the websites I'd read told me by the second trimester I'd be over the nausea. Not a chance.

We arrived in the hotel lobby and stood around. I snapped some photos of the mustard-coloured floor tiles and white-washed walls, and I listened to the chatter of a group of German tourists who were pointing and exclaiming in loud, grunting delight at a photograph of the bright pink unfinished church, La Sagrada Família, on the wall. I wandered into a small court-yard filled with dark metal tables and chairs, and photographed that too. A loud squawk made me jump. A huge blue-and-red parrot perched in an ornate cage to my left. He spent the fol-lowing days yelling at passersby, and through our breakfasts in the courtyard, he screamed in semi-Spanish to those of us unfortunate enough to end up close to him.

The owners of the hotel were from Panama, Ms. Devlin said. They'd called the hotel Colón after their home city, apparently a violent and dangerous place. As she was conversing with them, I tried to understand what they were saying and was disappointed not to be able to pick up a word. I had thought I was good at Spanish, but when real Spanish-speakers said anything, I was out of my depth. The rest of our group was giggling and chat-ting—all of us were excited and buzzing with the prospect of so many days away from home and parents and responsibilities.

CLEO AND I HAD A SMALL ROOM TOGETHER ON THE FOURTH FLOOR of the hotel. It had two austere single beds covered in thin brown blankets. Just over the street was a bar that boomed loud pop music, and as we settled in for the first night, both of us were kept awake by the sounds of people laughing and yelling outside. We lay there quietly, and I just enjoyed thinking about all we were supposed to be doing during the week ahead.

There was a beep, then Cleo whispered, "I just got an email for you from Griffin on my phone."

She threw over the phone and I read it.

Love U baby. Sleep well. Dream Spanish dreams. Sorry we couldn't talk yesterday—Mom having a bad time. Can't believe I'm not going to see you for a WEEK!!!! Did you get my text?

I checked my phone and emailed him back on Cleo's.

No—my phone isn't working at all. Sorry. It's great here—warmer than we thought it would be, and full of flowers. Spring comes earlier here, I guess.

Tired, and busy day tomorrow. Ms. D has a full itinerary—which I'm excited about. Cleo's phone is working fine (of course!), so find me here.

Thinking of you.

Love, Bird

THE MORNINGS WERE FULL OF GUIDED TOURS TO VARIOUS BUILDINGS, which I photographed like crazy, and the afternoons were devoted to three-hour Spanish lessons that left us all exhausted.

After supper and an evening lecture, Cleo and I barely had the energy to talk to each other, let alone go out.

Griffin and I sent a few emails to each other on her phone, and he told me he'd checked in on Dad, who seemed to be doing okay. Griffin was always so sweet and thoughtful, but as the week went on, I heard from him less. He didn't even reply to my last email. As the week was coming to an end, one evening lecture was cancelled, so Cleo and I got dressed up and slipped down the hotel corridor to secret freedom.

The night was aromatic with spring flowers and with the leaves of the large basil plants that the hotel owners had in pots outside the front door. The mildness of the air and the bouquet of stars above made me feel like we were a million miles from my life in London. Joy bubbled up inside me like sparkling white wine. We stood outside the bar and Cleo grinned at me.

"I love this," she said.

A couple of guys came over and, in Spanish, offered us cigarettes. I was glad to understand what they were saying. Somehow during the week, the babbling, unintelligible sounds had become clearer.

Cleo took a cigarette, smiling at the skinny dark-haired guy handing them out. I refused.

The other guy, who had a moustache and a flat cap jauntily perched on his head, opened his mouth to speak to me. His teeth were surprisingly white and straight. He said, in Spanish, "Where are you from?"

To my delight, I could answer him easily. He offered me a bottle of beer, but I declined. He shrugged and carried on asking me questions, most of which I could understand and answer. I wondered what I might look like to someone walking past, for here I was speaking Spanish, dressed in a cute designer dress of Cleo's mum's collection, animated and happy. That was it: I was happy.

TOP TIP 21: BE HAPPY

After a while, we went inside with the guys, Miguel and Pedro, joining a group of their friends. The music was loud and the bar sparked with flashing lights. Everyone was sweaty and dancing. Cleo and I danced together and laughed at the guys who were circling us. Miguel, the one with the white teeth, and Cleo started kissing at one point and I pulled back a bit. One of their friends put his hands on my waist but I spun away. I was glad not to be thinking about guys or having to deal with them, and I put my hands up toward the ceiling to feel the music pulse. Happiness surged through me again and I could feel myself smiling.

As we sneaked up to our hotel room, I let out a huge yawn. "I'm so tired," I said. We stumbled into our beds and lay there in the dark. "We should do that every night," I whispered.

She said, "It was fun."

"I mean it—why can't we just have fun all the time?"

"Uh, I don't mean to bring you down, but you're, you know, having a baby." She threw a pillow at me. "Go to sleep," she said.

"I can't."

She was quiet, then said, "You're right. I can't sleep either. I love it here. I could live here forever."

"Here?"

"Yeah, that's right, stuck in this room with you forever. No. I want to live in a foreign city, like here, and speak foreign languages. Maybe study in Barcelona, or Madrid, or Berlin, or Paris. I don't know." She sat up and I could see her eyes glittering in the soft dark of our room. "It's so great. Exciting."

She fell silent and I pictured the life she had ahead of her. The weight of the baby inside me was suddenly immense. Just like that, I made my decision.

I said, "I'm thinking . . . well, I might . . . no, I am. I think I am. For sure."

"What?"

"I'm going to give the baby up for adoption," I said, testing out the words.

She sat bolt upright, enthusiasm spilling everywhere. "You are? Really? That's great. Really great. Good for you."

I threw her pillow back and said, "We'll get a place together when we finish university—live in Spain. Meet some people," I added slowly, fatigue overwhelming me.

"Do you want to talk about it more? About giving up the baby?"

I lay looking up into the dark. "What's there to say?"

ON THE LAST DAY, WE WENT TO LA SAGRADA FAMÍLIA, THE BEAUTIFUL pink church synonymous with Barcelona (according to Ms. Devlin). The towers pointed like bejewelled fingers right up into the blue of the sky. Totally photogenic. We admired it from the outside first of all, and even the people in our group who were normally too cool to enjoy the morning tours seemed impressed. Then we began to climb the stairs, which spiralled up into one of the tall towers. I puffed my way up about fifty steps and then began to feel dizzy: the late night, the exertion, the pregnancy . . . My head began to spin and I sat heavily. Ms. Devlin, who was just behind, bent over me with concern.

"Bird?"

I caught my breath. "I'm fine. It just that I'm . . ." I stopped. I wasn't going to spoil the holiday, not when there were so few hours left. "I'll just wait here," I said.

She frowned momentarily, then nodded.

I smiled up at her. "It's great being here," I said, knowing suddenly that I couldn't pretend for much longer that none of this was happening.

CHAPTER 17

THE FLIGHT HOME WAS MASSIVELY DELAYED BECAUSE OF TECHNICAL problems. We spent most of the day being shunted from one plane to another, and even Ms. Devlin had lost a little sparkle when we finally got back to London at 11 p.m. Cleo's dad dropped me off at home and I tiptoed up the stairs.

My dad was sleeping, but he'd left me a note.

Saw the flight was going to be really late. Waited up, but it kept getting later and later. Cleo's parents called and told me they'd bring you home, so I've gone to bed.

Hope you had a good time.

Love Dad

I tumbled into bed, too tired even to text Griffin, woke up early, squeezed into some clothes—I seemed to have got a load bigger during the holiday—did some homework, got straight to work on the Internet looking up Adoption Services, made a call, then wrote the email that was on my mind.

Mon 28 Feb

Dear AllTheAnswers,

I did it. I set up an appointment with Adoption Services so they can come and see me. I spoke to someone called Nicole. She's the only person I've been honest with for ages. She's coming in two weeks and there is an information package being sent. I've decided adoption is the best choice. It's the right decision for me; everyone says so and agrees with me, and I know it's for the best—I'm only seventeen. I just wish I didn't feel so weird all the time.

It's making me cry writing this.

I don't know why I'm crying so hard. This is the right thing for the baby and for me. The baby will grow up happy and safe in a perfect family. And I'll be able to get back to my life. To my friends. My website.

A

Dear A,

What you're going through is hard. You're making a decision that only you can make. You know what will be best for this baby. I claim to have all the answers, but the answer to your dilemma is one only you can know.

When I advise people, I try to remind them to follow their heart. You need to give yourself time to make this decision.

Keep writing to me,

AllTheAnswers

I texted Griffin but he didn't reply—even though we hadn't seen each other for a week. I tried knocking on his door, but he wasn't there to walk me to school—his mum said he'd already gone. She seemed totally fine. Griffin was right; maybe she wasn't as bad as I'd thought.

I walked to school alone. I was exhausted from the trip, but I wasn't going to miss classes. I was surprised to see Cleo when I got in. I figured she'd take the day off. She gave me a big hug and we pressed in close to the lockers in the school corridor. The first bell hadn't yet gone and she was watching me gather my stuff.

She said, "God, I'm sooo tired. Did you do your essay on *King Lear*?"

"Really early this morning, like at 6 a.m. I never do homework last minute. I wrote about the part when he goes mad."

"The part where King Lear takes his clothes off?"

I giggled. My good mood from Spain was lasting.

She said, "Better to do it last minute than not at all, but I figure with the flight delays I'll get away with not having done it. Have you spoken to Pete since we got back?"

"Pete? No. Why would I? You know it's all over. I told you."

"Just, I guess, you lied about it so well before, I just wondered if you were still seeing him."

I pushed my locker shut. "Stop it, all right?"

She sighed and put a perfect blue nail up to her lips. "Your secret's safe. You know that. But you do have to tell Griffin. Er, unless he's blind, he's going to notice soon. You're pretty round already."

"Doesn't this top hide it? I can't believe how some girls don't show until they're like six months along and I'm not even eighteen weeks yet."

She surveyed me critically. "Um, yeah, I guess it's covered enough. Sort of."

I sucked in my tummy. I already had the button of my jeans undone. I said, "You know, I haven't heard from Griffin since we got back. It's weird. He's not answering his phone and he didn't call last night. I'm expecting to see him any minute."

"Does he know we're home?"

"He should. I hope he's okay." A finger of worry tickled my neck. "Perhaps he thinks that we get back a different day, and that my phone still isn't getting his messages. He hasn't emailed you instead, then?"

"Well, my stupid phone stopped working yesterday and I haven't been online. Hmm, even the last couple days in Barcelona I didn't check. Then I was too tired last night and too rushed this morning. I feel like I . . . I'm just so *unconnected.*"

I said, "What's wrong with it?"

She shrugged. "I'll get Xavier to have a look at the stupid thing later."

I said, "Griffin's probably caught up with things with his mum."

"You know, you have to tell him. Really, Bird, you're getting bigger, and although it could be just fat if you didn't know—"

"I get it, Cleo."

My back was to the passing hordes of students. Someone came up behind me. Glad for the interruption, I pivoted, only to find horsey-faced Neen Patel leaning close to me. She was standing with a group of girls and said loudly, "She is. You can tell, look." She pointed at my belly and the other girls laughed. One of them sneered at me and said, "Whore."

My heart shunted the blood through my body. Red heat went all the way to my fingers and toes. Cleo stood there open-mouthed, showing two rows of perfect teeth, and I was reminded of the boy, Miguel, in Spain, the thrill of the music, the sweaty dance floor.

Cleo launched herself into action. "What did you say?" she yelled.

The girls huddled together defensively. The tallest one, Simone McLeod, yelled, "She's the one who's having a baby."

"What do you know about it?" Cleo shouted.

"It's true," cried another girl with glee. "Miss Perfect's knocked up."

I grabbed Cleo and pulled her down the corridor. She started yelling at the girls, calling them names, but I yanked her into the girls' toilets.

"Did you tell anyone?" I asked before I could stop myself. "You must have."

She turned her huge brown eyes on me and her pupils widened with surprise, then hurt.

"I'm sorry. Of course you didn't tell anyone," I said. "I'm just shocked."

"I can't believe you'd even think I would," she said, and she looked down at her bright blue nails. "God, Bird."

"I'm sorry, okay? Sorry. I just don't know how they know."

"I can't believe you had to ask. Of course I didn't tell anyone."

With a sickening lurch I remembered the horrible conversation in the park with Pete before we went to Spain. Could he? Would he?

Just then, Kitty Moss came past the open door. Her bright blonde curls were up in a high ponytail and her red lipstick made her mouth shine like a fire extinguisher. "Slag," she said through her vivid mouth. And she walked away.

Everyone knew.

TOP TIP 22: WHAT YOU DON'T KNOW *CAN* HURT YOU

Griffin. I had to tell Griffin.

I had to tell Dad.

The teachers.

This was really happening.

How could Pete have done this to me?

I heard the first bell as I pushed my way through the mocking faces of everyone around me. My heart was racing. I marched out of the school building, trying to keep my head high. As I passed the park opposite school, I could feel my cheeks burning. I thought of Pete and his metallic-grey eyes when they looked at me. I felt desire. And something else. Hatred. I hated him for ruining my life. *Hated* him.

I walked home as fast as I could. Before I could stop myself, before I had time to think, I hurried into the living room.

Dad was staring at the photo of Mum on the wall.

My throat was tight. "I have to tell you something," I managed to say.

He didn't seem to hear me. "I have a new idea for an aluminum water bottle. You could personalize it with an engraving, meaning you'd keep it. You'd never have to buy a water bottle again. They're bad for the environment. Can you engrave aluminum?"

I'd recently read the same idea in a magazine, but I didn't have the heart to tell him. I said, "Dad, please listen."

He looked at me and his eyes were bleary with lack of sleep. The silence was agony. He'd never see me the same way again. I was nearly crying. "I'm sorry, Dad."

"What's wrong, honey? Why aren't you at school?"

"I'm . . ." It was so hard. "I'm having a . . ."

"What?"

"Baby."

I could see shock in his hazel eyes. As if he'd been punctured, he deflated on the sofa. He spoke very quietly, not looking at me.

"You stupid, stupid girl."

I put my hand to my cheek like I'd been slapped.

He pushed himself up using his hands against the sofa. He made to head out of the room, his heavy body moving slowly.

"Dad," I sobbed. "Please."

He stopped and rotated back to me. His lips were pressed together.

I stammered, "It w-was an accident. I . . . I just—"

Vitriol erupted from him like he'd sprung a leak. "You just *what*?" he yelled. "You were just so busy pretending to be the perfect daughter that you accidentally had sex?"

My cheeks heated up. "I never pretended anything."

"You sit there checking Oxford University online and get me to help you fill out your job application, and all the while you're sleeping with your boyfriend like that would be okay? You thought I'd just be fine with that? What's wrong with the women in this family? Cheerful old man, me, hey? I don't care that my wife left me and my daughter is a little slut. Oh no, rely on me to just roll with the blows." He took a gasp of air. "Bird, you're supposed to be the good one in the family. All of it's meant to be worth it because you're going to do a better job of your life than me. Than your mother. She gave it all up." He yelled louder, his face turning red and his hands gesturing about him like fireworks. "She gave it all up *for you*. And I worked like a dog so you could have everything."

Stupidly, I rose to the bait and didn't keep my mouth shut. "What, Dad? What did you do that was so great? You worked yourself half to death for failed businesses and a broken marriage. This is not all my fault."

"Failed businesses? What are you talking about? I have *ideas*. And as for your mother, you seem to have forgotten that *she's* the one who left *me*. I didn't ruin the marriage. Don't you dare blame me, young lady. I'm not the one who's pregnant, am I?"

I tried to backtrack—I was just making everything worse. "I'm sorry, Dad. I didn't mean it. I just—"

"Just what? Didn't you say this already? I'm still not hearing any answers, Bird. You thought I'd give you a hug and tell you everything was going to be okay? A pat on the back and then we'd go on like you hadn't just ruined your life."

"I'm giving the baby up for adoption."

"Oh, are you? You've got it all worked out, have you? Just give it away, that'll sort things out. That's what's wrong with you, Bird. You think life's so easy. Simple solutions to difficult problems. That's always been your mistake."

"Dad, please. I'm so sorry."

He looked me up and down. His voice became very soft again. "I'm such a fool. I've been so blind to you and your mother."

"It's not you. It's my fault."

"I'm so disappointed," he said, and to my horror a sob broke from his chest. "Just get out of my sight."

"Dad—"

"Seriously, get out. Go to Cleo's. Or Griffin's."

He stormed out of the room and I heard the back door slam. He was probably headed off to his shed to stare at his sketches of solar bricks or whatever. I stood there shaking.

The phone rang then, the sound like a fire-blanket being thrown over me, blocking my distress from flaring up inside. The ringing propelled me into action and I ran to grab the phone. It was some telesales guy trying to see if we needed new windows. What a crazy world. How could people be talking about windows as my universe was shattering? I couldn't summon words, so I gently returned the handset to its cradle, hanging up on the guy mid-spiel.

Trying not to cry, I took in quick, short breaths. Then I ran to the back door to follow Dad. I had to talk to him. I yanked open the door and blinked in the bright morning sunshine. Griffin stood outside like a terrible apparition. I jumped, horrified to see him there. He looked like he hadn't slept in weeks, big purple lines under his washed-out eyes, his skin pale and his black hair greasy.

"Griffin," I said, steadying myself against the door frame. "What are you doing here?" It was a stupid thing to ask.

"Is it true what they're saying? It can't be true. Tell me it's not true. It was up on *Facebook*, Bird . . ."

I searched for words. Someone had put it up on Facebook. Oh my God, everything was ruined. Facebook? I put my hand over my mouth to stop myself from throwing up.

"A *baby*?" he said.

"Griffin . . . I . . ."

"I don't understand," he said.

My insides heaved. "I'm going to give it away," I said, desperately, like that would help.

He put his hands to his face and spoke through his fingers. He said, "I love you. Forever. We've always known that we love each other, but . . ." He gestured at my belly, which was churning.

My words rushed up like vomit. "I didn't know how to tell you. I was paralyzed, completely stuck. I just . . ."

He stood there as if he hadn't heard. For one second . . . two.

I said, "I'm sorry. I'm so sorry."

He said, suddenly sarcastic, not like him at all, "*I'm sorry, Griffin. I'm not ready for sex. Not with you, Griffin, so don't rush me.*"

"Griffin, don't."

"*I* was *pushing* you, was I? You didn't want to *rush*."

No words came from my mouth. A cloud obscured the sun and Griffin's face was brought into bleak focus by the greying of the light. His sarcasm finished, suddenly he sounded confused. "Is this really happening? Jesus, Bird, it's public knowledge but you didn't think you'd tell me? Do you know what it felt like reading that about you—*about us*—online?"

"I'm sorry." I could not undo what I'd done. "I should have told you."

"How? Who? Who is he?" He was desperate. "Bird?"

I shook my head. "It's too late."

He became insistent. "Who is he?"

"It won't help, Griffin."

"You won't even tell me that? You lied to me, made me feel like it was me ruining everything—"

"It doesn't matter who he is—"

"I can't believe you'd do this." His face pleaded with me to change what was happening. "Bird?"

I shook my head again. "I'm sorry."

He drank me in with his last look. And then he swallowed hard. He turned his back and walked down the path, and I knew, because I know him so well, that he was crying.

I ARRIVED AT CLEO'S LATER THAT EVENING. SHE ANSWERED THE DOOR in a shirt-dress and leggings. "How've you been?" she said, her eyes worried. "I've been trying to call you all day. Like thousands of times." She cast an eye over the small rucksack at my feet. "Seriously, this is bad. I saw it on Facebook—I can't believe I didn't read it when we were away. I wasn't checking anything like that—you know, being disconnected is supposed to be a good thing for Internet addicts like me, holidays, whatever. Did you get my messages? Did you see it online? Griffin *must* have read it." I knew she was rambling because everything was so awful. "Did you see Griffin? What about your dad?"

"I didn't know where else to go, C." I choked back a sob. "My dad's so angry. Griffin hates me. I've ruined everything. I need— Can I stay here?"

"Hey, hey, come in." She grabbed me in a huge hug. I stood there crying. "I'll just ask my mum."

"I'll wait."

She nodded and headed up the curved staircase. I could see myself in the mirror in the hallway. I looked wretched, my body bloated, my hair a frizzy mess. My cheeks were pale and a little mascara darkened the flesh under my eyes. Cleo came back downstairs.

"She says it's okay. Your dad had already called. Told her about, you know . . ." She pointed at my tummy. "Mum says just until you work things out with your dad. It's not that she doesn't love having you here, but she thinks you and your dad need to sort it out."

"This just gets worse every day. How could I have been so stupid? At least Dad cares enough to call your mum."

She said, "Of course he cares. He's just angry. Come and chill out. The spare room at the back is always all set up for, uh, longer-term guests. Unless you want to share a bed with me for the next week or so . . ." She led me up the stairs.

I thought how many times I'd longed to live at Cleo's gorgeous house, how often I'd felt like her house was way better than our cozy home, but now more than anything I wanted to be where I belonged. Cleo directed me to a small, sweet room on the same floor as hers. The walls were papered with rose patterns and etched with golden ferns. I sat heavily on the single bed.

"Thanks, Cleo," I said, dissolving into tears again.

"You don't like the room?" she tried to joke.

"I've made such a mess of things," I said, sobbing.

CHAPTER 18

SCHOOL BECAME A NIGHTMARE. NO ONE WAS SPEAKING TO ME except for Cleo, and although I'd never been one of those girls who hung out with a gaggle of friends, I didn't realize how much I would miss the easy *hello*s and *how's it going*s? from the other students. Now they just looked at me like I was a creature from a different planet. As for Griffin . . . well, it was unbearable. He vanished from my life as if he'd never existed. His bedroom curtains were always drawn, and if I caught a glimpse of him at school, he hurried away. All of our history together was destroyed.

I tried to call Dad every day but he wouldn't take my calls, although Cleo's mum said he was calling her to make sure I was okay. The more angry he was with me, the more angry I was with Mum. I ignored her calls and frantic emails, acting like she didn't exist.

Even though Cleo offered to go with me, I went to my second scan alone. A mistake. I looked at the baby kicking its legs and punching its fists but I could hardly see, I was crying so hard.

"Do you want to know the sex of the baby?"

I shrugged.

"He's a boy," the doctor said.

A boy. *A boy.*

The baby kicked on the screen again, a full hard kick, which I could see but couldn't yet feel.

A son.

AND SUDDENLY, THREE DAYS LATER, ON THE MONDAY MORNING WHEN someone from Adoption Services was due to visit me at Cleo's, I felt the baby move. It was like a fish swimming through my gut, or a shudder of a tiny earthquake. I rested my hand, feeling for another movement, but the baby was still again.

I concentrated on a question in Miss Take-Control's inbox. It had been sitting there for weeks, and today I was finally going to answer it—probably too late for 96tough-chick, but hopefully it might help someone else.

Mon 15 March

Dear Miss Take-Control-of-Your-Life,

I had a baby when I was 15 and I gave it away for adoption. I'm 19 now and I still wonder about my little girl and when it's her birthday or mother's day I cry. Her birth parents and my parents decided I wouldn't be involved in her life because I was a bad influence when I was younger—into drugs and stuff—but

I miss her every day and I'm different now. I want her to know I love her but I don't want to ruin her life. She doesn't know she's adopted, I don't think.

96tough-chick, 19

I began to type:

Dear 96tough-chick,
You've been through a lot. It's normal to mourn a loss like the one you have suffered. I don't know what the legal implications are of the adoption you agreed to, but I think if you talk to Social Services they'll be able to direct you as to next steps. Your concern for your daughter shows you are very mature. You'll need to be strong as you navigate your way through this, but you've already shown how strong you are.

From one teen to another . . .

Miss Take-Control-of-Your-Life

I wasn't going to cry. I shut down the computer and drifted downstairs at Cleo's. Everyone was out—Cleo at school (I was pulling another sick day), and her parents at work. At five to ten, I was waiting in the plush front room watching out the window. The social worker had said over the phone that this was to be just a preliminary discussion. I played her name over in my mouth. *Nicole.* As I let the syllables slide in my cheeks, I saw a busty blonde come up the drive. Her hair needed to be touched up at the roots, where the brown was coming through. She wore no makeup, but her full lips and baby blue eyes were pretty without. Her white shirt and black skirt made her look a bit like a waitress. She caught sight of me in the window, hitched up her large lime-green shoulder bag, and her smile travelled all the way to her eyes.

As I opened the door, fresh morning air burst in along with Nicole. She shook my hand in her own warm one. She beamed at me.

"How are you feeling? You look wonderful."

"I'm okay," I said. "Less tired than I was. Do you, um, want a cup of coffee or tea or something? We can go to the kitchen."

"Absolutely. Wonderful. Tea. Lovely. Lovely house, gorgeous."

Up close, I could make out small wrinkles around her mouth as she smiled. I made us both tea and watched her as she admired the landscaped garden through the wraparound windows and commented on a painting by some semi-famous artist.

"This isn't where I normally live. My dad kicked me out."

"That must be hard," she said. "Have you tried to talk to him?"

I rubbed my temples and changed the subject. "So once I've decided, is that it?"

She rummaged in her huge bag and laid out some pamphlets on the kitchen table. Last thing she pulled out was a clipboard with a pen tied to it by a string. You're"—she checked her papers—"eighteen weeks pregnant, right?"

"And a half."

"This is a preliminary meeting, as we already discussed. We're having it because you're thinking about giving your baby up for adoption, is that right?"

I cupped my hands around my mug. It was a perfect temperature in my grasp but I could not drink it.

She continued, "The way this works—if you decide to go ahead—is that you fill out these forms I give you. Then we meet again. I'm going to ask you some questions in a few minutes, just to establish that you've thought about everything. And to answer your first question, no, nothing will be fixed until after the birth, but we can discuss potential families together."

"I don't know if I want to do that."

"We can decide that together too. I'll be your point of contact and your support, but you'll need to go to counselling as well. We can work out when suits you."

"I have school. I don't know if I have time."

"We'll make time. It's all to make sure this is the right decision and the best thing for you. And for the child."

"It's the right thing. Definitely," I said.

"The way it works here is that the once the baby's born we'll talk over the decision again. You can't sign any papers until the baby is six weeks old."

"But he doesn't come home with me. He goes to the other family—not home with me for those six weeks. I don't even have anywhere to live. My dad's pretty angry about everything, but I'm hoping to move home once the baby's—you know, gone."

She smiled. "The baby won't come home with you if that's what you want. We can find an interim situation. What about your mum? Can we talk with you and her together at some point?"

"Not yet. If that's okay."

"There's time. Will your parents be able to be involved in this? We'd like to explore all possible options for a family for the baby. Is there someone in your family who might take your child? We can, if you like, have a family group conference—your family and the family of the father of the baby, although that may not be necessary."

I was hardly listening. "This was a mistake. I screwed every-thing up. I had a great boyfriend but I slept with someone else and now everything's ruined."

She sat quietly, her blue eyes patient.

"I should maybe have had an abortion, but I couldn't go through with it. And now I feel like my whole life is out of my control. The baby keeps getting bigger and I'm getting bigger and everyone knows and I just want all this to be over. I want my life back how it was."

"Have you talked to the father of the baby about what your plans are?"

I felt the blood rush from my cheeks. "Do I have to get his permission?"

"We'd like to contact him, if possible, to get some informa-tion about him. Health checks, background information. For the child. We don't have to do it right now, though." She made a note on her papers. "It's important to explore all the options, Amy. More adoptions are open now. You could have some con-tact with the child."

"It all sounds so complicated." My voice was small.

"Are you ready to answer some questions now?" She smiled at me brightly. *Efficient* was the word that popped into my head.

I wondered how many times she'd done this. I wondered about the babies moving to new homes. I wondered about the other women and girls giving up children. My heart hurt so much it was hard to draw breath.

"Go for it," I said. But what I wanted to say was *Can I change my mind?*

A COUPLE OF DAYS LATER, I HAD TO SLIP HOME TO GET SOME NEW clothes. I was sick of having to borrow Cleo's stuff. I tried to choose a time when I thought Dad would be out, but it was hard to predict anything with his weird work schedule.

I sneaked along the path, averting my gaze from Griffin's house. I was a stranger in my own life.

I opened the door quietly and called out, "Dad?" but there was no answer. My phone beeped. Voicemail.

Ms. Finch? It's Jake Angar. If you would be available to come in for an interview this Saturday, March 19, we'd like to have a trial run at a family portrait later that day.

Finally. I'd assumed they'd forgotten or found someone else.

I rested my hand on the baby bump and wandered into the living room. I imagined myself going in for the interview on Saturday and getting a job. Cleo's mum wasn't going to let me stay forever, so I needed money to pay rent somewhere. Rent. Adoption. I rubbed my face with my hands. The logistics of the whole thing threatened to overwhelm me.

The front door clicked open. Seconds later, Dad cleared his throat behind me. My heart juddered. Then I said, half turning from the window, "I'm sorry. I was just here picking up some stuff."

"Bird."

My heart flickered with hope. "What can I do, Dad?"

He said, softly, "I feel like I don't even know you."

"It looks like maybe I got the job. I thought they'd forgotten, but they want me to try out this weekend. I can save some money and find a place. Get out of Cleo's mum's hair."

"You haven't thought about this," he said. "A baby isn't . . ."

"I've thought about nothing else."

"You haven't considered all the options."

"I'm going to give him away."

"He's a boy?" Dad said, then went quiet.

I turned away. Back out the window a plane slowly unzipped the sky with a white vapour trail. I thought about the passengers far above, looking down at the soft puffs of cloud, the squares of land, the toy houses below. For a moment I returned to Spain in my mind.

I faced him. "I don't know what else to do, Dad."

"If you wear a baggy top, they probably won't realize you're pregnant at the photography studio."

"I've given up pretending."

"Get the job first," he said.

He just wanted to deny all this was happening. "Okay, Dad."

"What about your mother? She said you haven't answered any of her calls."

"You know I'm not speaking to her," I said.

"You don't know, do you?"

TOP TIP 23: ALL FAMILIES HAVE SECRETS

I frowned. He looked old suddenly, grey around the edges. He said, "She was pregnant with another baby when you were two."

The words hung between us like mist. "What happened?"

"It wasn't . . . it wasn't her fault; these things happen. Your mother blamed herself. She had a fall and it caused a late miscarriage, you see, and she took it very hard. Very hard. She so wanted . . . always wanted another child. We tried again. Another miscarriage. Then another. After the fourth, we gave up. We always thought we'd have two children but . . . well, we never did. This"—he glanced at me—"is not exactly how she thought another child would come into our lives."

All the sounds in the room had been sucked out. I thought of Mum all those years, so sad. And now here I was, pregnant with a baby I didn't want. "Why didn't anyone ever tell me?"

"I don't know." He wouldn't meet my gaze. "Are you going to follow my advice about the job?"

"Yes." I asked, quietly, "Do you think I could come home?"

"Bird," he said, "I can't even look at you right now. Your mum and I have worked things out with Cleo's mum for now, given her some money. Obviously, your mum would prefer you were with her, but she understands. You know what she's like. We all need some time apart."

With that, he left the room and I broke down.

ON THE MORNING OF THE INTERVIEW, I WANDERED FROM CLEO'S house over to the photography shop. It was getting warmer and late spring flowers stuck up their colourful heads. I kicked over two purple crocuses. Their petals smeared into the ground and immediately I felt bad. I was so mired in my screwed-up, ridiculous world that I had to go round squashing pretty flowers. Thank God for my website. At least I was still Miss Take-Control in one area of my life.

Arriving at the shop, I checked my watch. I was on time. I

smoothed down my relaxed-fit shirt and maternity skirt—both gifts from Cleo. The skirt had a secret expanding waistline that hid the baby pretty well.

The doorbell chimed into the quiet foyer as I entered. Stunning photos lined every wall: weddings and babies and families, and gorgeous images of urban landscapes. I thought of my Empty Streets project. Whoever had taken these would maybe be able to help me improve my own photos.

A tall, slim man with glasses and a goatee appeared. He wore Converse trainers, corduroys, a light T-shirt and a black suit jacket. Cool chic. He reached out a hand to shake mine. I felt suddenly encouraged.

"So," he said, "you want to book photos of the baby when it comes?" He gestured at me with a broad grin. "I get ladies coming in all the time who are so excited they just want to book shots, but I always tell them to slow down, wait—once the baby comes you might be a bit too exhausted for photos. Certainly for the first couple weeks. When are you due? A few months?" Without stopping speaking he flicked open a diary. "We could book you in for the end of August or early September? Don't ask me how I know when. I just *know*. I had my own little one a year ago." He pointed up to a photograph of a sweet chubby baby. "So does September eighth work?"

I wished I could dissolve. I mumbled, "Um, Jake Angar?"

"Yep. Oh no, hang on, you're not"—he scanned his diary—"Amy Finch?"

Suddenly unable to raise my eyes, I said, "I'm here for the interview."

"Oh, Amy." He rubbed his palms against his cords. "It's not

that you're not talented. I loved your pictures. But I need some-one long term." He slapped his hand to his forehead. "You have no idea how hard it's been to find a good assistant. It's taking ages and I had to get rid of the first two."

"I'll work hard. I promise. I really need this job."

He forced a smile. "I, uh, look, it's just not the right time."

TOP TIP 24: RIGHT AND WRONG AREN'T ALWAYS EASY TO TELL APART

"I would be perfect." I knew I was begging.

"Seriously, I don't think you've thought about this. You're not going to find it easy to have a job with a newborn."

"I'm giving the baby away."

His tone changed. "Look, Amy, I'm, uh, I'm really sorry."

I could see in the thinning of his eyes that he was disap-pointed in me somehow. He figured I was a stupid teenager. He was judging me. What happened to *lady*, the word he'd used to describe me when he thought I was booking a shoot?

I wanted to ask him if he was allowed to discriminate against me like this. Surely there were laws or something to protect pregnant women so they could get jobs. But I was too ashamed. It was too much. I twisted away so I could get out of there before I wept.

CHAPTER 19

Fri 1 April

Dear Miss Take-Control-of-Your-Life,

I'm apprehensive about my future. My parents and my teachers all pressure me. I'm hardworking, so they all want me to keep going with my education after my exams and become a lawyer. I feel like I've been sheltered by school my whole life and I want to explore the world, perhaps do a project with a volunteer organization abroad. I don't want to let them all down, but I want to say that it's my life.

Felicity345, 18

This was the sort of question I used to find easy to answer. Now I typed out the right responses, feeling like a fraud.

Dear Felicity345,

It's totally normal to feel apprehensive about the future, especially when it feels like it's set in stone. You're right. It's your life, and by being honest with yourself about what you want, you show your family and your teachers that you're independent and strong. But you have to be honest with them too.

Tips to Take Back Control

Research some other options for the next year—there are loads of resources in school libraries about this sort of stuff—and show them to your family.

Show them how you plan to pay for it.

Tell them how important this is to you.

From one teen to another . . .

Miss Take-Control-of-Your-Life

I looked over my answer. It was the right thing to say, but it felt like I wasn't the one writing it. I was a *liar*. I sounded calm on the page when in real life I was trembling. But I couldn't confess to Felicity345 that I wasn't even a tiny bit in control of my life.

TOP TIP 25: BEING FREAKED OUT AND TERRIFIED IS NOT THE END OF THE WORLD—IT'LL PASS

I climbed into the single bed in the rosy room at Cleo's house and fell into a restless sleep. Sometime in the night I woke up to the baby moving. It kicked at my hand as I rested my fingers on the hardening balloon of my belly. I wondered if the baby was dreaming like I'd been dreaming. Do babies dream in the womb? I'd dreamed I was about to climb Everest. I stood at the bottom of the mountain and looked up to the clouds above. There was a sharp peak far, far away, jutting into the sky like a solitary tooth in a baby's mouth.

I said, "I can't."

TOP TIP 26: LIFE CAN BE AS LONELY AS A MOUNTAIN, AND AS DAUNTING

I WAS MELTING. THE WEATHER WAS FREAKISHLY HOT FOR APRIL. Unbearable. My thighs rubbed together under my dark green dress. It was like a sack. The short sleeves showed off the thickness of my wobbly arms. I'd gained so much weight and was way bigger than I'd expected, and than any of the women I'd looked at on YouTube as they sailed through their first five months. As I waddled along the corridors of school I wondered if I'd ever get my body back the way it used to be.

Kitty sneered at me one day, "You're so fat *already*."

I ignored her, so she gave up and left.

Cleo came over and kissed me on the cheek. "You look so pretty. Glowing."

"I look fat. And everyone thinks I'm a slag. And I'm going to fail all my exams. And I can't imagine ever having a life again. Moan, moan."

"You were so little to start with, you were bound to get, you know, big." Her fingernails were yellow and black.

"I *knew* I was extra fat. Interesting nails," I said. "Like bees."

She wrinkled up her nose. "I know. Who does yellow and black?"

"At least you can stay awake to study. I'm worried, Cleo. I can't take my exams. I keep falling asleep on my homework. I wish I could handle a latte."

She wasn't listening. She pulled a torn-out newspaper article from her pocket. Underneath the headline was Cleo's *name*.

It was about a band. "You wrote this? When did you do all this? I didn't even know you'd been to see these guys. Were they good? Hang on, don't tell me," I said when she tried to speak. I read, "*Opening with a thin sound, unsure and shy, but finishing with explosive anarchy, Diet Nations grabbed hold of the stage halfway through and made it their own . . .*"

When I got to the end, I said, "Wow, Cleo. It's great. It's so, I don't know, so well *written*. I can't believe you got something published in the paper. I didn't know you were even *interested* in writing for newspapers."

Cleo shone with pleasure. "I'm a girl of many talents."

"I can't believe I haven't even noticed what's been going on with you. We're living in the same house!"

"You've been busy."

I was about to reply when all the muscles around my swollen tummy tightened like a corset being tied.

"You okay?" she said.

"I think I had a contraction."

Her eyes grew wide. "What do we do?"

"I don't know."

"What did it feel like?"

"Tight. Weird." I rubbed my belly and said, "It stopped as suddenly as it started."

"It's probably Braxton Hicks. Fake contractions. Your body is preparing itself for the baby. They can come and go for weeks."

"Fake contractions?"

"I read about them on the Internet. I've been trying to keep up with the pregnancy week by week, you know."

I turned to her. "You're, like, the best friend ever. You know that, right?"

"Yeah, yeah, enough of that. How d'you feel now?"

"It's stopped. Nothing's happening now."

"Good, that's good."

"So the baby isn't coming?"

"I don't think so. We'll wait and see. Let's skip English. We can go to the doctor if you're worried."

"I think I'm fine. I should read those sites."

"I still think we should skip." She leaned through the open door into the classroom. "Mr. Bennetts, I have to take Bird to the nurse."

I couldn't hear his reply. But Cleo said in an exaggerated whisper, "Do I *have* to explain, sir?" My cheeks grew hot. Cleo swung back out the door, grinned, spun me round and guided me down the corridor.

"Let's go sit outside," she said. "Here, have this." She gave me a chocolate bar from her bag.

TOP TIP 27: CHOCOLATE ALWAYS HELPS

EASTER CAME AND WENT AND THE DAYS BLURRED INTO EACH OTHER.
The next meeting with Nicole was pretty much like the first one, just with more details. She gave me stuff about the new family and asked me to read it, but it stayed on the floor next

to my bed at Cleo's house. I didn't book an appointment with the counsellor. Several people wrote in to my website, but I didn't answer their problems. Mum stopped calling but sent frequent texts telling me she loved me. I guess she'd decided a new approach might work better. School started again. The weather grew colder and then hotter again, and the worst April of my life turned slowly into May.

One lunch break, I took a walk in the park across from the school. I was sitting by myself on a bench in the shade of a tree when Pete came over and sat next to me.

"How's it going, Amy?"

"What do you think?"

"You don't need to be so angry," he said.

He'd told everyone I was pregnant. God. I should hate him for blurting out my secret, but the baby wriggling inside me made me feel connected to him.

He said, "Are you okay?"

I looked at him and started laughing. I laughed so hard, tears sprang to my eyes and I knew that in about half a second I was going to start crying and getting hysterical. I said, trying to calm down, "Pete, just leave me alone, would you?"

He clenched his jaw. Got up. Walked away.

I sat very still and watched him. I wished I had my camera with me so I could photograph the image. His outline made a Pete-shaped exclamation mark against the bright sky. He'd made a Pete-shaped exclamation mark in my life.

I wished I could ask him to come back and tell me everything was going to be all right.

But it was too late for that.

CHAPTER 20

Wed 4 May

Miss Take-Control,

my best friend is sooooo mad at me because i told our teacher she was being abused. i was trying to protect her but now she wont believe me and she hates me. i got everything wrong.

SuzyBlue, 17

Dear SuzyBlue,

You were in a difficult situation and you did what you thought was right.

<u>Tips to Take Back Control</u>

Don't be too hard on yourself, even though your friend is really angry.

Remember, she's dealing with a lot. Tell her how sorry you are, but tell her too that you were trying to protect her.

Keep saying it. As time goes by, she may forgive you. If she can't, understand that there is more going on here than your friendship—she might not be ready to be friends for some time.

From one teen to another . . .

Miss Take-Control-of-Your-Life

I read over what I'd written. Forgiveness. SuzyBlue needed to forgive herself, and her friend needed to forgive her too, but I wasn't sure either girl would be able to do it. I rubbed my arms, feeling suddenly shivery, then I posted my reply. I flipped from my website to my personal inbox.

Dear Bird,

Your mother and I have decided that you should move back to the house. I'm still very angry with you and very disappointed, but she feels that you should be under this roof.

I wish I wasn't so angry, and you must understand I do still love you, but this course of events has been very difficult for me to live with.

I expect you back this evening. I will be away at a solar energy conference.

Your father

I shut down my laptop and folded it up, chucking it into my small rucksack. I rubbed my hands over my out-of-control curly hair. I'd pictured moving back home as some sort of wonderful reunion with hugs and *I love you*s, but Dad wasn't even going to be there.

Later that evening, I unlocked the front door to my empty house. I wandered from the front room to the kitchen and then up the stairs to my room. Across the way I could see Griffin's window, curtains wide open. He wasn't there, but I couldn't help but remember all the times we'd spoken to each other through those panes of glass. I drew my curtains.

I looked at the printout from Oxford University I'd pinned on my corkboard. With a rush of anger, I ripped it down and tore it into tiny pieces. I tore off the quotations and the inspirational messages. I ripped down the photograph of myself smiling into the distance and threw it away. The corkboard was empty.

TOP TIP 28: A SILLY SONG CAN STOP YOU FROM GOING CRAZY

Hickory, dickory, dock,
The mouse ran up the clock . . .

The clock struck midnight and I was wide awake. Ominous night filled my bedroom. The baby moved inside me, small flutters and then two hard kicks.

I tried to imagine the baby—its eyes, hands, tiny feet—but only other people's babies came to mind.

The clock struck one . . .
Two . . .
Three . . .
Four . . .

My legs cramped and I had to get up to pee and then I drifted off, but the baby wriggled and woke me. I heard a soft footfall in the living room and I wondered if Dad was home. But what if it wasn't him? Fear jolted me like an electric current. Not fear for me: fear for the baby. I lay there, stiff and frightened, waiting to hear any other noise. I held my breath until I worried that the baby needed air. I tucked my phone in my hand, ready to call for help. The baby kicked me, harder than before.

A moment later, I heard a creak in the corridor by the front door. I sat straight up, the covers falling off my body so I was exposed. Someone *was* in the house, but it didn't sound like Dad. Even when he tried to be quiet, he moved far more loudly than this person. Silently, I put my feet onto the carpeted floor, pushed myself off the bed and tiptoed to my door. My heart thudded like the baby was kicking me repeatedly, except he was still now, frightened too. Or sleeping, oblivious. I stubbed my toe on the doorframe. Wincing, I listened for the intruder. Silence. But I *knew* someone was there. As if to confirm my suspicions, there was another creak.

Cautiously, I peered at the upstairs corridor from my room. Strange shadows lurked like huge dark bats hanging from the ceiling. I padded along to the top of the stairs, smelling my dad's aftershave, all spicy and warm, as I passed his room.

My heart was so loud, I was convinced the intruder would hear it. I imagined a great hulking man in the living room—perhaps he was stealing the TV. I imagined what he would do when he saw me, shivery in my nightgown, pregnant and vulnerable. Another soft footstep came from the kitchen. A light flickered on.

My heart fluttered to the top of my throat.

I flipped open my phone. I yelled, "I'm calling the police."

The kitchen door opened. From within came a surprised voice. "Bird? Did I wake you?" A woman's voice. My mum's voice.

Fury replaced fear like I'd been injected with it. "What are you doing here? You scared the crap out of me."

She came into the hallway, fragile and childish somehow in the semi-dark, illuminated only by the kitchen light behind her.

I cried, "Why are you *here*? This isn't your house anymore."

I could see her willing herself not to correct me. It *was* her house. Never Dad's. If it had been Dad's, he would have invested it in the business. I felt my throat constrict. I wondered how Mum had survived worrying about money for all those years.

"You scared me half to death," I said. "What are you doing here? I nearly had a heart attack," I added.

She said, "I'm sorry. I'm really sorry. I didn't mean to scare you. Your father told me to come by so you weren't on your own tonight, but I knew you wouldn't want to see me, so I waited until you were asleep."

"It's five in the morning."

"I've been here since about midnight. In the living room, reading. We just wanted to make sure you were safe."

"I'm *fine*. I'm not a kid."

She appraised me. "No, no. You're not." She rubbed her neck. "Your father tells me you're giving the baby away."

"I don't want to talk about this."

"I think it's a good idea. You'll be able to carry on with your life."

"Yeah, okay. Good night." She made to speak but I lifted a hand to stop her. "Really, Mum, I just need to sleep."

The mouse ran down,
Hickory, dickory, dock.

I couldn't sleep, though. I was too keyed up. And I couldn't help thinking about the babies Mum had lost. I switched on the light. Tears blurred my vision but I pulled a pen and paper from my desk and began to write.

I don't know what to say. I look at the empty page and my heart feels like it's ripping in two. I want to explain why I'm doing it—why I'm going along the adoption route. Although sometimes I want one thing, sometimes another, I have a list of practical reasons.
This isn't what I want to say. What do I want to say?
Why is this so hard? Why can't I do this?
What am I doing? I hardly know myself anymore.
I'm sorry. I'm really sorry.
I don't know what I'm doing. I feel kicks in the night and I am sick with what I'm doing. But I don't know how else to . . . I don't know what to say. I. Don't. Know. What. To. Say.

I gave up and collapsed back onto my bed. I fell into a woozy, anxious sleep.

When I awoke, Mum was gone. She'd left me a fruit salad in the fridge.

THE NEXT DAY, I WAS SO TIRED I COULD HARDLY THINK AS I WENT
from class to class at school. At one point I stumbled and leaned
against my locker. When I looked up, Griffin was staring at me,
his vivid blue eyes filled with pain. His hair was wet—he must
have come from gym class and just had a shower. I attempted a
smile. He pushed his hair from his face and his gaze ran down
over my body. I wanted to say something to him but there were
no words left. His lips puckered like he'd eaten something bitter. I could almost see his heart breaking all over again. He
turned away.

Cleo came up to me and said angrily, "What's *with* you?"

I knew immediately from her tone that she was furious.
"What?"

She leaned against a locker. "I have to talk to you."

"What's up?"

She wouldn't look at me. "So, um, you didn't tell Griffin."

"What?"

"That Pete's the father."

Oh no. I steadied my shaking hands. "Griffin found out?
Pete knows? How?"

"Nathan was being a jerk to Griffin all through Art. Calling
him Big Daddy and pretending to rock a baby. Griffin finally
just snapped and yelled that the baby wasn't his. Then Pete
went completely white. Like all the colour had been taken from
him. Pete said, *Not yours? You sure?* Then Kitty made a joke,
saying, *What, do you think it might be yours?*

"Suddenly Griffin got it. He said, *You?* But although it was a
question, it wasn't, and I was sitting there trying to work out
what to do or say. Why didn't you tell him? Why would you

231

treat him so horribly? Didn't you learn from lying to him the first time round?"

I stammered, "I didn't . . . didn't know how. And then more and more time kept going by and he wasn't speaking to me and . . ." I looked at her beseechingly, willing her to understand. "I didn't know how to deal with it."

She pushed herself off from the locker. A group of girls slowed to watch as she yelled, "Who *are* you? It's like I don't even *know* you."

TOP TIP 29: GETTING ANGRY WHEN SOMEONE'S YELLING AT YOU WILL JUST MAKE EVERYTHING WORSE

"I didn't say I'd tell Griffin everything. You have *no* idea what this is like."

"I do my best. I helped you through every step of this. You lived in my house when you had nowhere else to go. I held your hand through the scan, stood waiting for you at the stupid abortion clinic. I read stuff on the Internet about babies. But all you think about nowadays is you. It's like everyone else has faded out the picture. You used to be so caring for other people. You used to care about *me*."

I couldn't speak.

"You're *so* screwing everything up. Yet you keep giving advice on your website like nothing's changed. But everything's changed." She brushed a hand over the space in front of her face as if she were wiping me away. "You know what? I can't handle you right now."

"Cleo, don't go," I called.

She pushed her way through the group of people gathering round us. "I don't think I know you the way I thought I did. You've changed."

I said, weakly, "Maybe I have. Maybe I was tired of being predictable."

"Well, I'm tired of you," she said. And she was gone.

CHAPTER 21

TOP TIP 30: STICKS AND STONES MAY BREAK YOUR BONES, BUT THE THINGS PEOPLE SAY HURT MORE

Dad (said with a look of disgust): *Griffin's not the father?*

Cleo: *I don't want to hear it.*

Griffin: *Pete?*

Pete: *Why didn't you just tell me?*

Mum (yelling at me down the landline): *You can't tell your father something like that and not expect me to find out.*

Kitty: *Slag.*

Mr. Bennetts: *Perhaps you should think about taking some time off school.*

Dad: *You've never even mentioned a Pete.*

Griffin: *It hurts so much, Bird.*

Mum: *You have to talk to me. I'm your mother.*

Dad: *And to think I was so angry with Griffin—it took every ounce of strength I had for me not to go over and kill him when I found out.*

Kitty: *Whore.*

Cleo: *I don't want to talk to you.*

Pete: *It's really my baby?*

Griffin: *Why him?*

Mum: *We can't go on like this.*

Dad: *I'm so . . . so disappointed.*

Cleo: *Just leave it for a while, Bird.*

Pete: *Don't walk away from me when I have the right to . . .*

Griffin: *I don't ever want to see you again.*

Kitty: *Slut.*

Thurs 19 May

Dear Miss Take-Control-of-Your-Life,

Hi. I just turned 15 and I'm worried about my friend. We've been best mates for ages but recently hes started hanging out with a different group of friends and ignoring and making fun of me when he does. They have a reputation for smoking a lot of dope and I think my mate has started . . . to fit in. I dont know if he is doing anything else but he seems all different. I dont really have any other friends and dont know what to do—perhaps I should try and b more like his new friends. He says such horrible things about me, I don't know if we're even friends anymore.

                                                                    Ben

Dear Ben,

You and your friend seem to have gone in different directions recently. You say you don't really have any other friends, but perhaps if you turn your attention away from this friend, you might see there are other people who are more fun to hang out with. Are there things you enjoy doing outside of school where you can make new friends? You might feel shy but I bet there are loads of other people who would like to get to know you. As for your best mate . . . well, it sounds like he's trying out stuff that is making him change.

<u>Tips to Take Back Control</u>

Talk to your friend about your concerns.

But don't try to be like his new crowd of friends—trying drugs to please someone else makes no sense.

If talking to your friend doesn't change anything, and it might not, let him be for a while.

Try to meet new people and find your own path by doing things that interest you.

From one teen to another . . .

Miss Take-Control-of-Your-Life

THE LAST COUPLE OF WEEKS OF MAY WERE THE WORST WEEKS OF MY life. I hadn't realized just how much Cleo had been there for me through all this. She was the only real friend I had left and now I'd screwed things up with her. I felt like crying all the time, but instead I kept my eyes down and got on with things in my classes.

My days were strange and quiet, my evenings quieter. No one called me or chatted with me online. I remembered a time when I was friends, or at least friendly, with everyone in my year. No one spoke to me anymore. It was like I was the woman in that book we'd had to do for English in September, *The Scarlet Letter*. What was her name? Hester? The one who wore the red letter *A* around her neck so people knew what she'd done and could judge her. My baby belly was my own scarlet letter.

When I woke up one gloomy morning at the end of May, Dad was standing at the door telling me it was time to go to school. Most of the time he hardly spoke to me, so I was surprised to see him. I half sat up, pulling the cover around me.

"Dad?"

He was quiet and frayed around the edges, like a worn piece of fabric ready to be thrown out. He told me one more time to get out of bed and then paused as if he had more to say. I thought about how we were so far from where we had been as a family six months ago. There was me, moving like I was swimming, pregnant, self-absorbed, hating school, hardly the daughter of his dreams. And then there was the absence of Mum: there was almost a Mum-shaped hole next to him where she should have been. She'd made him louder and larger than life. Without her he was like an unplugged TV. He pressed his lips together.

I asked, "Are you going to work on your solar-brick business today?"

"I sold the business."

"When? Why?"

"I've been kidding myself for years. No wonder your mother left me."

"That's not true, Dad." As I spoke, I felt as if a tiny pebble had dislodged from my throat and was tumbling down.

"It was too much for me. I need to have smaller dreams."

"But—"

He shook his head. "You need to get up," he said.

"What are you doing instead?" I asked.

"Bird, you're late." He left.

I hauled myself out of bed and stared at my blank corkboard. I knew with a sickening certainty that I really *was* going to give up the baby. It was the right decision. It was the only way to get my life back in my control. The only way. I wanted to go to Oxford University, right? I wanted to take photographs of ancient spires and cobbled streets, or people boating down the river. I wanted to sit in seminars and listen to professors talking about intellectual things.

The plan had been to go to Oxford *with Griffin*. That was when the two of us had been in love. Then the realization punched me in the gut: Griffin and I had *never* been in love. We just went from being friends and neighbours to dating . . . but along the way I forgot to fall in love with him. I wanted to call Griffin and chat like we used to. More than that, I wanted to go and see Pete. He'd tried to talk to me when he found out about the baby, but I'd shut him out. Perhaps that was a mistake—perhaps he would understand; perhaps he would be someone who could listen to me through all this. I rested my hand on my swollen baby bump. The baby kicked. I fingered my phone. I was about to dial Pete's number when I stopped myself.

Instead, I switched on my computer and stared at the empty screen. I wanted to write a letter to the baby, a letter that explained why I was giving him away, a letter that gave him some hint of who I was and of how I wanted him to live.

Not a single word came to mind.

CHAPTER 22

Mon 6 June

Dear MissTC,

I usd to hang with a group of 3 girls and we were best friends but they made all these plans for the summer to go on holiday with one of their families and my parents wont let me go so now things are weird and we dont hang out together . . . well . . . we do but they're always talking about the summer and Im left out.

How can I make new friends . . . Im shy with new people but my old friendshps are sooooo over.

Lonely, 14

I missed Cleo so badly, tears stung my eyes. I wiped them away. I could try to help Lonely at least. She didn't need to know I was the loneliest girl in the world right now.

Dear Lonely,

Huh, when I read your question, I got the feeling your friendship with these three girls isn't so obviously over. It seems to me that if you're all still hanging out like normal *maybe* the feeling of being left out is coming from you. It totally sucks that you can't go on this holiday with them, but that doesn't mean you can't hear about it and share in some of the buildup.

Tips to Take Back Control

Find something your parents will let you do this summer—go to the pool or do an activity that sounds fun so you have something of your own to look forward to.

Try to meet some new people—when you feel shy, be interested and ask questions (people love talking about themselves). Be open and be yourself. And remember, the new person might be just as shy as you.

From one teen to another . . .

Miss Take-Control-of-Your-Life

BY EARLY JUNE, OUR SCHOOL HAD SHIFTED INTO EXAM MODE. BECAUSE we were in the sixth form, we didn't have to keep normal hours, and it seemed the teachers were pretty pleased I wasn't regularly in school anymore. They'd been trying to persuade me to stay home for a while. Study leave, they called it. It made my life even lonelier than before.

One afternoon I was walking home from my Spanish Literature exam. I headed down the hill and was turning onto my tree-lined road, listening to the birds tweet and various dogs bark. It was completely empty of people. I wished I had my camera to photograph it. The line of the empty street leading off into the distance looked like a road map to a certain future.

I reminded myself that once I gave the baby away, everything would go back to normal.

I pushed open the front door of my house and stepped into the cool corridor. It felt even emptier than the street. I went through to the kitchen. It was dim in there because of the shade provided by the bushy trees out back. I ran my hands over the recipe books stacked haphazardly on the small bookshelf, and then I pulled out an old, tattered book. It was one my granny had left in the house—one I remembered her using.

I decided not to study for once. Forget the exams, I felt like cooking.

TOP TIP 31: THIS RECIPE MAKES THE BEST FLAN IN THE WORLD

⅔ cup sugar
4 eggs
2 (3 oz.) packages cream cheese, room temperature
1 (14 oz.) can sweetened condensed milk
1¾ cups milk
½ teaspoon vanilla extract

Preheat oven to 350 degrees F. Boil a kettleful of water. Heat sugar in a medium skillet over medium-high heat until melted, clear and light brown.

The kitchen was quiet apart from the gentle hissing of the sugar. I turned on the oven and filled the kettle to let it boil.

I put on the radio, but I didn't like the song, so I turned it off again. The quiet came back louder.

Stir occasionally so that sugar will melt evenly.

I stirred the sugar until it was brown and clear. I remembered Mum used to make this dessert. Dad and I would hover around her, trying to dip our fingers in the hot saucepan. She'd beat us off with the wooden spoon, telling us we'd burn our fingers. I was amazed that hard white granules of sugar could turn into such seductive golden liquid. It was so easy for everything to change.

Spoon syrup over bottom and around sides of a 1½ quart glass baking dish. Set aside to cool.

The evening turned the sky pinker, and a gorgeous summery light fell into the garden. Last year on a night like this, Cleo and I would have been out somewhere, perhaps having coffee together, sitting at an outside table of a café, or perhaps we'd have been getting ready to go to a party. Or Griffin and I would have been lying around, looking at the sky, comfortable together. Friends.

Combine eggs and cream cheese in a blender; blend until smooth.

The sound of the blender shattered my thoughts. I watched the eggs and cream cheese mixing together.

Add remaining ingredients; blend just until combined.
Pour into prepared baking dish.

I wondered what it would have been like to have a brother or sister. I imagined how Mum must have felt losing those babies. I laced my fingers, resting my hands on my belly.

Place in a larger pan; add boiling water to come halfway up outer sides of dish.

I'd taken everything for granted. My friends, my family, my life.

Bake 1 hour, until knife inserted in flan comes out clean.
Flan may still quiver in centre.

The whoosh of the baby's gymnastics made me lean against the counter. I switched on the oven light and watched the flan bake. It was funny how time didn't seem to matter anymore. I knew I should be studying or dealing with my website, but I just wanted to stand with my hand on my big bump and do nothing. Very Zen, or whatever. Just letting life go on around me without trying to make it perfect. It felt good.

Remove from water; cool on rack. Cover and refrigerate.
To serve, invert onto a platter.

When the flan was done, I flipped it onto a plate and watched the syrup drip down the sides.

Makes 8 servings.

Dad came in. He said, "That looks delicious."

"I felt like cooking. My exam didn't go well."

"How did we get to this?" he said suddenly.

Tears glossed my vision. "Would you like some?"

He opened the cutlery drawer. "After you," he said, giving me a spoon.

The flan was creamy and sweet. He watched me eat, cleared his throat and said, "I thought I might clean out the spare room. Set it up as an office for you to use once you've, you know, given the baby away. When you need to study. Get you ready for Oxford. Give you your own space. I don't know."

"That would be great. I mean, thank you." I rested my hip against the warm oven. "I wish I wasn't, um, putting you through all this." I added, "You know I'm sorry, right?"

TOP TIP 32: IT REALLY ISN'T TOO LATE TO SAY SORRY

He studied his thumb, picking at a hangnail. "What's happening with the baby's father?"

"Nothing. We're not really talking."

"And the, um, social worker. Your adoption lady? Don't I need to be involved somehow? I'm your father."

"I don't have to sign anything until six weeks after the baby's born. I haven't— They want me to think about some details, lots of stuff . . . have another meeting, a family meeting maybe . . . go to counselling, but I've just been sort of waiting. I dunno . . ." I moved my weight from foot to foot.

He frowned a little, his expression unreadable.

I said, "Do you want me to help you turn the spare room into an office?" I passed him the flan.

He took it. "We'll get through this," he said.

"I've been so stupid. I got so many things wrong with you and Mum. With Cleo. With Griffin. Mainly with Pete."

"I don't understand how you got mixed up . . . involved with this other boy."

"I'm not sure. I was following the *plan* with Griffin . . . and I just . . ."

"I know my dreams and crazy ideas might have made you want to be the opposite, but you're too young for a plan."

I wanted to tell him that I loved his dreams and crazy plans, but he was still talking.

"Your mother's more restrained. Controlled. Now. But she was a free spirit when we met, full of crazy hopes herself. I think I took all the air. And then we lost the babies. Things went downhill from there. Grief can be relentless, but it wasn't grief alone that destroyed us. It just exposed how unhappy your mother really had become . . ."

He dropped his gaze and scuffed the floor with his heel. His feet were bare. I remembered being little and looking up to my giant of a dad. Everything seemed so easy then, like he had all the answers.

"I am really sorry, Dad. This"—I gestured at my tummy—"hasn't helped any."

"It's not what I hoped for you."

"I know you want me to go to Oxford University. Conquer the world."

He rested his hand on my forearm. It was the first time he'd touched me in months. "I don't care if you go to Oxford, silly girl. I just want you to be happy."

"I will be happy there," I said.

"*Being happy doesn't mean everything is perfect,*" he said.

"Sure it does."

"It's a quotation I read on the Internet, so it must be true." He glanced up at the ceiling. "Hmm, I should probably clean up there. I have no idea how your mother managed to keep this house running so smoothly. So"—he squeezed my arm—"the rest of the quotation goes something like, *Being happy means you've decided to accept the imperfections and get on with it anyway.* Oh, I can't remember it exactly and I can't remember who said it. Anon, I think. Clever guy," he joked. "I do have one more quotation—"

"Since when do you like other people's quotations?"

"Since you took them down off your corkboard. I missed them. Here it is: *Most people are about as happy as they make up their minds to be.* Abraham Lincoln said that. I like it." He passed the flan back to me and I took a big, wobbly mouthful and licked the spoon clean.

"It's good, huh?" Dad said.

I nodded.

He patted me on the shoulder. "I'm job-hunting for the rest of the day. Maybe later you can help me with my application."

I reached up to kiss him on the cheek, and he smelled of his spicy aftershave. He put his arms around me, and just like that we were hugging.

He pulled away first and said, "Okay, Birdy, I've got things to do."

"Dad, you know what you said, what Abraham Lincoln said, about making up your mind to be happy? You're right." I pulled out my phone.

As he wandered out he said, "Of course I'm right. I'm your father."

I flicked through to Pete's number and, before I could stop myself, keyed it in.

He picked up on the first ring. "Amy?" he said.

"Uh-huh."

He was quiet, waiting.

"Pete, I need to see you."

"I've been wanting you to say that for months," he said.

My heart jumped. It wasn't too late. I felt like I was flying.

He said, "I can meet you at the park in, like, fifteen minutes."

"Fifteen. Okay."

I ARRIVED IN THE PARK AND PERCHED ON THE BENCH OVERLOOKING the small lake. The water reflected the blue sky, and it was so still the trees opposite were perfectly mirrored. Pete came sauntering across within a couple of minutes. He wore a black T-shirt and he had a tan, making his sandy hair look blonder. It suited him.

He lifted one hand to wave. I felt a blush through my cheeks on seeing him. He smiled and said, "How you doing?"

I patted the space next to me. He sat and I instantly felt the heat of his presence.

"How did the exam go for you today?" I said.

"Hard. I was kidding myself this would be a new start. I'm just not that sort of guy."

"What do you mean?"

"It was supposed to be, you know, a new school, new family, everything. Anyway, what did you want? I thought we weren't speaking," he said, turning to me. His eyes were open and honest.

I realized how little I knew about him. I realized how much I'd based on rumours and reputation. What an idiot I was. I could smell the cigarette he'd just smoked and I longed to kiss him.

TOP TIP 33: DON'T JUMP TO CONCLUSIONS ABOUT SOMEONE

I said, "I wanted to see you. We need to talk. First, I wanted to say that I should have told you."

"Why didn't you?"

"I screwed up so badly, Pete."

He stared off at the lake.

"I wanted to be in love with Griffin."

"Yeah." He spoke to the water in front of us. "I wanted you to look at me the way you looked at him. You know, with respect."

My insides twisted up. "I should have told you about the baby. I never—" My voice cracked. "I never slept with Griffin. Only you."

He studied me seriously. "What do you want me to do?"

This close, I could make out that small, silvery scar above his lip. I said, "Nothing."

"I don't want to be like my dad," he said. "I can, you know, be responsible. I know I didn't exactly show you that . . . I got things wrong with you, Amy."

"I was so angry with you. Why did you tell everyone I was pregnant? When I got back from Spain, everyone knew. You told *everyone*."

"It wasn't like that. I was upset. I talked to Kitty when you told me at first. I was angry and it came out. I told her not to tell anyone."

"It was on *Facebook*. I've been so . . . so *mad* at you."

"You never trusted me. Or us. I'm not that bad, you know."

I stammered, "I just figured Griffin was the perfect guy."

He leaned closer. "Not for you," he said.

A breeze came between us, light and summery. "I know."

He put his hand on mine. "What can I do to help? You know, with the baby?"

"I'm—" I choked up. "I'm giving him away."

His jaw tightened. "Do I get a say?"

"What do you want?"

He pulled his hand from mine and leaned his head back to look up at the blue sky. It framed his face. "I don't know. I'm too young for all this, I know that, but I should be helping you decide this stuff."

"I've already spoken to the adoption worker. She'll want to speak to you too."

"Sure. Okay. If that's what you want."

"I feel so out of control, Pete. I hate all this."

He half stood and reached into the back pocket of his jeans. "I got you something for Christmas." He presented me with a small, flat box. "A while ago now. You never wanted it before, you know."

I tore off the paper. Inside lay a silver chain with a teardrop-shaped silver pendant.

His lips curled up in his lazy smile. He said, "It reminded me of you."

"God, Pete, I . . ."

He sat back on the bench and I leaned forward. I was going to kiss him—it felt right and I was going to follow my heart. I was just about to place my lips on his when he held up a hand so his finger rested on my mouth.

"Amy," he said softly.

"What? What's wrong?" I murmured into his warm finger.

"It's too late. I'm back with Kitty Moss. She's, you know, not so bad . . . well, apart from the Facebook thing. I'm not the guy I used to be. I'm not going to mess her around."

I pulled back, stung. "She's so mean to me. God, anyone else would be better."

"Yeah. She doesn't like you very much," he said, looking down at the ground. "I feel bad about that. If I'd ever thought you'd come around, I wouldn't have started it with her. I wouldn't. But you made it so clear I wasn't good enough for you. She never made me feel like that."

"What's this, then?" I gestured at the necklace angrily.

"I'm still the baby's dad. I—"

I said, "No, I'm being stupid. Of course you don't want to be with me. Look at me. I get it."

He raised his voice. "No, you *don't* get it. You never did get it. You always thought you knew what was going on in my head. You always assumed you knew who I was. But you never did."

"I'm sorry," I said quietly. "You're right. I just wish I hadn't waited so long."

He slumped back. "Yeah," he said, "me too."

TOP TIP 34: DON'T CRY BECAUSE IT'S OVER; SMILE BECAUSE IT HAPPENED. AND IF YOU CAN'T DO THAT, FORCE A SMILE ON YOUR FACE AND SOB INTO YOUR PILLOW LATER

I said, "Can we at least be friends?"

He considered my offer. "You could do with a friend," he said. "Seems like no one's talking to you."

I laughed. It was the first time I'd laughed in ages. "Yeah, well, I'm not Miss Perfect anymore."

He said, "I like you better this way."

"I thought you liked me before." I raised an eyebrow.

He smiled.

I tugged my camera from my bag. "I want to take a photo of you."

"Sure."

"You look great against the sky." I angled myself and snapped a photo. Outlined by the blue he looked even more handsome than usual. "It might not be easy for me to be friends with you," I said from behind the camera.

"Why's that?"

"I mixed up being friends and being a couple when I was with Griffin. I never had the right sort of feelings for him. Now it's the other way round. Being friends with you when I have, you know, feelings . . ."

"Yeah. Happens to girls around me," he joked. "They can't control themselves."

"Oh, I'll be able to control myself," I said. "Control is my middle name."

"Sure," he said. "If you say so."

CHAPTER 23

Mon 20 June

Dear Miss Take-Control,

Im broken-hearted. I loved this guy but I let him go and its too late to be with him. Ive ruined my life.

HaleyB

Dear HaleyB,

I have a confession to make to you. To everyone, really. Miss Take-Control-of-Your-Life was the worst name for me. I was just Miss Take. MissTake. A big Mistake. I've been so sure of myself, telling you all how to live, fully believing we all have control over our lives, but I realize my whole website is based on a lie. We don't have control over our lives. We just have control over *how* we take things.

You could be me, HaleyB. I messed up a relationship with a guy I really like, all the while breaking the heart of my boyfriend because I was never brave enough to tell him we weren't right together. I ignored my best friend and now she hates me. I'm not even speaking to my mum, although she did exactly what I should have done months ago: she followed her heart. I was too caught up in my own mess to see that she might be better off.

And if I'm really being honest, I should tell you that I'm pregnant. Huh. Me. Miss Not-So-Perfect-After-All. Miss Definitely-Not-in-Control-of-Anything.

So this is an apology to all of you. An apology for me being so sure of myself while doling out advice. I should have come clean and told you ages ago that I don't know the answers. I just don't. I should have come clean and told you that all the advice I've been giving, I haven't followed at all.

I'm sorry,

Amy

TOP TIP 35: ADMITTING YOU CAN'T KNOW IT ALL IS SCARY FOR A CONTROL FREAK (LIKE ME)

I shut down the website. I didn't have time to think about it anymore—I had to get ready for my first prenatal class. Pete promised to be there for the next one, but Kitty had told him she didn't want him to go with me this time. I longed for someone to be there by my side, and that made me miss Cleo. I texted her—not that she ever replied.

I'm still sorry. And I miss you. Wish you were around today. Life without you in it isn't as good. Amy xxx

I decided to walk to the hospital rather than get the bus. I'd been walking every day to relax. I wandered along, stopping to look up at the bushy trees. Birds scattered in flight from the branches, calling to one another. Pink clouds floated above, tinged with the warm morning light. The baby was wiggling inside me, his movements less pronounced than they used to be as he slowly ran out of room. I felt that summer had slipped into my veins. Soon all this would be over and I could get on with my life.

A car horn beeped, making me jump.

Cleo waved from the open window. She said, "What are you grinning about?"

"It must just be hormones. And the fact it's so sunny."

"Your dad said you'd walked this way. Apparently you've got a class today, for . . . you know."

I nodded.

"I passed my test."

"You passed! Congratulations!"

"Get in. I'll drive you."

I looked at her smiling up at me. I said, "I'm really sorry I was so self-absorbed. You were right about—"

"We are *absolutely* not ever mentioning that again. Okay?"

"Why today? It's not like I haven't been calling you and texting you forever."

"I dunno. That text was different—I just realized I didn't want to fight with you anymore. Plus I saw your website. It made me feel very sorry for you."

"I am really sorry. I meant every word."

"Stop. No more. Promise you won't bring it up again."

"Okay," I agreed. "If that's what you want. Deal."

"Now get in the car. We've got a class to get to. Are you going to invite me to come or what?"

"You want to?"

"Sure," she said. "We can't have you looking all lonely and teenage and pathetic all by yourself. You'll give other teenagers a bad name."

"I'm not pathetic," I said.

"Now you've got me, you're not," she said. "Now get in."

THE CLASS COMPLETELY FREAKED ME OUT. EVERYONE WAS THERE with a boyfriend or a birthing partner or their mum, and when I glanced over at Cleo as all the pregnant women huffed and puffed and practised breathing, I could see she was just as freaked out as me. Then they showed a horrifying video and I would have started crying if Cleo hadn't gripped my hand and given me this look that made me burst into laughter.

The woman running the class raised her eyebrows and said, "Birth is a beautiful experience. No need to be afraid."

I looked briefly back at the screen. What I was seeing was *not* in any way beautiful. Cleo had her face dipped down, so I couldn't see her expression, but I could tell from her shuddering shoulders that she had the giggles.

By the time we were eventually released from the room, the pair of us were in hysterics. "Oh God, Cleo," I said, trying to control myself, "there's no way I could ever do that."

She took a breath and looked at me seriously. "I could be there, you know. As a birthing partner or whatever it's called."

"I—" I paused. I suddenly wanted my mum and I wished I'd answered one of her calls or replied to one of her texts over the last few months. "I just don't know, Cleo. I can't even think about that right now. But thank you." I reached out and squeezed her hand. "So how's Xavier?"

"You would be very proud. I told him I never wanted to see him again."

"Really? That's great."

She tucked her arm in mine. "You and me, we're going for coffee, or whatever it is you're drinking—camomile?" She giggled. "We have a lot to catch up on. Then, after that, we're going to your house to pack the bag that woman told us you need for the hospital. I can't believe she didn't put makeup at the top of the list of *essential* items for a girl in labour."

AFTER ANOTHER ONE OF OUR RELENTLESS EXAMS A FEW DAYS later, Cleo and I walked back to my house together. Since the prenatal class, we were back to hanging out all the time. She was carrying my bag over her shoulder, and as we swung into my street, she said, "I can't believe school's nearly finished for the year."

"I know. Great. What are you doing this summer, besides Jamaica?"

"Um, writing a little. I figured I'd try to do some travel stuff and see if I could pitch it somewhere."

"You already sound like a pro."

"And I'm thinking about which university I'm going to apply to," she added. "Hey," she said, "what's up?"

"Nothing. You know."

She came to a stop and put her hands on her skinny hips. "You're thinking about Pete Loewen again."

"No." I swiped at her. "No, it's not him. Although what he sees in that stupid Kitty Moss is totally beyond me."

"All right, all right, don't start that. I mean, sure, she's blonde and pretty, not pregnant, willing to follow him round like an adoring pet."

"She is not pretty. She's gross," I cried. "But the not-pregnant thing is probably attractive."

"So what is it?"

"It's stupid. I just think a lot about the baby. I still want to, you know, keep it."

She slapped a hand against her forehead. "How will you do anything you want to do if you do that? What about Oxford?"

"Yeah, you know, I'm just not so sure about that anymore. I feel like my big plan might not have been such a great plan for me—"

I was cut off by a terrifying scream coming from Griffin's house. We both gasped as the front door was yanked open and his mum hurtled along the path yelling, "No, no, I won't. You can't make me."

Her hair was wild and tangled and she wore her dressing gown. I put my hand to my mouth in shock as she fell to her knees at the gate and began to rattle it. "Let me go-o-o," she screamed.

Cleo pushed past me and hurried over to Griffin's mum, just as Griffin came out the house. His hair stuck up and his eyes were circled with purple exhaustion. He didn't even see me. He called to Cleo, "I'm phoning the hospital."

She nodded and crouched down in front of Griffin's mum, murmuring softly. I watched them stay like that, Cleo soothing Griffin's mum, Griffin speaking into the phone.

When the ambulance arrived, I quietly slipped into my house. Thank God Griffin was finally getting some help. I suddenly wanted to call my own mum, but I went into the living room and sat for a while looking out the window, watching Cleo hold Griffin as he leaned against her, sagging like a fallen tree, then watching the two of them head into his house and close the door. The baby performed a slow somersault, oblivious to the complicated, scary, beautiful world outside.

TOP TIP 36: BE GENTLE WITH YOURSELF

CHAPTER 24

Mon 4 July

Dear Miss Take-Control,

I loved your last post and how honest you were but then you havent written for 2 wks. Where RU?

JJJ

Thurs 7 July

Dear MissTake,

You are definitely the worst advice columnist in the world but I love ya anyways. Uh, come tell us how to live, or how to screw it all up!!!!

BessT

Thurs 7 July

Dear Amy,

Come back come back come back.

HeavenSentGirl

Wed 13 July

MTCofYLife,

Luvd wot u said. Ur the best.

Pumpkin54

Sun 17 July

Really missing reading your posts—are you reallyreallyreally never going to start up the site again???

I flipped through the comments on my website, a slight smile playing on my face, then I shut the computer down. I was huge and uncomfortable as I got into bed, and I tossed and turned for ages. In the end I wedged a small pillow under my belly and finally fell asleep.

TOP TIP 37: YOU WILL FIND A WAY

AT ONE IN THE MORNING, A RUSH OF WATER BROKE FROM MY BODY. I sat up, half awake, not sure what was happening. I clambered as quickly as I could out of bed. "Dad," I yelled. "Dad. Something's wrong."

He found me hunched over the bed, my head on my hands, my pyjamas soaked. "What should I do?" I wept. "I think the baby's coming. It's early. Oh God. I'm only, like, thirty-six weeks." I was crying. "I'm frightened, Dad. I'm really scared."

"You'll be fine. Just . . . fine." His eyes were as wide as an owl's. "I'm calling your mother."

I didn't argue.

He helped me downstairs, and I sat on the front step, with the warm night full upon me, crying and leaking water, while Dad got the car out of the garage.

The baby kicked.

As I got into the car, Dad slammed the passenger door onto my head.

"I'm sorry," he yelped.

I started laughing.

WE DROVE, THE NIGHT PASSING US BY. HE SWERVED TO A STOP. "WE forgot the bag," he said, panic transforming his features so I hardly recognized him.

"You didn't forget. It's here at my feet," I said.

AS WE ARRIVED AT THE HOSPITAL, DAD USHERED ME FROM THE CAR. "I'll park. Go inside."

More water spilled from me as I stepped out. Two ambulances sat to my left. Big looming vehicles, empty, for the moment, of any drama. My own drama filled the space. This is really happening, I thought. I shuffled inside the hospital.

BRIGHT LIGHTS AND A SYMPHONY OF VOICES. A NURSE USHERED ME
from Casualty to a small room surrounded by green curtains.

"Where're your charts?" the nurse asked.

I pulled them out of the bag, grateful to Cleo for packing everything so well after the prenatal class.

"Your waters have broken. We're getting you up to Maternity. You're thirty-six weeks, three days, right? You're early, but not too early. Happens often with younger mothers."

"Thirty-six weeks. Will the baby be okay?"

She filled in some forms. "Any pain yet?" she asked.

I shook my head.

MUM PUSHED BACK THE CURTAIN. WE SIZED EACH OTHER UP, THEN SHE
rushed over and pushed my hair back from my face, kissing my forehead.

"How's it going, sweetheart?" she asked.

I was nearly crying. "We need to call Pete and Cleo. Tell them."

The nurse interrupted. "You need to take her to Maternity."

I lowered myself into a wheelchair while Mum got directions.

Two fingers of pain crept from the small of my back and pinched suddenly deep in my belly.

"Now it hurts," I gasped.

The nurse said, "You'll do fine."

MUM WHEELED ME SILENTLY ALONG THE CORRIDOR. HOSPITALS WERE all corridors, it seemed. Mum said, "Please let me stay with you."

I didn't speak.

She said, "We can talk after."

I reached my hand back to squeeze hers.

THE PAIN WAS WORSE. DEEP AND LOW. I COULD HEAR MYSELF MOAN-ing but I didn't feel connected to my own voice.

Between contractions, ten minutes apart, I walked round the room I'd been given. I would stay here until *active labour*. I vaguely remembered the phrase from the class, but I wasn't sure what it meant. We waited. And waited. Until the contractions got closer together. Mum sat on a plastic chair, flipping through yesterday's paper. I could tell she wasn't reading it.

Dad arrived. He was sweaty and wild looking. "It took me ages to find you. Hospital has terrible signs. Is the baby here? Did I miss everything?"

Mum and I both laughed. "Not yet," she said.

Dad looked at me. "You okay? That boy and Cleo are in the hall—do you want them in here?"

I shook my head. "Pete and I decided he wouldn't be in the room. He's not as tough as he makes out. Oh God. Another contraction's starting," I moaned.

I leaned against the wall and grunted. Oh God. The pain. The pain. The pain. I had a sudden vision of myself holding a baby, the moonlight falling through the window, the baby crying, me shifting my weight from foot to foot. It scared me, but it seemed worse to let the baby go. How could I give my child to strangers?

MY PARENTS LEFT WHILE A NURSE CHECKED ME. "ONLY TWO CENTIMEtres dilated," she said.

I lay on my side and noticed my pillow was damp with tears.

"Do you want to try the tub?" she said. "It'll help with the pain."

I followed her down a hallway into a large room with a bath. She turned the taps and I dropped off my robe, realizing with a flush of embarrassment that the nurse was still in the room. But then another contraction started and I didn't care that I was naked and she was helping me into the water.

She smiled at me. "Call when you want to get out."

SOMETIME LATER I WAS BACK IN THE ROOM. ALONE. I COULDN'T LOOK after a baby alone. No way.

Mum came in and said, "How are you doing? I remember all this when I gave birth to you."

"How long did it take?" I asked during a pause in contractions.

"I'll tell you later." She smiled.

"God, that long?"

"Look, Bird, have you decided if you want me to be here?"

"For the birth?"

She said, "I want to. You're my daughter."

"I didn't mean it when I told you I'd be a better mother than you. I'm giving the baby away—" My voice broke. "You'd never have done that. Never."

"It's okay. Don't think about it now."

"I don't know if I'm doing the right thing. Giving the baby away."

"Don't think about it."

"Yes," I said.

"Yes, what?"

"Yes, please be here with me through this."

SOMETIME LATER AGAIN, I WAS FOUR CENTIMETRES DILATED AND THE nurse got Mum to wheel me through to the active labour ward. It was a bigger room. They wanted to strap me with monitors to watch the baby's heartbeat, and so I had to lie down. Somehow lying down made the pain worse.

The nurse asked if I wanted an epidural.

I agreed. "I can't take any more."

THE ANAESTHESIOLOGIST SAT BEHIND ME AND TOLD ME TO STAY PER- fectly still. Fear shuddered through me and then I held my breath. The needle was in and the drug slid into my veins.

"The pain will stop in about twenty minutes," he said. "Okay, you can move now."

I turned to him. "I think I love you," I said.

He said, with a smile, "I hear that all the time."

I LOOKED AT THE CLOCK. THE TIME MADE NO SENSE. I PUZZLED OVER where the hours had gone. Then I slept.

I AWOKE TO MUM STROKING MY HAIR. A NURSE CAME IN. SHE CHECKED the monitors and then rushed back out. When she came back, a doctor and another nurse came with her. The doctor asked me to lift up my robe.

"What's wrong?"

"The baby's heartbeat is dropping. Get onto all fours. It might help."

I did as I was told while they all gawped at the monitor. The baby's heartbeat came back up.

And

then

began

to

slow

again.

Another doctor came in. "I'm doing an ultrasound. I'm not sure what's wrong."

THE BABY WAS ON THE ULTRASOUND SCREEN AND THEN HE WAS GONE.
Everything was happening too quickly.

"Is the baby okay?" I begged. "Is he okay?"

Mum had gone white. Her eyes were big and childlike. She held my hand. "You're doing great," she kept saying.

A doctor leaned over me, her breath sweet and warm, as if she'd been drinking hot chocolate. "The baby needs to come out now."

"Now?" I said.

"He's too far up and you've started to bleed." Her eyes locked onto mine. "The placenta may be separating." She said, "I recommend a Caesarean. Now."

I was crying. "Just make sure the baby's okay."

THEY WHEELED ME ON MY BACK TO ANOTHER ROOM. MUM HURRIED
along next to me. I could hear her panting. I saw Dad as we flashed along the corridor. His mouth was wide open.

He yelled, "*It is easy to be brave from a safe distance.* Aesop said that." He punched the air. Then I was wheeled away.

THE ROOM WAS VERY BRIGHT. WHITE. THERE WERE MANY PEOPLE IN
there. I could hear voices and someone had put on classical music.

Everything was out of my control.

The same anaesthesiologist came back. He explained the drug he was going to use. It would be stronger, he told me, and I would feel only pressure but no pain as they performed the operation.

"Is the baby okay?" I begged.

"Just breathe," he said.

I WAS LYING DOWN. SOMEONE WAS TOUCHING MY ARM LIGHTLY.

"Can you feel this?"

A CURTAIN WAS RIGGED UP THAT STOPPED AT MY NECK. IT MEANT I
couldn't see my body. The ceiling was so white.

MUM STOOD NEXT TO MY HEAD. I COULD HEAR THE DOCTORS TALKING.
I gazed up at Mum, my tears falling fast and salty.

I COULD SMELL BLOOD AND I COULD FEEL THEM TUGGING AT ME.

Wait.

Breathe.

Hope.

Wait.

Hope.

Breathe.

Then I hear you cry.

CHAPTER 25

"HOW IS HE?" I SOBBED.

"He's fine. He's great," the doctor called back. "He's doing great."

Mum was crying as they laid you on me. You were wrapped up in a blanket, your tiny face so close to mine that I couldn't see you properly. Your features scrunched against the bright light.

THEY WERE CLEANING UP. I COULD HEAR THEM FAINTLY IN THE BACKground. But I could only look at you.

You.

There was nothing but you.

TIME SLIPPED PAST. I WAS IN ANOTHER ROOM, YOU ON THE BED with me.

I could not sleep for looking at you.

Your tiny, hungry mouth. Toothless as a baby bird.

Your tiny fingers.

I put my hand to yours and you squeezed.

DAD CAME IN. "HOW'S IT GOING? EVERYTHING OKAY? THEY COULD DO with better signs here at the hospital. Maybe I'll talk to them about that. I could work something out for them." He stopped himself. His lips turned up in a rueful smile. "Ignore me. Are you okay, Bird?" Then he asked Mum the same thing.

But he didn't listen to our answers. He'd stopped speaking. He'd seen you.

He came over and put his hand on your head.

His hazel eyes were glazed.

He said, "He's beautiful—" His voice cracked.

LATER I SAID, "COULD SOMEONE GET PETE? AND CLEO?"

I LAY WITH YOU ON MY CHEST. YOU WERE SLEEPING. I STUDIED THE sticky swirls of hair on your head. Your ear, so perfectly formed. Your lashes, long, blond-tipped. Perfect. It was the right time for such a word.

PETE TIPTOED INTO THE ROOM AND CAME OVER TO ME, RESTING HIS hand on my shoulder. We stared at you. And stared. After a while he held you. I watched the two of you together. I cried a little.

"He's a baby," Pete said.

I giggled.

"I can't believe how tiny he is, Amy."

Later, Pete kissed me lightly on the cheek and left.

Time passed.

DAD WAS TALKING ON A PHONE IN THE CORRIDOR JUST OUTSIDE THE room. He said, "Yes, bring him. That would be fine."

Cleo came into the room. She put her hand on my forehead, and then moved her hand to your face. "He's gorgeous. How are you? Are you okay? It took forever. Pete and I were here. How was it? Did it really hurt? God, no, don't tell me. Is it as bad as they say?"

"Really bad. But the epidural, *God*. Amazing."

"What happens now? You know, with the adoption worker?" She turned her gaze to me. "You don't have to, you know, give him up if you don't want."

"How do you always know what I'm thinking?"

"I'm your best friend."

"God, am I crazy?"

"So crazy. Now stop talking and let me look at this baby." She bent over me and kissed you on your forehead. You reached a tiny hand out to hold her finger. "He likes me. You like me," she said to you. "So cute. Anyway, I brought someone with me. He's waiting outside. I should let him have a turn."

Cleo left and *Griffin* came through the open door, pulling it closed behind him.

I swallowed hard. "I wish I hadn't treated you so badly."

He shrugged.

"I should have been braver," I said. "I miss you as my friend."

"We'll be friends again one day. I just need time to move on." He gave a funny half-smile, and then looked at the baby. "He's sweet."

"Thanks."

"My mom had to go into hospital a few days ago. She's not doing very well."

"Do you want to talk about it?"

"No. Not now."

"Are you okay?"

He pushed his hair from his forehead. "I will be," he said.

I WAS ALONE WITH YOU. TIME PASSED. YOU WERE AWAKE. YOU WERE hungry. You cried. A nurse showed me how to change you. She taught me how to hold you so you could latch properly—it was weird and wonderful. She stroked under your chin so you would suck. I didn't tell the nurse that you weren't going to be staying with me, that I didn't need to know how to feed you. I didn't say a word.

I RESTED WITH YOU IN MY ARMS, SENSATION CREEPING PAINFULLY back into my body. I looked at your tiny face. I couldn't imagine giving you to someone else. I couldn't imagine letting you go.

NICOLE, THE ADOPTION WORKER, CAME IN. BRIGHT AND BREEZY. SHE smiled and said, "How are you feeling?"

I flushed with anxiety. You squirmed against me.

"Are you okay?"

I shook my head. "I'm not going to sign anything right now."

She gave me a long, gentle look. "No, no. You don't have to sign anything, remember. That's not why I'm here. There's no rush. I'm just seeing how you're doing. I'm here to support you, remember? And I wanted to meet your beautiful baby." She turned to look at you in the bassinet and tickle you under your chin.

"Nicole, I don't know what I want to do."

"That's fine," she said. "Take your time. As I said, I'm supporting you with whatever choice you make." Soon after, she slipped out.

THE DOOR OPENED AND I LOOKED UP TO SEE PETE STANDING THERE. "You're back," I said. "He's sleeping."

"It's you I wanted to see." He chewed his lower lip. "So, uh, I was thinking about the baby and about you and I was reading your website and I put this together." He scrabbled in his back pocket and handed me a folded sheet of white computer paper. "I, uh, printed all these out. I thought maybe we could give this to the baby. You know, before he goes to some other family—"

His voice caught and I looked up at him. It seemed like he might cry.

"What is it?"

"Just read it."

I opened up the sheet of paper and began to read.

- You never know what's coming next—embrace the unexpected.
- Do what you love.
- It's called a comfort zone for a reason.
- Sometimes you're lying when you say nothing at all.
- Snow sucks.
- You *can* regret what you haven't done.
- Secrets breed lies.
- Temptation is just too tempting.
- Even the best parties aren't always fun.
- Swim or sink.
- Life is not fair.

"Pete," I said. "These are my Top Tips."

A small smile played on his lips. "Yeah, I know. I thought they were pretty good advice for the little guy."

I read on.

- Sometimes when nothing seems to have changed, everything has.

- You don't always know yourself as well as you think you do.
- The truth comes out in the middle of the night.
- Some secrets are too hard to keep.
- Trust your instincts, even if they make no sense.
- You have to make your own decisions.
- When you make a decision, say it out loud.
- Be honest with your best friend.
- Mums can always tell when you're lying.
- Be happy.
- What you don't know *can* hurt you.
- All families have secrets.
- Right and wrong aren't always easy to tell apart.
- Being freaked out and terrified is not the end of the world—it'll pass.
- Life can be as lonely as a mountain, and as daunting.
- Chocolate always helps.
- A silly song can stop you from going crazy.
- Getting angry when someone's yelling at you will just make everything worse.
- Sticks and stones may break your bones, but the things people say hurt more.
- This recipe makes the best flan in the world.
- It really isn't too late to say sorry.
- Don't jump to conclusions about someone.
- Don't cry because it's over; smile because it happened. And if you can't do that, force a smile on your face and sob into your pillow later.
- Admitting you can't know it all is scary for a control freak (like me).

I burst into tears.

Pete joked gently, "You cry a lot."

"Yeah, giving birth does something funny to your hormones." I smiled at him. "I have two more tips that I thought up but didn't put on the site."

I found a pen in my overnight bag and wrote them carefully below the list Pete had printed out.

• Be gentle with yourself.
• You will find a way.

Pete looked at what I'd written. "Those are good."

I swallowed hard. I read over the list.

I tried to imagine you reading it, far away from me.

I said what was on my mind. "I . . . I don't know if I want to give him away. I don't know what to do, Pete."

"Yeah, I was sort of— I was . . . feeling the same thing. He's so—"

"We can't look after a baby."

He looked out the window. "You seem like you'd make a pretty good mum."

"It's crazy."

"Yeah, but crazy isn't always a bad thing." He turned his grey eyes to me.

I said, "Perhaps you should have been the one writing the Top Tips. You've got a lot of sensible things to say."

"You're the list maker." He sat on the edge of the bed. "I'll do my best to help, you know."

I watched him. I *did* know.

For the first time in ages, I knew what I wanted. I turned to look at you sleeping. I thought of all the advice I'd been giving everyone else but not following myself, all those Top Tips.

You pushed a small baby hand up into the air.

I wanted *you*.

Exhilaration and fear shivered over my body like a cold sweat. My life was over. My life was beginning.

I thought of something else I wanted to tell you one day. Face to face.

NUMBER 38: HOLD ON WHEN THE RIDE GETS BUMPY

Pete leaned over and held your tiny outstretched hand.

NUMBER 39: IT'S YOUR LIFE. LIVE IT

You opened your eyes.

EPILOGUE

Dear AmyAdvice,

I really love my boyfriend but he wants us to take our relationship to the next level, and I'm worried because I don't know whether I really want to. I know I love him and I think he loves me, but I'm not sure it really feels right—does that make sense? All my friends have lost it, most of them forever ago, and my best friend thinks I'm being stupid for waiting. And I'm really worried if I don't make my mind up soon, my boyfriend will find someone else, although I don't think he's that kind of guy, but I don't really know. I don't know what I want.

What should I do? Tell me soon before it's too late . . .

Really Confused.

By the way, I really love this website. I really love the way your new Tips For Teens section lets anyone put up their own tips and advice.

Dear Really Confused,

Theres a lot of pressure on U right now. But U don't know if you love UR boyfriend or not, U dont know if he loves U or if he just wants U for sex, U don't know whether to trust UR friends' advice or to trust UR own intuition and UR not sure what to do. Make him wait.

GigglyGirl

Really Confused,

Do NOT let any man push you when you're not ready. You could end up pregnant or with HIV—use protection.

CarefulLaydee783

Dear Really Confused,

If he loves you, he'll w8.

Brianne, 15

Dear Confused,

Im a guy and I think ur boyfriend sounds like a jerk . . . ur friends should be on ur side. Thats my advice.

Steve, 16

Dear Really Confused,

It's okay to be unsure.

Most of us live our lives thinking we're totally in control of everything that happens to us. Actually, life is outside of our control. Scary but true. Right now, you can't control your feelings of uncertainty. So *be* uncertain. Let your boyfriend know that you're not ready to make a decision, and that you won't be rushed.

I'm telling you this from experience: trust your instincts even if they make no sense.

And remember, you *know* best. It's your life after all.

AmyAdvice

IT'S BEEN REALLY HARD SOMETIMES. LONELY. SCARY. YOU HAD COLIC and didn't stop crying for months. I quit school completely. I watched my dad sign for the divorce. I've been isolated, tired, overwhelmed.

I have a part-time job in a supermarket—dull, dull, dull. Mum looks after you when I work—her job with the wedding photographer is flexible. She and I have spent a lot of time together this year getting to know each other all over again. But you and I live with Dad (I never asked Mum how she ended up without her own house—some things are too hard to talk about). You got the spare room. Dad's not so full of crazy dreams. It makes me sad sometimes when I remember how excited he used to get about stuff, but we've all had to be more grounded since you came along.

You're in a Jolly Jumper right now. You look over at me with your slate-grey eyes. You laugh. You jump. Your feet leave the ground. You're flying. I remember how much I used to want to fly. Huh. It seems so long ago.

Cleo and I don't get to hang out as much anymore. A few months after you were born, she started seeing Griffin. They're crazy in love. Griffin is so happy and I've never seen Cleo like this. Turns out everyone could see they were perfect together, except for me—but then, I was pretty self-absorbed at the time.

Cleo's going to university at Manchester Metropolitan. She's studying English and journalism. Griffin has a place there to take neuropsychology, and so they'll move up there together at the end of the school year—just after your first birthday. They both promised they'd come to your party.

I'll miss them.

Recently I set up a website for other teenagers who want to talk about sex, and for those who get pregnant. I give advice—whatever they decide to do with the pregnancy—and give them a space to communicate with one another. This means anyone logging in can give advice to anyone else, and then I throw in my thoughts too. It's not always easy to know what to say—sometimes the questions people ask cut very close. But I decided to use my own name for it, AmyAdvice. Miss Take-Control-of-Your-Life wasn't exactly the right way to describe me anymore. Dad has a job with an online company. Something very boring, but it means he can help look after you while I'm at school. I'm studying photography at a local college part time. My exam results were easily good enough to be able to apply to Oxford, but, turns out, Oxford isn't really where I want to go. Even if you were older and I could figure out the logistics, there are other universities that specialize in fine art with photography, which is what I'd like to study one day. For now, the photography class is pretty great. I'm going to base my photography project for class on a quotation I have up on my corkboard.

The best-laid plans of mice and men | Often go awry.
Robert Burns (paraphrased from the Scottish)

Mum and I have a great photography subject now. You. She comes over and we take photos together; she shows me what she learned at the studio. Sometimes I fantasize about setting up my own photography business, taking photos of weddings and babies. We'll see how it goes. I'm still pretty good at making lists and plans, but babies, turns out, don't always respect those plans.

And then there is your dad. He takes you out on weekends. When he comes over you light up, your smile filling your whole face. He and I have stayed friends. It's not always easy, especially as he's still with Kitty and I can't stand her. But he's a good dad to you. Like he promised he would be.

You might think I'm harbouring a crazy dream where Pete and I end up together and we become one happy family. I'm not saying I wouldn't like that, but some things you just can't plan. All we can do today is to be a good mum and dad to you. I'm starting by writing all of this out. Not for you to read, but to help me understand how we got here. Writing all of this out helps me remember where I got my list of things I want to tell you—the list that Pete and I plan to give you one day when you're older. The list has thirty-nine things on it. Pete thinks there should be forty. He doesn't know that there already are.

You've just started to fuss, little man. I'll whisper to you the most important thing I want to tell you as I scoop you up in my arms.

NUMBER 40: LOVE IS WORTH THE RISK

ACKNOWLEDGEMENTS

Thanks, Lynne and Hadley. Thanks, Sarah and Allyson and everyone else at HCC.

Thanks, Carol, Michael, Jocelyn, Juna and Community Relations. Thanks, everyone at Saskatoon Public Library, for the terrific residency.

Thanks, Holly Calder, for directing me to the recipe.

Thanks, Barbara Hansen. The recipe Bird uses on page 241 is from her book *Mexican Cooking*. Find more recipes at EatMx.com

Thanks, Cassandra and Karen, for answering my calls.

Thanks, Jen, Richard, Natalia, Tim-Tim, Alexia and Adrian, for lots of fun.

Thanks, Emile, for printing. Thank you, Nicole, for holding the baby.

Thanks, Jocelyne Martel, both times.

Thank you, Mum, for all you've done. Thank you, Paul.

Thank you, Dad, for reading, advising and more. Thank you, Liz.

Thanks, Anneke—you're the best. You are too, Jack.

Thanks, Yann. You know why.

Q&A WITH ALICE KUIPERS

What inspired you to write *Forty Things*?

When I initially came up with the idea, I was pregnant with my first child. I wanted to write a list of things that would be good rules to live by, things I wanted to tell my baby when he arrived in the world. I'd been toying in my mind with the idea of a teenage advice columnist, called Bird. She just kept appearing on the page when I'd sit down to write. I realized it was her story to tell, not mine. Her list of forty things gave me the structure I needed, and so the novel was born.

What was difficult about writing the novel?

Bird isn't me, and so her decision process about her pregnancy isn't the one I went through. Bird's pregnancy is unplanned, and she has difficult choices to make. The choice she makes is right for her, and hopefully readers agree. But I also hope that readers don't feel Bird is telling anyone else how to live. Sure, she starts the book thinking she has all the answers for everyone else, but by the end she comes to realize that her way of living is only one way of living, not the only way of living. It was difficult to get the right balance when I wrote this book— I wanted to tell Bird's story, but I didn't want to endorse one choice over the other.

The other part of the book that was tricky was getting the advice columns to sound right. I asked people to help me come up with particular problems and then to write their own letters so the voices would be distinct.

In the novel, Bird and Griffin have a complicated relationship. Why do you think she stays with him for as long as she does?

Bird is the type of person who finds it hard when her vision of the world doesn't work out. I tried to hint at this by giving her photography as a hobby. When she takes a photograph, she's trying to make order out of her world—except the world isn't an orderly place that can be controlled. She's so sure that Griffin is the right guy for her that, even when it's obvious he isn't, she can't give up the security he provides.

What are you working on now?

I'm working on another YA novel and a book for young children. The novel is still in the mysterious, murky phase. The picture book is called *The Best-Ever Bookworm Book by Violet and Victor Small*.

What writing tips do you have for aspiring authors?

I have three main tips that I give (and check out my website, www.alicekuipers.com, for regular prompts and writing advice):

1. *Read*. The more you read, the more you see what the written word can do. There is so much potential with language to tell the stories you want to tell.

2. *Don't be afraid to make mistakes*. Writing should only appear effortless in the final stage, that of the finished book. Before that, writing is difficult—words come out all wrong, paragraphs get mixed up, whole pages need to be deleted. That's all okay. It's part of the process.

3. *Believe that what you write is worth it*. So what if you don't get published straight away? I didn't get published for years, and lots of the words I wrote during that time have only been read by me. You are your book's first and best reader, so enjoy those projects that never get shared. Publication isn't the only goal.

Read an excerpt from Alice Kuipers' riveting new novel,

ME AND ME

It's Lark's seventeenth birthday, and although she's hated being reminded of the day ever since her mom's death three years ago, it's off to a great start. Lark has written a killer song to perform with her band, the weather is stunning and she's got a date with gorgeous Alec. The two take a canoe out on the lake, and everything is perfect—until Lark hears the screams. Annabelle, a little girl she used to babysit, is drowning in the nearby reeds while Annabelle's mom tries desperately to reach her. Lark and Alec are closer, and they both dive in. But Alec hits his head on a rock in the water and begins to flail.

Alec and Annabelle are drowning. And Lark can save only one of them.

Lark chooses, and in that moment her world splits into two distinct lives. She must live with the consequences of both choices. As Lark finds herself going down more than one path, she has to decide: Which life is the right one?

My birthday: morning

"I like surprises," I say, as I strap myself in.

Alec turns his dark gaze to me. "Good. You ready?" He seems folded into his truck, huge in the front cab.

"I think I'm ready. I, uh, I noticed the canoe." And the orange roses between our seats, filling the space with their heady scent.

Alec jars the truck into drive. I glance at his silver thumb ring and notice the way the cuffs of his rolled-up sleeves are slightly dirty, as if he's been hauling stuff or doing yardwork. I love his outdoorsy look, his clothes from those stores where they have tents set up in the backroom. Makes him look like he's ready to chop down trees or build a fire. I can feel every movement of his foot on the pedals, the way his hands hold the wheel. I want his hands on me like that.

"Those are for you." He juts his chin at the roses and smiles over at me.

"Thanks." I lift them to my nose. They smell of summer and of the past. A reel of the cemetery plays in my head.

Lucy:

Where are u?

                                                              Lark:

                                                                ???

Lucy:

Breakfast, right?

B4 I work?

I was going to practise tarot reading

on u for ur birthday . . .

She sends a photo of herself at D'Lish, where we both work. Her strawberry blond hair is done in loose braids. She's pulling a pouty sad-face.

                                                              Lark:

                                    Sorry!!! Going on a date.

Lucy:

Now? Who with???

Lark:

Last-minute decision.

Alec messaged last night.

He brought a canoe. Forgive me ;-)

Lucy:

Alec Sandcross? Nice!

I know how you feel about birthdays

but 17 is a BIG DEAL

Lark:

Stop!

Lucy sends a snap of herself sticking out her tongue.

Lark:

Tonight instead? Meet me and the band.

They have something planned.

Lucy:

I'm already coming after work.

Txt me later.

As Alec drives, he bites his bottom lip, which is pierced in the centre with a silver stud. Cute habit. I've seen him do it in class, when he's figuring something out. I wonder if he's noticed what

I'm wearing; I pick at the meant-to-be-there rip in my pastel green jeans. My leather boots come close to the knee. My pale shirt has tiny pink flowers peeping out from beneath my long black hair, which is loose.

He pulls onto the highway, and soon the city falls away. "I think you're going to enjoy today." The prairies stretch out like a vast ocean before us. I drum my hands on my knees to the radio—Seafret—and then I'm thinking in lyrics. *Wanna give your heart to me. The fire in the woods. Cut down, cut down just one tree* . . . I note the words on my cell.

"So, you canoed before?" He checks his rear-view mirror and overtakes a car in front of us.

The song tugs at me. "I've got a lyric idea. Sorry. Can I just finish this?"

"Oh . . . sure." Alec falls quiet, hand on the wheel, staring ahead.

The words are flowing; sometimes it happens like that, and a whole song appears where seconds before there was nothing. Whenever this happens on a date, boys think it's a challenge. They want my full attention. But Alec just drives. Time flashes by. It's as if I've dived into deep water and I'm exploring a coral world, blue and beautiful. There's a psychologist that we learned about recently who talks about *flow*. I get it when I'm in the zone like this. I only emerge when Alec pulls the truck into the lot at Pike Lake.

Songs almost never appear all at once. This one came out fully formed, so I'm feeling a little pumped.

"All done?" he says, turning off the ignition.

"Yeah. Sorry about that."

"It's cool. But now you're done, let's go." He grins, unfolds himself from the truck and shuts his door.

I jump out too. The lot fronts the beach, a thin strip of sand that runs along the treeline for three hundred metres or so. Beyond the beach is the silk-calm lake. I breathe in deeply, meditating on the clear view. The fresh breeze gives me goosebumps.

The place is almost deserted. Through a line of pine trees, I spot a couple and a small, blond child. I realize that it's the Fields family. He's *the* Martin Fields of Fields' Studios, which was why I took a babysitting job with them six months ago. Except he was always at work, so I hardly saw him. Whatever. I fell in love with his little girl and worked for them for about two months, before they decided to hire a full-time nanny instead.

"Annabelle?" I yell.

She turns and whoops but then pauses, as if suddenly shy. Suzanne—her mom—pushes her wild, curly hair from her face and waves hello. She walks over. Annabelle follows.

"Hi, Lark." Annabelle tips up her chin. "I'm nearly five now."

"Wow! You grew up. Soon you'll be older than me!" I count to five.

She giggles, and her blue eyes meet mine.

"Want to help me load the cooler?" Alec calls from the back of the truck.

Suzanne nods in the direction of their two canoes, which are already at the edge of the lake. "We're hitting the water too."

"Come find us out there."

"Mom?" Annabelle asks.

"Sure. Though I'm not sure we should disturb your privacy."

I smile. "No, come and find us on the water. Seriously. Sorry, Alec, I'm coming." A gust of cool wind ripples the water. I wave to Annabelle. From across the beach, Martin is still talking on his cell.

Back at the truck, I heft the cooler with Alec, the weight straining my muscles. "What are we eating?"

"By the end of the day," he says, "you'll be awestruck by my gourmet cooking skills. Now, help me get the canoe off the top."

We carry it down to the water. Then, suddenly, I'm diving back into the song I was writing—one of the opening lines would work better if I added a word near the end to change the rhythm. *Wanna give your heart to me, the fire in the woods, cut down, cut down, just one tree* . . . We slide the canoe into the water. It thunks against the sandy ground and cold water slops over my pant leg.

"I've . . . I'll just be a moment, promise." I slide my cell out of my back pocket.

"Okay. If you want. But I'm going to show you something amazing." Alec waggles his eyebrows.

"Is this 'something amazing' out on the lake or something you can do?"

"I am, indeed, talented"—he winks to show he's kidding—"but no . . . no, you write your song."

I tuck my phone away. "This better be good," I say, smiling.

A gull swoops overhead, a long way from the ocean. I pull off my shoes and socks. The icy water makes me gasp. The canoe wobbles as I climb in to join him and slip on my life jacket. The bottom of the canoe is hot from being in the sun on the roof of the car. The temperature contrast on my feet unfurls something in my chest. I ease fully into the moment.

"I wish I could sing," Alec says. "It must be awesome to be able to express yourself like that."

"Everyone can sing," I say.

"Not true."

"Okay." I sit on the front bench and turn back to Alec. "Not *exactly* true. But what I mean is that everyone can do *something* well. My mom taught me that." There she is. My mom. Even when I forget all about her, she's still watching over me. She left me a video. In it she tells me she's *always there*. Once I wrote a song with that as the hook.

Alec passes me a paddle, and I dip it into the water. The sound of the splash makes me think of ice cream, of summer, of holidays on the lake when I was a kid. In mutual but not uncomfortable quiet, we head along the side of the lake. When I glance back at Alec, he smiles languidly. My heart does a pancake flip. Alec points out a beaver that glides by in the shallows.

A little while later, he interrupts the silence to say, "My dad used to take me on the water. He thought fishing was good for, I don't know, turning me into a man. 'Cept I hated it, which drove him insane. I couldn't stand being cooped up in a small space—I wanted to swim, kept jumping in. Disturbing the fish. He used to yell at me, which was . . . well, not exactly relaxing." He steers the canoe toward a small inlet, where the reeds hide us. His voice floats forward to me. "We don't go on the water together anymore. And it's weird, but without him around, I don't mind the small space. Maybe that's because you're here."

We both stop paddling and let the canoe drift. My paddle drips freezing water over my knees. I swivel so I can see him. He leans his head to one side and smiles. His paddle is still in the water, and he occasionally re-angles it, making a deep ripple.

I point at the piercing in his lip. "Did it hurt?"

"I was, like, thirteen. I got into trouble. Big trouble. Call it rebellion."

"You seem like a good student. Into nature and stuff, not drugs and parties."

"Not that sort of rebellious." He has placed his paddle across the canoe and now rests both arms on it. "So, have you canoed much before?"

"We canoed and camped every weekend during the summer when I was little. Dad doesn't look like it now." Alec stays quiet while I speak. "He has a heart thing, so he can't really exercise now. It means he's put on some weight, and he isn't so outdoorsy anymore, although he loves yardwork."

"What sort of a heart thing?"

"They don't really know. If he runs or gets his pulse up, I guess, his heart kinda skips."

My heart is skipping now. I don't want to talk about this. But I say, "It sucks. Some sort of scarring, maybe. I always think it's a broken heart 'cause of my mom." I lean back into paddling. My arms feel the pull of the water, and I fill my body with the sensation.

Alec seems to get the topic isn't my favourite, because he doesn't push; everyone at school knows what happened to my mom. Instead, as he paddles he shifts to a new subject.

"How long have you played guitar?"

"Since before I can remember. Dad got me a ukulele when I was tiny, because I wanted a guitar so badly, but a ukulele is smaller, easier to start with. But tell me about you. I mean, stuff I don't know from class."

"What do you know from class?"

I lift my oar and turn back to him. Boy, he's cute when he looks at me like that. I say, "Um, you've been living in Edenville as long as me. Like, forever. You live with your parents. You work at Eb's Outdoors. You aren't good at math. You are super good at history."

"I am too good at math."

"Whatever." Smiling, I tilt my face up to the sun. It means I'm not looking when Alec stands up. The lurching of the canoe makes me grab the sides. "What are you doing?"

"Fancy a swim?"

"Sure. But I don't have a swimsuit."

"Neither do I." His eyes are alight.

"Ah. The amazing thing you promised," I deadpan. "Alec Sandcross gets naked and goes for a swim."

"No, that's not it." He pulls off his shirt. My eyes travel over his tanned muscular arms and six-pack. "There maybe isn't anything amazing . . ."

I splash water at him. "You lied to stop me writing. I thought that might be the deal."

The canoe tips but rights itself as I wobble to my feet.

"Okay then, the amazing thing . . . is that you're going to take your clothes off too," he says.

I unzip my life jacket. I hesitate and check around. The Fields family can't be seen, and the water is glassy quiet. Alec smiles his lazy smile. Then I do it. I pull off my shirt. Thank God I'm wearing a decent bra.

Faltering and goofing off, suddenly we're giggling as he crouches and tugs off his jeans and I do the same—tricky in a canoe. We're stripped down to our underwear. The sun is amazing-warm against my skin. He steps closer along the canoe, causing it to wobble again. I bet he's gonna come up to me and kiss me.

Instead he turns to the water. "Come on."

A shout stops us. "Help! Oh my God, someone help me!"

It's Suzanne. I thought we were far from everyone, but I catch a glimpse of her flailing in the water just through the reeds.

And a red life jacket.

Annabelle!

She's floating face down on the other side of the canoe from Suzanne. Alec and I glance at each other. Alec dives and I jump. The water is as cold as death. I lift my face to orient myself, pushing hair out of my eyes, and then, focused, I knife through the water.

Now Annabelle is about ten metres away from me. Suzanne still flounders in the reeds.

"Help her!"

Just then, Alec cries out. I glance back. He's about ten metres behind me, *blood* pouring from his temple. His eyes are glassy.

"I banged my . . . I . . ."

He's sinking. "Alec!"

"I can't get to her!" Suzanne fights the reeds that have entangled her.

I turn back. I'm halfway between Annabelle and Alec. I have to save them. Alec is going under. Annabelle is face down. I can't breathe. Pain radiates through my chest. I tread water, frantically looking one way and then the other.

I do not know who to choose.

Suzanne screams, "Lark! DO SOMETHING!"

But *I can't*.